JUST A GIRL WITH A GUN

JUST A GIRL WITH A GUN

Maxim Jakubowski

First published by Telos Publishing
139 Whitstable Road, Canterbury, Kent CT2 8EQ,
United Kingdom.

www.telos.co.uk

ISBN: 978-1-84583-228-5

Telos Publishing Ltd values feedback. Please e-mail any
comments you might have about this book to:
feedback@telos.co.uk

British Library Cataloguing in Publication Data.
A catalogue record for this book is available from the
British Library.

1
Of Guns and Amber

To celebrate her fifth murder, Cornelia treated herself to a tattoo.

Her first tattoo.

It had been an easy kill. Bloodless. Fast and uncomplicated.

Her target had been a swarthy, pockmark-cheeked, and balding foreign businessman of Mediterranean appearance and she had initially accosted him at his hotel bar. If it had proven necessary, she would have followed him to his room with the unspoken promise of sex, and even delivered had it been impossible to do the deed before getting down to the nasty. But he was already half drunk and kept on making regular visits to the nearest toilet in the lobby to relieve his bladder, and she had taken advantage of one of his absences to slip the pill into his glass. He downed the drink within seconds of returning to the bar and promptly ordered another round for the two of them. Cornelia was just drinking Coca Cola. She had never enjoyed alcohol and didn't believe in forcing herself to taste things she didn't like. She had even reached the stage where, as a parlour game with friends, she would on occasion, blindfolded or not, distinguish between Coke and Pepsi. After a sip of each. Not a skill that could be advertised on a CV, but then neither was the fact that she was an efficient and ruthless contract killer.

Cornelia knew precisely how long it would take for the pill to take effect and excused herself from the clumsy flirtation a few minutes later and left the man sitting at the bar stool, already perspiring heavily, under pretext of some previous arrangement.

She departed the hotel, legging it through the lobby in

dark glasses she had kept in her purse and a dark green silk scarf wrapped around her hair, in case anyone should later wish to investigate the CCTV recordings.

She took refuge in an artisan café just across the road, and was casually leafing through the book she had brought along to read while keeping a keen eye on the hotel's entrance.

Half an hour later, an ambulance raced along the street and the paramedics rushed into the hotel. A further 30 mins along, she confirmed the kill on her phone as the stretcher bearing the body bag was carried out before the ambulance moved away, its siren no longer screeching.

Job done.

She texted her handler. Just the letter X. A code they had agreed on.

The payment reached her bank account before she'd even finished her coffee and brushed the remaining crumbs from her cupcake, from the tabletop.

She calmly kept on reading to the end of her chapter and then returned to her own hotel, where she had booked a room just as a matter of contingency and was asleep within minutes.

Her flight home was not until late afternoon.

She walked through the twisting streets of Tallinn's walled centre killing time, admiring some of the amber pieces in the many jewellers and souvenir stores catering to mostly the tourist trade. When her mother was still well, she had loved amber and had accumulated quite a collection: necklaces, brooches, all forms of jewellery that amber could come in. Then, Cornelia could not afford much amber. Now it was too late to acquire any as presents.

Her mother's collection lay in a couple of drawers in her SoHo apartment, useless, too painful a memory and Cornelia was unlikely to wear any of the valuable pieces.

She took a detour through yet another, narrow cobbled alley and came across the neon sign of the tattoo parlour and, on an impulse, walked inside. The thought of having a tattoo had never crossed her mind before today. Unlike most teenagers she had never even craved to have her ears pierced and body modifications had been far from her thoughts when she was younger and was never much of a rebel anyway.

A burly attendant greeted her in Estonian. He had a shaved head, was barrel-chested under his tight, black heavy metal T-shirt, but his eyes were sea-blue and particularly striking and conferred a strange sense of innocence or trustworthiness, contradicting his biker appearance.

'I only speak English,' Cornelia indicated. Although that was an untruth as she was fluent in French and Italian and even had a smattering of German.

'Welcome, then.'

'I think I want a tattoo …'

'You think?'

'Well, yes … I actually hadn't thought of it until I passed your storefront.'

He looked nonplussed, weighing her up, uncertain whether she was playing a joke on him or was exercising a strange foreign sense of humour he couldn't quite understand.

He looked her up and down.

Tall, blonde, slim, curly-haired. Not his usual type of customer.

'What sort of tattoo? We have all sorts.' He picked up a few folders in which he kept his main designs.

'Something small.'

'A bird, a name, a flower?'

'No.'

'OK.'

He could see she was deliberating. It wasn't as if the young woman was shy or hesitant. There was a steeliness about her, but also a sense of mischief. Something he couldn't quite pinpoint. A coolness, a sense of distance. He looked her up and down again. Of danger, too. She wore an unbuttoned leather trench coat and a sleek dress underneath it that seemed sewn across her lean body. Her legs went on forever and she was wearing perilously high heels. Like a fashion model, but with a perverse aura of intelligence.

She stood there, still only half past the store's doorway,

her grey eyes somehow peering into an unknown distance.

She stepped forward, looked around at the walls festooned with outrageous designs: tattoos, an assortment of Mexican *Día De Los Muertos* images, dragons and other exotic or mythological creatures, flowers, baroque or elaborate rococo patterns.

'Something small.'

'Size presents no problem.'

'Discreet.'

'You're the customer; you choose what and where.'

'Good.'

'I have a female assistant. She is really talented, particularly for small scale work. As good as me. She will be here in a few minutes, if you prefer a woman to work on you.'

'It makes no difference.'

Cornelia realised she had an embarrassment of choices if this was the day she was to be inked for the first time.

She remembered a friend from her early days as a stripper. Wallace, she recalled. Her whole back was dominated by a beautiful Māori tribal pattern, a living canvas that went down from the nape of her neck to the curve of her arse and realised she wished for something as memorable but on a smaller scale. More intimate.

And then a thought flashed across her mind. Her fourth kill. Her first overseas assignment. A brute in Amsterdam known for trafficking women. Once she made his acquaintance, she quickly decided she would have been as content to do the job without pay. He had his girls tattooed, but as property. Two had numbers above their genitalia, and a third girl she had seen had the words 'whore' inked on her rear, with the central 'o' marked by her anal opening. She had almost been sick when she had been shown the desecration as the guy, whose name she could no longer remember, or maybe didn't wish to, was trying to cajole her into joining his fold and was talking up her glittering career prospects. She had played along for a few days to justify her cover, until the right occasion manifested itself.

She had slit his throat.

Slowly.

Then watched him gurgle his way to death.

Although to this day, she guessed, the women whose bodies he had disfigured still had to live with their permanent marks.

Cornelia came to a decision.

'I want a small gun.'

'A gun?' The tattoo artist appeared bemused. He had incorporated weapons into overall patterns before: swords revolvers, but he hadn't expected the tall blonde to come up with that particular choice.

'Yes, but a small one …'

'What sort of gun? Something specific or generic?'

'I'm not sure.' Cornelia had only a limited experience of guns. None of her kills so far had necessitated one, although she had trained on a range both recently and in her youth. She had never owned one.

She closed her eyes and recalled the weight and the surface texture of the SIG Sauer P938 subcompact with anodized aluminium frame she had recently trained with, how it had fit snuggly in her hand, like a natural extension of herself. Not too heavy or light.

'I know which one.' She pulled out her iPhone and googled its image, turning the screen round towards the tattoo artist. 'This one.'

He gave the gun a quick look. 'I think I can do that; it's manageable.'

'Good. I'd like it this size.' She held two fingers apart to indicate how big she wanted the image.

He quoted a price.

She agreed on the spot. She had no idea if it was right, but it was not a matter of cost for Cornelia.

He pointed to a large black leather chair towards the back of the store, which reminded her of a dentist's throne.

She moved towards it, slipping out of her trench coat, and draping it over a nearby trestle table across which a pile of assorted catalogues was strewn. He turned his back on her and reached out for his instruments. That skin-tight dress of hers was sleeveless so he had full access to her arm.

Prepping his coil gun and ensuring he would have enough ink, he asked: 'Just the outline, or will you want it filled in?'

'Filled in. Black ink.'

'Left arm or right arm? Close to the wrist or higher up?'

'Neither.'

He finally turned back towards his new client.

She was still standing by the chair.

'Ankle?'

'No.'

'Oh …'

She looked him straight in the eye, a distinct note of irony piercing the steel grey of her gaze.

'I want it somewhere much more private. So that only I am aware of its presence. And, naturally, those I allow to witness it. On very special occasions …' Her lips curled into a brief smile.

She looked down her body.

'Below.'

Umru Peerna thought he understood her meaning. He had practiced his art a couple of times on breasts. It always gave him a special thrill, he remembered.

'It will be painful. It's not an area of the body where the skin is predisposed to being broken, pierced so to speak.'

'Temporary pain does not bother me.'

'I won't charge you more than we initially agreed.'

'I hope not.'

She moved to the side of the heavy, elaborate chair and slowly rolled up the lower half of her dress, first unveiling the pale fullness of her porcelain white thighs.

The tattooist's throat tightened. He had expected her to pull down the top half of her clinging garment. He held his breath.

She pulled the fabric further up with little hesitation and revealed her sex.

He held his breath.

She was fully shaved. Or depilated. Her mons a gentle hillock parted by a slit through which a thin sliver of pink peered through.

'I want the gun here.'

She pointed down to an area just an inch above the crease formed by the birth of her leg and separating it from her crotch.

She sat down, holding her legs slightly apart to facilitate his approach.

'You are quite certain of this?' he asked.

'Absolutely.'

He took the tattoo gun in hand and knelt in front of her open thighs, first placing a cushion on the linoleum floor to both protect his knees and stabilise his position.

He couldn't quite keep peering at her gape.

'A SIG Sauer it is,' he said and switched the motor on, glancing, one final time before he began piercing her delicate skin, at the photograph he had just a moment previously printed out of the gun's model she had called up on her iPhone, which would serve as guideline for the initial pattern of the actual tattoo.

She barely twitched when the needle broke through her skin for the first time.

His nose was just a few inches away from her sex and he imagined he could smell the delicate musk floating towards him but reasoned it was more the scent of soap or fragrant bodywash than any genuine secretion.

He tried to switch his mind off altogether and concentrate on the job at hand. It wasn't easy. Her beauty and total lack of self-consciousness made him hard. As the needle of his instrument continued assaulting her skin, she never even flinched once, and remained totally silent during the whole process.

Halfway through, his trainee, Jannika arrived for her shift. Because of the nature of the work, he was tracing the pattern of the revolver on Cornelia, he had locked the store's front door, but Jannika had her own set of keys. She walked in, witnessed the initially surprising spectacle of her boss buried between the blonde woman's thighs and was taken aback but remained silent. She approached in silence, curious as to the nature of the tattoo being carved into the client.

She had briefly imagined it might be a flower, but was shocked when she recognised the gun's outline.

But what made more of an impression was the bareness surrounding the woman's cunt. It was such an extreme form of nakedness. She had seen hairless vaginas before, in photos and porn clips, but this was the first time in real life. There was an eerie beauty about this woman's aggressive smoothness and Jannika decided on the spot that she would shave herself tonight!

Just about an hour later, the job had been completed.

Cornelia was given instructions into keeping the area where the tattoo had been needled into her flesh sterile and how to clean it and keep it clean for a week or so.

She pulled the dress back down to her knees, slipped her high heeled shoes on again and paid in cash, and left the two Estonian tattoo workers still entranced by her poise and total lack of outward emotions.

As she passed the parade of amber shops and made her way out of the walled city to the hotel on the main road to the port where she had stored her overnight bag, and had arranged for transport to the airport, Cornelia could still feel the sting of the tattoo gun around her sex and floated on the high it cushioned her with.

For her next kill, she decided, she would gift herself again with a rare book, as she had done on the four previous occasions she had completed a job satisfactorily.

A single tattoo would suffice.

And she had no appetite for piercings. Anywhere.

2
Killing Villanelle

Cornelia hated Villanelle with a vengeance.

She had been eliminating assigned targets for a year already when the TV series *Killing Eve* had been broadcast, and Cornelia felt the portrayal of the hitwoman by Jodie Comer was an affront to her professionalism.

She had no need for fancy accents, masquerading as a clown, wearing rococo dresses, or hiding in suitcases. This dislike was intensely personal and had the unfortunate if talented actress ever accidentally crossed her path, she would have been in great peril depending on Cornelia's mood of the day.

She took her job seriously.

She took life seriously.

And, of course, death.

When her father was still alive, he had regularly taken her as a teenager to firing ranges when they had taken rural family holidays in the Kentucky mountains or the Adirondacks in their camper van and she had taken an odd, perverse pleasure in the handling of deadly weapons and all the discipline it entailed. But it had always been a hobby and she never had the slightest thought that one day it might form an integral part of her future.

The problem with Cornelia was that, even this early in her life, she had no profound thoughts of the life ahead. She saw herself as a blank canvas. Was bright but had no ambition. Was fatalistic and devoid of any desires or wants. In her inner core, she knew she was a survivor and would have no worries carving out a life of some sort for herself. Her family were middle-class, her father an executive engineer in the power industry and her mother a retired educator. He died when she was only fourteen and Cornelia was surprised how little she was affected. It wasn't as if they hadn't been close but there was a strict limit to the affection she was capable of lavishing on others. Her mother had long ago been a teacher and when she was diagnosed with early onset dementia, there was something of the inevitable about it, the main inconvenience proving the cost of the care home she was obliged to find. It wasn't as if she didn't love both her parents but, in her heart, Cornelia knew that life was never fair and you had to survive with the cards you were dealt and there was no point complaining.

Cornelia didn't 'do' relationships.

From an early age, sex was just an exchange. Of favours, of fluids, just hydraulics basically. Feelings did not come into it.

She attended a prestigious university and passed all her exams with flying colours. She had job offers in the six figures from a choice selection of top of the range companies in the financial sector and industry, but had no interest in pursuing a high-flying career of any kind. To keep up the repayments on her student loans, she initially took a job in a bookshop, where she picked up the expensive habit of book collecting. At the time, it had felt a better option than drifting into the McJobs of the low gig economy.

Men were always complimenting her on her looks, claiming she had a body to die for, moved with a unique brand of sultry sexiness and when she became aware through a fellow collector in London with whom she corresponded, that a rare, late F. Scott Fitzgerald short story collection had appeared on eBay, albeit without a dustjacket, she decided she needed the book badly enough and had to raise the cash to acquire it fast. She had long been captivated by the 'wanted' ads she was always coming across in the free broadsheets on street corners for exotic dancers and the leaflets copiously distributed close to the clubs that littered the roads leading to LAX and the downtown area. She loved music anyway, and it turned out those ballet lessons she had disliked as an awkward teenager had at least taught her poise and equilibrium. So, what difference would it make whether she performed dressed or undressed? She considered the stripping option as a possible craft, and it was much more appealing and relaxing than dancing for tickets in crumbling dance halls past their sell date, let alone escorting. Cornelia took pride in her somewhat skewed sense of logic; she had never been overtly emotional, unless she had surrendered heart and soul to a story in a book where the characters felt so much more real than most of the folk she chanced across in civilian life. Her rare acquaintances often told her there was a chilling coldness that surrounded her like a shroud, which neither pleased nor displeased her. It was just the way she was engineered.

She hesitantly answered one of the ads, and soon found herself stripping in an upmarket joint close to the airport. Following her shift at the bookstore. After all this was the final volume to complete her set of Fitzgerald titles. *Flappers and Philosophers*. None of the other books she owned by him were actual first editions but she now saw the prospect of gradually upgrading her collection to firsts. Within weeks she had given up her job at the shop and was stripping full time.

It was an occupation that suited her. She could switch her mind off when she was dancing, had no qualms about men watching all her intimacies and whatever it triggered in their minds and bodies. Unlike many of her fellow strippers, she followed the bar's rules of engagement to the letter and systematically refused to engage with any customer beyond her stints on stage, unlike most of the other performers, despite the many opportunities that arose. She was disliked by the other women who also worked there, who found her remote, snooty, cold, and the fact didn't bother her in the least. Very quickly she was fielding offers to perform at better clubs and forged an enviable reputation for herself and was making good money from generous tippers and admirers.

Her mother's diagnostic had come just half a year after

her father's passing, but she had managed to live on her own, unassisted, despite the occasional fall, with the help of friends. She lived two hours away from the city so Cornelia would only see her on occasions when she was not dancing over the weekend when the shifts and attendant perks were more remunerative.

But in time she began to deteriorate. Cornelia would come upon her talking to herself in the mirror or back at the newsreaders or anchors on the television set, or imagining the presence of strangers in the garden who were evidently not there. A torrent of increasingly disturbing episodes as her mind accelerated the process of breaking down in incremental stages characteristic of the inexorable progress of the dementia.

Then she began to forget her toilet habits, innocently leaving unpleasant mementoes around the family's home and Cornelia knew radical steps would have to be taken.

In the same week, a fairly rare title by an author she collected assiduously had surfaced on the market; an early proof with substantial handwritten annotations by the writer which had been carried through to the final published version and substantially changed the original plot and the fate of some of the fictional characters involved. This not only made any copy of the advance reading proof valuable, but the changes visibly jotted down in the author's hand had created a unique artefact.

The book was priced well beyond her means but, with hope against hope, she had asked the dealer, with whom she had done business before, for a fortnight's grace so she could attempt to raise the money; the antiquarian seller had agreed – she had until now been a reliable customer in addition to the fact he had taken a shine to her.

Cornelia had briefly pondered, not for the first time, doing some escorting but quickly calculated the cost of the book would even then prove out of her reach, let alone factoring in future care costs in the home she had located. Her mother's health insurance would only cover a small part of the cost and their respective savings would not finance the move beyond an initial six months.

Cornelia began to think of more creative ways of raising further cash.

Legally or illegally.

She hinted about her need for fast cash to the doormen and baristas of the clubs where she was working. They, she assumed, were the closest to matters best left in shadows. Made it clear she was not seeking sex work but something else, although she was uncertain what it might be, but she was open to suggestions. Maybe a friend of a friend of a friend would come up with an idea, a lead?

The initial approach from the friend of a friend of a casual acquaintance involved peddling drugs and she categorically turned the offer down.

It was Samuel Trimlin, a long-time bouncer at the Zanzibar Lounge – a lower league place she had once worked in before graduating to classier joints, which had a reputation for rough edges to say the least – who came up trumps. He was a tall and lean guy with 60s rocker hairstyle and attitude to match, but generally a friendly sort. He claimed to have been on the road for various rock bands, including The Who in their, and his, heyday.

'You look good and proper for a dancer. As if butter wouldn't melt in your mouth.'

He'd accosted her in the car lot behind the club where she'd just completed a set. She knew of him, as he often frequented the bar after his own duties across the street. There were several gentlemen's clubs along the twisting roads that circled LAX.

'Thank you, kind sir. But I'm not seeking sex work.'

'So, I was informed. A waste if I may say so, you'd be perfect, both innocent and naughty. And not your usual run of the mill escort. But you could pass for an upper-class one and that's where the rub is.'

He explained.

A man with a penchant for willowy blondes and a

penchant for hookers would have to be lured into a motel room.

'I did say, no sex …' Cornelia interrupted him.

'I know.'

'So?'

'Then we want him dead. We'll supply the means, if you know what I mean. You use sex, or the promise of it, purely as a bait. The lure.'

He was impressed by her deadpan expression. She didn't display any element of shock. Just absorbed the information quietly, not even manifesting a hint of surprise. The woman was coolness in motion.

'I see … How much does it pay?'

He quoted an impressive sum. Worth several weeks of care home costs. And maybe even the rare book proof she coveted at the Heritage Bookshop on South Riverside Drive.

'Tell me more,' Cornelia asked.

He did.

Should she mess matters up and get caught or hurt, she would have to shoulder the full blame. Even in prison, they would have ways to reach her and ensure her silence. This was a basic rule.

It made sense to Cornelia. 'Why me?' she asked, 'Surely you have access to guys with more experience?'

'We have. But the target won't expect you. We are aware of his weaknesses.'

No, she had no desire to know what her future victim had done to deserve his assigned fate. It was none of her business.

'I'm glad you answered that. Had you not we would harbour doubts about your attitude.'

This, she understood.

'Must I make it look like an accident or a suicide?'

'No, that will not be necessary. We want his case to be an example to others not to cross certain lines and anger my employers.'

Cornelia spent a whole day with Trimlin in a motel

room close by the airport where he gave her rudimentary lessons on the facts of death. How to avoid CCTV, the type of gloves to wear to avoid leaving DNA traces, all the sort of basic know-how she'd read about in books, thrillers, or forensic true crime volumes which she was already an avid reader of, even though these types of volumes were not among the ones she collected. She was a classic fiction girl, through and through.

She was provided with a thin dossier; a dozen photocopied pages at most, which she had to memorise. Photographs. Of the target, his habits, where he drank, ate, played. Once she had done so, she had to hand the documents back.

'Do you have your own gun?'

'No, I don't own one.' Although they had checked she could use one.

'Good. If you require one, we will provide an untraceable one.'

'With a silencer?'

'Yes.'

But she had already made up her mind she had no wish to use a gun on this initial occasion. It felt too crude. She would improvise.

He asked her what she would need.

She made a list. A short one.

She was given a week to get the job done.

Cornelia agreed.

She made her approach three days later.

She deliberately spilled the contents of her glass at the bar he was drinking at, just a few meters away from the man she was hoping to kill. It was not coincidentally a glass of Pernod, a beverage she disliked with a vengeance but, as indicated in the dossier, one he enjoyed. He promptly offered to get her a replacement and this gave her the opportunity to start a conversation.

Everything afterwards went like clockwork. Men were so easy to predict, ruled by their cocks rather than their brains.

She wasn't even wearing anything particularly sexy. That evening. Just a pair of skinny jeans and tight white T-shirt. She didn't want him to think she was on the game. She pretended to be a local art student when answering his questions. She was still in her early 20s and could easily pass for one. It was too easy; how could he not realise that her intentions were bad? She was half his age, more than half his size, and with a beer belly growing outwards at an exponential pace that meant he couldn't have had sight of his balls when standing in a decade or so. How could she ever have been attracted to him? But the minds of some men just won't accept reality.

She agreed to join him at his nearby apartment.

She stood behind him as he unbuttoned his shirt and slipped the piece of piano wire from the rucksack she had brought along and garrotted him. She had the element of surprise on her side and by the time he even thought of putting up some form of resistance, the damage had been done, his carotid slashed and the outcome immovable.

Her first kill.

Clean and effortless.

As she saw herself out of the apartment, she felt supremely calm. Showed no trace of fear or guilt. It was just a job, wasn't it? He probably deserved to die, didn't he. She was not prone to nightmares and the money was good enough to assuage her already relaxed conscience.

She settled a further half year of fees in advance with her mother's care home. Before her credit expired, she had deteriorated so badly that she was no longer capable of recognising Cornelia when she visited, let alone anyone else, and had lost the power of speech, babbling away like a child, words full of nonsense, as her desperate brain struggled for some sort of vocabulary. Lacking mobility. Having to eat her food mashed as she sometimes forgot how to even swallow solids. She barely lasted a few more weeks.

Cornelia mourned her in her own, silent way. Continued stripping and the next time she was approached for a hit, readily agreed.

She knew she was good at killing people.

Why not fine-tune that particular skill?

One more rare book for her collection. She was professional and careful not to get caught on security cameras, leave fingerprints, or allow anyone to witness her presence on the scene or the vicinity of the crime. Other assignments followed. The death broker always supplied the weapon, which she disposed of afterwards although she decided after the first handful of hits that she should not restrict herself to guns only, and began using other methods so that she didn't adhere to a specific trademark.

Her collection of rare and antiquarian books kept on growing. In the wake of bodies strewn in her path.

3
An American in Paris

Cornelia took the RER from Roissy-Charles De Gaulle. A taxi would have proven easier and more relaxed after the 7-hour plane journey, but she knew she had to remain as anonymous as possible. Cab drivers have a bad habit of remembering tall, lanky blondes, particularly so those who did not wish to engage in needless conversation and reveal whether it was their first time in Paris or was she coming here on holiday? It wouldn't be the last time she was asked whether she was an actress, a model or someone famous.

Because she knew there were countless CCTV cameras sprinkled across the airport and the train terminal, she had quickly swapped outfits in a somewhat insalubrious toilet shortly after picking her suitcase up from the luggage carrousel, and by the time she walked on to the RER train, she now had a mauve scarf draped around her blonde curls and wore a different colour scheme altogether from her flight outfit. It was far from fool proof, but at least would serve its purpose in muddying the waters in the eventuality of a later, thorough investigation.

The commuters on the train to Paris looked grey and tired, wage slaves on their mindless journey to work or elsewhere. A couple of teenage Arab kids listening to rap - or was it hip hop – on their iPods glanced at her repeatedly, but her indifference soon got the better of them and she wasn't bothered until the Luxembourg Gardens stop where she got off.

After researching the area, she had booked a double room in a small hotel there online the previous day. Its windows overlooking the Panthéon. She checked herself in under the false name on her spare passport, a Canadian one she'd seldom used before. She took a shower and relaxed before taking the lift to the lobby around lunch hour and noticed someone new had taken over at the registration desk from the young woman who'd earlier checked her in. She calmly walked back to her room and stuffed some clothes into a tote bag and went down to the lobby again and left the hotel. Fifteen minutes later, she registered at another hotel, near the Place de L'Odéon, this time under her real name. This booking she'd made by phone from New York a week or so before. She was now the unremarkable occupant of two separate hotel rooms under two separate names and nationalities. Both rooms were rather noisy and looked out onto busy streets, but that was Paris, and anyway she wasn't here for a spot of tourism. This was work. She settled into the new room, took a nap, and just before the evening walked out and took a cab to the Place de L'Opéra. There was a thin jiffy bag awaiting her at the American Express Poste Restante. Here, she retrieved the key she had purchased back in Brooklyn Beach from a Russian connection she occasionally used. She then caught another taxi to the Gare du Nord, where she located the left luggage locker which the key allowed access to. The package was anonymous and not too bulky. She picked up a copy of *Libération* at a nearby news kiosk and casually wrapped it around the bundle she had just retrieved from the locker and walked over to the train station stairs to the Métro and took the Porte d'Orléans line back to Odéon. In the room, she unwrapped the package and weighed the SIG Sauer in her hand. Her weapon of choice. Perfect. As if it had been pre-ordained.

The Italian girl had always preferred older men. Some of her friends and other fellow students at La Sapienza, Rome's University, had always kidded her, saying she had something of a father fixation, and indeed her relationship with her gastro-enterologist Dad was prickly to say the least, seesawing between devotion and simmering anger. At any rate, he also spoiled her badly.

But boys her age seemed so clumsy and uninteresting, coarse, superficial, so sadly predictable, and she found herself recoiling instinctively from their tentative touches all too often. Not that she knew what exactly she wanted herself.

Whenever asked about her plans for the future, she would answer in jest (or maybe not) that she planned to marry an ambassador and have lots of babies. When Peppino –the name she would use for her much older, foreign lover to make him difficult to identify for her parents – queried her about this, she would add that the ambassador would also be a black man, a big man in both size and personality. Her older lover would smile silently in response, betraying his own personal fears and prejudices, only to point out that she'd be wasting so many opportunities by becoming merely a wife. After all, this was a young woman who by the age of 22 had a degree in comparative literature, spoke five languages, and would surely make a hell of a journalist or foreign correspondent one day.

Her affair with the man she and her friends affectionately called Peppino had lasted just over a year and he had been the first man she had fucked. To her amazement, he had become not just a lover but her professor of sex; unimaginably tender, crudely transgressive and the first time she had come across a guy who understood her so well their contact when apart became almost telepathic. However, he was also more than twice her age, lived in another country and happened to be married, which sharpened her longing and her jealousy to breaking point. The affair had proven both beautiful and traumatic, but eventually the enforced separations from Peppino could not be assuaged by telephone calls, frantic emails, and mere words any longer. For her sanity, she was obliged to break up with him. Even though she loved him. She had a life to live, adventures to experience; he had already lived his life, hadn't he? Now was her time. The decision was a painful one and he naturally took it badly. Not that her state of mind was much better, wracked by doubts, heartache, and regrets by the thousands as both Peppino and she could not help recalling with deep pangs of regret their days and nights together, the shocking intimacy they had experienced, the pleasure and complicity, the joy, and the darkness. Sleepless nights and silent unhappiness followed in her wake and she agreed to visit a girlfriend from her Erasmus months in Lisbon who lived in Paris -ironically, a city he had always promised to take her to.

It was a wet spring day and a thin layer of rain peppered the Latin Quarter pavements with a coating of damp melancholy. Her friend Flora had departed for the countryside and her grandparents' villa and left the Italian girl on her own for a few days. Initially, she had looked forward to the prospect but now found herself particularly lonely. When she was not busy and frantically exploring the city with Flora, all those beautiful but painful memories just kept on creeping back.

She was sitting reading a book at the terrace of Les Deux Magots, sipping a coffee, half-watching the world pass by, women who strolled along with distinct elegance, young men who looked cute but would surely prove dull in real life she thought, when she heard the seductive voice of the bad man across her shoulders.

'That's quite a wonderful book, Mademoiselle,' he said. 'I envy you the experience of reading it for the first time. Truly.'

Giuly looked up at him.

He looked older. How could he not be?

Cornelia much preferred ignorance. A job was a job and it was better not to have to know any of the frequently murky reasons she was provided an assignment.

Had the target stolen from another party, swindled, lied, killed, betrayed? It was not important.

Cornelia knew she had a cold heart. It made her work easier, not that she sought excuses. She would kill both innocent and guilty parties with the same mindset. It was not hers to reason why.

She had been given a thin dossier on her Paris mark, a half dozen pages of random information about his haunts and habits and a couple of photographs. A manila folder she had slipped between her folded black cashmere sweaters in her travelling suitcase, to which she had added a few torn-out pages from the financial pages of the *New York Times* and a section on international investment from the Wall Street Journal to muddy the waters in the event of an unlikely snap examination of her belongings by customs at either JFK or Roissy. He was a man in his late forties, good-looking in a rugged sort of way which appealed to some women, she knew. Tall-ish, hair greying at the temples in subdued and discreet manner. She studied one of the photographs, and noted the ice-green eyes, and a steely inner determination behind the crooked smile. A dangerous man. A bad man.

But they all have weaknesses, and it appeared his was women. Always markedly younger than himself. It usually was. Did men ever change? Cornelia sighed. Kept on studying the information sheet she had been provided with, made notes. Finally, she booted up her laptop and went online to hunt down the 'clubs échangistes' her prey was known to frequent on a regular basis. They appeared to be located all over the city, but the main ones were clustered around the Marais area and close to the Louvre. She wrote down the particulars of Au Pluriel, Le Chateau des Lys, Les Chandelles and Chris et Manu, and studied the respective web sites. She'd been to a couple of similar 'swing' clubs back in the States, both privately and for work reasons. She'd found them somewhat sordid. Maybe the Parisian ones would prove classier, but she seriously doubted it. Cornelia had no qualms about public sex, let alone exhibitionism -after all she had been stripping for a living for several years now and still enjoyed the occasional gig and greatly enjoyed the sensation - but still found that sex was an essentially private communion. But then, she'd always had a particular relationship with and perception of sex, and at a push would confess to decidedly mixed feelings about it.

Would sex in Paris, sex and Paris, prove any different, she wondered?

She rose from the bed where she had spread out the pages and photos, switched off the metal grey laptop and walked pensively to the hotel room's small, pokey bathroom. She pulled off her T-shirt, slipped off her white cotton panties and looked at herself in the full-length mirror.

Focused on her miniscule tattoo.

And shed a tear.

It came unbidden. Out of nowhere, for no reason.

As if embarrassed, she quickly wiped it away.

Even a killer's soul can have a bad day, she reckoned.

Nothing she should be worried about.

Yet.

4
Paris Swings

The bad man had no problem seducing the young Italian woman. He had experience, fluid assurance and elegance. Anyway, she was on the rebound from her Peppino and a vulnerable prey. Had her first lover not warned her that no man would ever love her, touch her with as much tenderness as he? And had she not known in the deep of her heart that he was right? But falling into the arms of the Frenchman was easy, a way of moving on, she reckoned. She knew all he really wanted to do was fuck her, use her and that was good enough for now for Giuly. She was lost and the excesses of sex felt as good a way of burying the past and the hurt. This new man would not love her; he was just another adventure on the road. So why not? This was Paris, wasn't it? And spring would soon turn into summer and she just couldn't bear the thought of returning to Rome and resuming her Ph.D. studies and being subsidised by her father.

She rang home and informed her parents she would be staying on in Paris for a few more months. There were muted protests and fiery arguments, but she was well-trained in manipulating them. She was old enough by now, she told them, to do what she wanted with her life.

'Respect me, and my needs' she said. Not for the first time.

'Do you need money?' her father enquired.

'No, I've found a part-time job, helping my friend's father with his statistical research,' she lied. It came easy to her, although she had no clue what statistical research might even entail.

The Frenchman –he said he was a businessman,

something in export/import – requested she move in with him and Giuly accepted. She couldn't stay on at Flora's without revealing the existence of her new relationship, and suspected it would not go down well with her friend.

At first, it was nice to sleep at night in bed with another person, a man. Feeling the warmth of the other's body, waking up to another naked body next to her own. And to feel herself filled to the brim when he made love to her. To again experience a man's cock growing inside her as it ploughed her, stretched her. To take a penis, savour its hardening inside her mouth, to hear a man moan above her as he came, shuddered, shouted out obscenities or religious adjectives and experience those unforgettable heat waves radiating from cunt to heart to brain. Of course, it reminded her of Peppino. But then again, it was different. No fish face to behold at the moment of climax with this new man, just a detached air of satisfaction, almost cruelty as he often took her to the brink and retreated, teasing with her senses, enjoying her like an object.

Day times, he would often leave her early in the morning and go about his work and Giuly was able to explore Paris, fancy free, absorbing the essence of the city in her long, lanky stride. For the first time in ages, she felt like a gypsy again, like the young teenager who would live on the streets of Rome and even enjoy sleepless nights wandering from alleys to coffee shops with a cohort of friends or even alone, drinking in life with no care in the world. In the Belleville, she discovered a patisserie with sweet delicacies, near Censier-Daubenton she made an acquaintance with a young dope dealer who furnished her with cheap weed, which she would take care never to smoke at the man's apartment off the Quai de Grenelle. As with Peppino, she knew older guys secretly disapproved of her getting high, as if pretending they had never been young themselves. Neither did they appreciate The Clash, she'd found out … Her favourite band. He would leave her money when he left her behind but she was frugal and never used it all or asked for more.

And at night, following her aimless, carefree

wanderings, he would treat her to fancy restaurants – she'd cooked for him a few times at the flat but he was not too keen on pasta or tomato sauce or seemingly of Italian food altogether - and would then carry her back to the bedroom where he would fuck her. Harder and harder. As she offered no resistance and her passiveness increased, the bad man went further. One night, he tied her hands. Giuly allowed him.

Soon, he was encouraged to test her limits.

She knew it was all leading in the wrong direction and she should resist his growing attempts at domination. But the thought of leaving this strange new life in Paris and returning to Rome would feel like an admission of defeat, an acknowledgement that she should not have broken up with Peppino, and broken his heart into a thousand pieces, as she knew she had. Maybe this was a form of penance, a way of punishing herself? She just didn't know any more. Had she ever known?

One dark evening, after he'd tied her hands to the bedpost and, somehow, her ankles, he'd taken her by surprise and despite her mild protests, had resolutely shaven away her thick thatch of wild, curling jet-black pubic hair and left her quite bald, like a child, which not only brought back bittersweet memories of her younger years but also a deep sense of shame and the fact she'd always strongly insisted Peppino should not even trim her, as he had sometimes been inclined to do. What was it about older men and their fixation on hairless genitalia? Were they all paedophiles at heart?

The next day, the Frenchman used his belt on her arse cheeks and marked her badly.

Sitting watching a movie that afternoon in a small art house by the Odéon was painful, as Giuly kept on fidgeting in her seat to find a position that did not remind her of the previous evening's punishment. Her period pains had also begun, as bad as ever; she'd once been told they'd only start improving after she'd had her first child.

That night, the bad man wanted to fuck her, as usual and she pointed out that her period had begun. He became angry. He would have been quite furious had she actually revealed that she had once allowed Peppino to make love to her on such a day and the blood mass they had shared was still one of her most exquisitely shocking and treasured memories. He brutally stripped her, tied her hands behind her back and pushed her down on the floor, onto her stomach and sharply penetrated her anus, spitting onto his cock and her opening for necessary lubrication. She screamed in pain and he gagged her with her own panties and continued relentlessly to invest her. Giuly recalled how she had once assured Peppino as they spooned in bed one night how she would never agree to anal sex with him or anyone. Another promise betrayed, she knew. She grew familiar with the pain. She had never thought it would be so easy to break with her past.

Later, as she lay there motionless, the bad man said:

'Next week, I shall continue your education. I'm taking you to a club and I want to watch you being fucked by a stranger, my sweet little Italian whore.'

Giuly couldn't respond. She was frozen. And in pain. When he left the apartment, he retrieved her set of keys from her handbag and locked her in. They were on the fifth floor and she had no other way out. Giuly sighed.

Cornelia watched her mark leave the building and head to his car. She had been observing him for several days now and was beginning to get an idea of his habits and patterns. She wasn't sure where the young Italian woman fitted in. She was pretty but always seemed lost, a soul in search of a life, following in his footsteps, somehow allowing herself to be pawed and pulled along as if it wasn't quite her destiny, her role in life.

This was a man who used women.

Another reason he should be punished.

Cornelia was no feminist. She was too fiercely individualistic for that. But there was something from afar that moved her about the Italian girl. His mistress. Or at any rate, his current one. This was not a man who appeared suited for monogamy or faithfulness.

He didn't deserve her.

It would make the hit more satisfying, Cornelia reckoned.

5
In the Country of Bodies

It was a night full of stars and the Seine quivered with a thousand lights.

The taxi had dropped Cornelia around the corner from Les Chandelles. She looked out for a decent-looking café and installed herself at a table overlooking the street, where she would be highly visible to all passers-by. She wore an opaque white silk shirt and was, as ever, braless. Her short black skirt highlighted her endless pale legs and this was one of the rare occasions when she had lipstick on, a scarlet stain across her thin lips. She'd ruffled her hair, blonde medusa curls like a forest, and slowly sipped a glass of Sancerre, a US paperback edition of John Irving's *A Widow for One Year*, sitting broken-spined on the ceramic top next to the wine carafe.

The bait was set: a lonesome American woman on a Friday night in Paris, just some steps away from a notorious 'Club Échangiste'. *L'Américaine*. She'd found out earlier, through judicious tipping and a hint of further largesse of another nature from the club's doorman that her target was planning to attend the club later this evening. The entrance fee for single women was advantageous but she felt she would attract less attention if she were part of a couple. She'd gathered on the grapevine that lone men would often congregate here before moving on the club, in search of a partner. As would single women seeking entry to the club.

The information was reliable and within an hour, she'd been twice offered an escort into the premises. She hadn't even needed to uncross her legs and reveal her lack of underwear. The first guy was too skanky for her liking, and altogether too condescending in the way he spoke to her in the slowly-enunciating manner some automatically do with foreigners. She quietly gave him the brush-off. He did not protest unduly. The second candidate was more suitable, a middle-aged businessman with a well-cut suit and half-decent aftershave. He even sent her over a glass of champagne before accosting her. Much too old, of course, but then there was something about Paris and older men with younger women. The water, the air, whatever!

They agreed that once inside she would have no obligation to either stay with him or fuck him, at any rate initially. Maybe later, if neither came across someone more suitable. He readily acquiesced. Cornelia knew she was good arm candy, tall and distinctive, a beautiful woman with a style all her own, and an unnerving visible mix of brains and provocation. She'd worked hard on that aspect of her appearance.

Despite its upmarket reputation, Les Chandelles was much as she expected. Tasteful in a vulgar but chic way; too many muted lights, drapes and parquet flooring, dark corners or 'coins calins' as they were coyly described on the club's website, semi-opulent staircases leading to private rooms and a strange overall smell of sex, cheap perfume, and a touch of discreet disinfectant not unlike the cabins of erstwhile American sex shop cabins or the tawdry rooms set asides for private lap dances in some of the joints she had once navigated through.

She spent some time at the bar with her escort and enjoyed further champagne, allowing him to gleefully demonstrate some of the nooks and crannies of the swing club, which he appeared to be a regular patron of. Now she knew the lay of the land. She offered to dance with him.

'Not my scene,' he churlishly protested.

'It warms me up,' she pointed out. He nodded in appreciation.

'Just go ahead,' he said. 'Maybe we can meet up later, if you want?'

'Yes,' Cornelia said.

From the dance floor, she would have a perfect vantage point to observe new arrivals as they trooped past on their way to more intimate areas of the club. She shuffled along to a Leonard Cohen tune and marked her area between a few embracing couples, embracing the melody with her languorous movements. She'd always enjoyed dancing; it had made the stripping bearable. Cornelia closed her eyes and navigated along to the soft music. Occasionally, a hand or another would gently tap her on the shoulder, an invitation to move on and join a man, a woman or more often a couple to a more private location, but each time she amiably turned the offer down with a smile. No one insisted, following the club's strict protocols.

Alongside the many, sultry French songs she had not previously known, Cornelia had already delicately shimmied to recognisable tunes by Luna, Strays Don't Sleep and Nick Cave when she noticed the new couple settling down at the bar.

Now she could take a closer look at them. The Italian girl couldn't have been older than 25 with a jungle of thick dark curls falling to her shoulders and a gawky, slightly unfeminine walk. Her back was bare, pale skin on full display emerging from a thin knitted top, and she wore a white skirt that fell all the way to her ankles, through which one could spy on her long legs and a round arse just that little bit bigger than she would no doubt have wished to have, an imperfection that actually made her quite stunning, what with deep brown eyes and a gypsy-like, wild demeanour that reminded Cornelia of a child still to fully mature. She wore dark black shoes with heels, which she visibly didn't need, as she was almost as tall as Cornelia. But there was also a sad sensuality that poured out from every inch of her as she followed her companion's instructions and settled on a high stall at the bar. The man ordered drinks, without asking the young girl what she wanted. Her eyes darted across the room, glancing at the other patrons of the club, judging them, weighing them, surveying the dubious scene in which she how found herself. It was evidently her first time here.

Cornelia adjusted her gaze.

The man squiring the exotic young woman was him, her target. The bad man. Her information had proven correct. As she watched the couple, Cornelia blanked out the music.

Less than an hour later, she had made acquaintance with them and suggested to her new friends they could move on to a more private space. Throughout their conversation, the Italian girl had been mostly silent, leaving her older companion to ask all the questions and flirt quite openly and suggestively with the splendid American blonde seemingly in search of local thrills. At first, the man appeared hesitant, as if the visit to Les Chandelles had been planned differently.

'I've never been with a woman before,' the Italian girl complained to the man.

'Would you rather I looked for a black bull to fuck you here and now with an audience watching?' he said to her. 'I'd actually had that in mind before we came across our charming new companion. But we now have much more interesting prospects, don't we?' It was no longer a smile but an unpleasant leer distorting his thick lips.

'No,' Giuly whispered.

'So, we all agree,' he concluded and pushed his stall away, and gallantly took Cornelia's hand. 'Anyway, you can do most of the watching as I intend to enjoy the company of our new American friend to its fullest extent. You can watch and learn; I do find you somewhat passive and unimaginative, my dear young Italian gypsy. See how a real woman fucks.'

Giuly lowered her eyes and stood up to follow them.

Once they had located an empty room on the next floor, Cornelia briefly excused herself and insisted she had to walk back to the cloakroom to get something from the handbag she had left there as well as picking up some clean towels, which their forthcoming activities would no doubt require.

'Ah, Americans, always keen on hygiene,' the bad man said and broadly smiled. 'We'll be waiting for you,' he added, indicating his young companion to begin shedding her clothes.

'I will undress too; the moment I return,' Cornelia said, turning round. 'Don't want to get them crumpled, do we? I so much prefer the feel of body against body. There's something absurd about people lovemaking still partially undressed, I've always felt. Like pantomime, no?'

'Perfect,' the man said, turning his attention to Giuly's slight, pale, uncovered breasts and sharply twisting her nipples while she was still in the process of slipping out of her billowing long white skirt. There were red and purple bruise marks on her butt cheeks.

When Cornelia returned a few minutes later, the bad man was stripped from the waist down and the Italian girl was sucking him off while his fingers held her hair tight and her head was forcibly pressed against his groin, even though his thrusts were making her gag and gasp for breath. He turned his own head towards Cornelia, a blonde apparition, now fully naked and holding a bunch of towels under her left arm.

'Beautiful,' he said, releasing his pressure on Giuly's head. 'Truly regal,' he observed, his eyes running up and down Cornelia's body. 'I like very much,' he added. His attention now centred on her groin. 'A tattoo? There? Pretty? What is it?'

Cornelia approached the couple. The man withdrew his penis from the Italian girl's mouth, allowing her to breathe easier, and put a proprietary hand on Cornelia's left breast and then squinted, taking a closer look at her depilated pubic area and the small tattoo she sported there.

'A gun? Interesting' he said.

'SIG Sauer, actually' Cornelia said.

There was a momentary look of concern on his face, but then he relaxed briefly and nodded towards the American woman, indicating she should replace Giuly and service his still jutting cock. Cornelia quietly asked Giuly to move away from the man so that she might take over her position. The Italian girl stumbled backwards to the bed. Cornelia kneeled.

As her mouth approached his groin, she pulled out the gun she had kept hidden under the white towels, placed it upwards against his chin and pressed the trigger.

The silencer muffled most of the sound and Giuly's cry of surprise proved louder than the actual shot which blew the lid of his head off, moving through his mouth and through to his brain in a fraction of a second. He fell to the ground, Cornelia cushioning his collapse with her outstretched arm.

'Jesus,' Giuly said.

And looked questioningly at Cornelia who now stood with her legs firmly apart, the weapon still in her hand, a naked angel of death.

'He was a bad man,' Cornelia said.

'I know,' the Italian girl said. 'But ...'

'It was just a job, nothing personal,' Cornelia said.

'So ...'

'Shhhh ...' Cornelia. 'Get your clothes.'

The young Italian stood there, as if nailed to the floor, every inch of her body revealed. Cornelia couldn't avoid examining her.

'You're very pretty,' she said.

'You too,' the other replied.

Cornelia folded the gun back inside the towels. 'Normally, I would have killed you too,' she said. 'As a rule, I must leave no witnesses. But I'm not big on killing women. Just dress, go and forget him. I don't know how well you knew him and suspect it wasn't long. Find a younger man. Go back to Italy. Live. Be happy. And ...'

'What?'

'Forget me, forget what I look like. You don't know me; you've never known me.'

Giuly nodded her agreement as she pulled the knitted top she had worn earlier over her head, disturbing the thousand thick dark curls. The other woman was in no rush to dress, comfortable in her porcelain nudity. Her body was also pale, but a different sort of pallor, Giuly couldn't quite work out the nature of the difference. But she didn't feel threatened.

The American woman looming above her and the dead man's body like a goddess of retribution. Her heart was beating wildly.

Cornelia watched her hurriedly dress.

'Return to Rome. This never happened. It's just Paris, Giuly. Another place.'

Back in the street, Giuly initially felt disorientated. It had all happened so quickly. She was surprised to see that she wasn't as shocked as she should have been. It was just something that had happened. An adventure. Her first adventure since Peppino. Under her breath, she whispered his real name. The Paris night did not answer.

She checked her bag; she had enough money for a small hotel room for the night. Tomorrow, she would take the train back to Rome.

The Louvre was lit up and she walked towards the Seine, and towards the darkness. At her fourth attempt, she found a cheap hotel on the Rue Monsieur le Prince. The room was on the fourth floor and she could barely fit into the lift. Later, she went out and had a crêpe with sugar and Grand Marnier from an all-night kiosk near the junction between the Rue de l'Odéon and the Boulevard Saint Germain. People were queuing outside the nearby cinemas, folk mostly of her own age, no older men here. She walked towards Notre-Dame and wasted time in a bookshop, idly leafing through the new titles on display. She would have dearly liked to have a coffee, but no Latin Quarter bookstores also served coffee, unlike her favourite haunt, Feltrinelli's in Rome where she had spent most of her teenage years. But she knew that if she walked into a café and took a table alone, someone would eventually try a pick-up line and disturb her, and tonight she felt no need for further conversation. So, she finally returned, head bowed, to her small room and slept soundly. A night without nightmares or memories.

The man in the Police du Territoire uniform handed her passport back to Cornelia.

'I hope you enjoyed your stay, Mademoiselle?'

L'Américaine candidly smiled back at him as she made her way into the departure lounge at the airport.

'Absolutely,' she said.

6
A Most Imperfect Gentleman

Hopley had returned home.

He'd taken a six-month sabbatical.

Just like an academic, which he sometimes pretended to be or appeared to be. Maybe it was because he sometimes wore glasses? He looked the part, which went a long way to convincing people he was one. Clothes maketh the man. As does a deceptively gentle demeanour, polite manners, and an air of sophistication which he carried lightly. His hair had turned grey in his mid-30s, a final touch in ensuring his public persona was unthreatening. He couldn't have engineered matters better.

But, when operational, he was very much a threat. He was a killer. And a good one at that, insofar as he had never been caught, let alone come under any kind of suspicion.

One with a splendid indifference for the failings of others and a man with a terribly cold heart.

He didn't kill at random and had nothing but contempt for serial killers. For Hopley, it was a job. One he was good at.

In fact, as much as he tried to understand or even identify with other murderers, he couldn't genuinely understand the mentality or motivations of those others who killed at random, for the thrill, for lack of morals. At a stretch he could appreciate why people committed acts of passion, though. Love was another of those great unknowns that had him wondering, an equation he hadn't yet properly solved.

For Hopley, crime was a profession.

He had enough money in the bank and the last job he had undertaken had proven unfortunately messy and he had felt, in the aftermath, the need to hit the 'pause' button.

As a freelance operator, with no obligatory ties to any patron, he wasn't tied down by any form of contract, had always had the choice of accepting or turning down jobs. Not a 9 to 5 man.

So, he'd gone travelling. Leaving a message on his answerphone to this effect.

He took a long cruise to the Far East, sailing down the Yangtze River, exploring Hong Kong and Vietnam, then descended on an assortment of beaches and fancy resorts and tried to enjoy his leisure time, soaking up the sun, enjoying local foods and just lazing around with no particular thing to do. He even bedded a few women along the way. One in Bali and the others in Funchal in Madeira where he was staying in a luxury hotel in the Lido area. They were sisters. That had been a first. They had certainly tired him out, but the experience had felt hollow. Almost a challenge to himself which by the time they departed his crumpled sheets, had left him feeling emptier than ever, even questioning the rationale for sex altogether. That had certainly not been the rationale of the experiment!

All three women his path had crossed had skills, looks, decent bodies and were lustful enough, but the experience had left Hopley unsatisfied, as if he were going through the motions of seduction and lust, doing things by the book, and the ensuing orgasms had been perfunctory, almost unnecessary. A routine that had to be completed to make sense of the couplings.

Leaving their bedroom or the women creeping out at dawn from his, he hadn't even bothered to go through the formality of exchanging addresses or telephone numbers. Neither did any of the women, who had by now realised that Hopley was not a long-term prospect of any kind and probably harboured a similar sense of disappointment.

No one compared to Ramona.

Or Elizabeth.

Or Lois.

All those other women that littered his past he had been unable to hold on to. He had tried. But he hadn't found the words, the sincerity that might have swayed them and they had no doubt seen through him and understood that his best intentions were not strong enough to sustain a lasting relationship and they had moved on with their lives, leaving him stranded on the access road to that elusive highway of happiness, of contentment.

Many years back, following his final stint in the army, when Hopley had first made a connection with the Bureau and was offered the opportunity to undertake wet work for them, he had made it clear he would not accept killing women, however guilty or problematic they might be. It was understood by his prospective employers and no such contracts were ever offered to him.

Nor children or animals, of course. Not that he had any love whatsoever for pets; he just felt they were not worth the cost of a bullet or any other effort to dispose of them. Not that anyone would pay a fee to eliminate a pet.

It wasn't as if he were sentimental. Just practical.

In the business he was in, you had to be, he reckoned.

But … Ramona.

It was some time earlier in the killing game that he had met her.

One of those unthinkable coincidences: they had been reading the same paperback, sitting in the departure lounge at La Guardia airport. Remarkable, he could no longer even remember the title of the novel that fortuitously brought them together.

It was a flight to New Orleans. He was on a job. She was on mid-term break and was meeting up with friends in the Big Easy. Her first time there. He had visited before.

They both looked up at the same time and could not help noticing they were both holding a copy of the same paperback in their lap as they waited for the call to board the aircraft. She smiled first. Hopley was similarly amused by the coincidence and did the same.

'What do you think of it so far?' she asked.

He had only just picked the book up from the nearby Hudson News store at the top of the concourse. Something to read on the flight. He recalled coming across an interesting review of it somewhere some months previously.

'I haven't even opened it yet. Just bought it. You?'

'I'm halfway through. It's good, although maybe not as gripping as the author's previous thrillers,' she said.

'I haven't read him before.'

'In that case, you should enjoy the book. Very twisty but a fast read. It grips.'

They happened to have been assigned seats in the same row of the aircraft. Although there was an elderly passenger seated between them.

Ramona asked the traveller in the middle seat if he preferred to be by the window seat and he quickly agreed to swap. Now they were next to each other.

'We can compare impressions,' she said.

'Why not?'

Hopley loved her openness.

She was studying accountancy at night classes but in the meantime was working odd hours as a supply teacher of maths at a New York private school run by Quakers, but quickly reassured him that she was not one herself. Had in fact no religious bone in her body.

He volunteered very little about himself.

Did not pretend to be an academic as she might have had too pointed questions for him to sustain the pretence. He vaguely indicated he was involved in publishing. Which intrigued her even more.

'What sort? Books, magazines, newspapers?'

'Just trade stuff. Very boring and uninteresting, but it's a living.'

'I'm Ramona, by the way,' she finally introduced herself thirty minutes into the flight.

'Hopley.'

'Is that a first name or a surname?'

'Both. Everybody calls me that.'

'So, a surname I guess. Haven't you a first name? Or a middle one even?'

'My parents couldn't afford a middle-name. And yes, I do have a first name. But I never use it.'

'Do tell. I can keep secrets.'

'It's actually the name of a famous character who has a book named after him. A rather old-fashioned name.'

Ramona giggled.

Pondered.

'Sherlock?'

'No.'

'Robinson?'

'No.'

'Ebenezer?'

'No and, he wasn't afforded the honour of his first name being evoked in the title, if you remember correctly.'

She continued to try names out on him and then threw her hands up in the air and gave up following a few further hopeless if humorous attempts at identifying the name.

'Come on. I won't tell. Scout's honour.'

Hopley took a long, slow sip of his plastic cup of tomato juice, deliberately teasing with her, dragging the suspense along, amused by the twinkle in her eye that reminded him of a child, although the rest of her was certainly in her mid-20s.

She licked her upper lip, as she waited for him to treat her with the great reveal.

He set his cup down.

'Silas.'

She laughed. Hopley saw she had a slightly crooked incisor. It moved him.

'Love it.'

'I don't.'

'I'll stick to my promise and the name will never pass my lips ever again, Mr. Hopley.' She over-emphasised the 'Mr', her broad smile betraying mischief.

'Just Hopley, please.'

'So be it.'

The conversation continued as the plane made its way south. One of those on/off dialogues where not much of consequence is said, but much lies under the surface in a falsely innocent way. Ramona had never been to New Orleans before but was apprehensive of the fact it had a reputation as a party city.

'I'm not a party sort of gal. A bit old-fashioned that way.'

'I'm sure you will still find a way to enjoy yourselves. You're meeting friends, that helps.'

'You?'

'Me what?'

'Are you travelling there for business or pleasure?'

Hopley was truthful. 'For business.' He was on a recce for a job. Had no intentions of doing the deed this time around but, as a matter of professionalism, had to get accustomed to the territory where he'd be working, familiarise himself with the lie of the land.

'Will you have any leisure time?'

'Maybe.'

He'd visited New Orleans once before, had witnessed New Year's Eve celebrations from the balcony of Tujague's, a restaurant close to Jackson Square, had admired the fireworks rising from the pontoons on the nearby Mississippi. He could no longer recall who he had come with. Hopley had mentioned the name of a couple of other eateries to Ramona.

The plane was banking down towards Louis Armstrong Airport. The stewards were giving out landing instructions.

'If you have time after your business dealings, maybe we could meet up for a drink? I'm staying at the Marriott on Canal Street. You?'

'I'm at the Prince Conti, in the French Quarter.'

'Is it nice?'

'It's small and cosy, but very central. I'm no fan of big chain hotels. Too impersonal.'

They landed.

'I've loved talking to you,' Ramona said. 'You're interesting.'

'You too.'

'Am I? I've been asking most of the questions. You've

barely asked me any.' She sounded amused by it, rather than annoyed. So many of the men she knew were the same and expressed little interest in finding out more about her, beyond the basics, but then they also only spoke about themselves. Hopley, on the other hand, seemed particularly reluctant to reveal anything about who he actually was. Certainly, no show boater and the very soul of discretion.

It was true. Hopley was guarded and even though she was attractive, he couldn't quite understand why she was interested in him. But the possible prospect of seeing more of this curious young woman had some attraction.

They parted in the luggage hall. She had a small suitcase but he only had hand luggage and did not suggest they share a cab into the city. Which disappointed her. She wanted to know more about this curious man of few words.

Two days later, Hopley had completed his homework and had a good notion of how he would set up the job on his next visit. He was ready to fly back to New York, but still remembered the young woman from the plane with both curiosity and amusement. Maybe he should try and see her again. But then, what was the point?

He was about to call the airline to find out when the next flight home would be and book a seat on it, when the phone by his bedside rang.

'It's Ramona, from the plane. Do you remember me?'

'I do.'

'My friends have gone on an excursion to the bayous. They're hoping to see some alligators. Not my idea of fun. Might you be free, your business done?'

Hopley didn't hesitate.

'Are you a vegetarian?'

'No. What sort of question is that?'

'There's a place called Tujague's on Decatur, almost opposite the Café du Monde. It's one of the oldest eateries in New Orleans, apart from the Napoleon House. Their beef brisket is out of this world. Join me there for dinner.'

7
An Affair of the Moment

They were sitting an ornate metal table by the empty pool in the inner courtyard of the hotel, having breakfast. Soft beignets overflowing with powdery sugar, freshly-squeezed orange juice for Hopley and coffee for Ramona.

She had spent the night with Hopley.

He couldn't recall with any degree of precision who had made the first move. It had just happened, something natural in the progression of their conversations, veiled looks and fingers tentatively grazing skin at the dinner table. As if it had been pre-ordained. Neither the seductor or the seduced.

They had walked back the few blocks to his hotel. By now the conversation they had sustained over food, flirty, ironic, detached and probing at the same time (at any rate from her side of the table) had ground to a halt and it felt as if it was now just an inevitable scenario silently unfolding.

The distinct smell of the Crescent City surrounded them as they stepped their way through it. Fragrant, a curious, if exhilarating, blend of rotting flowers, stale beer and the lingering potpourri of spices floating suspended in invisible clouds.

He had been surprised by how easy it had been conversing with her, not that he had done much of the talking, carefully economical with any facts and the true reasons for his presence in the city. They had both found out that neither of them had made much further progress with the book that had somehow brought them together.

'So, we'll have to find something else to talk about, then …'

'Feels like homework to me.'

'Promise not to grade you …'

They'd glanced at the menu. Not the usual New Orleans fare. No jambalaya or crawfish to be seen. It had an almost European feel to it. Although Ramona was attracted to the gumbo.

'So, you're sure about the brisket?' she asked.

'I'm told it's heavenly. Blends to perfection with the horseradish sauce,' Hopley said.

'I'll take your word for it. I'm not a great meat eater generally.'

'Neither am I. Actually, I could live on fish and seafood.'

'Something else in common!' Romona said.

'I hope you're not taking notes. Building a dossier on me, maybe.'

She had a lovely, open smile.

Hopley made a note to himself to not fall for her too seriously.

Because he knew she was exactly the type of woman who ticked his boxes. Beautiful but without a single ounce of aggression, a hint of being lost somehow in her own dreams or maybe past; a sense of vulnerability that echoed deeply inside him. There was something profoundly relaxed about her demeanour, a lack of complication. Too many women he had known, if briefly, had been dangerous packages of neuroses behind their glossy exterior. And the one thing Hopley avoided like hell were complications. Even as he was guiltily attracted to them, maybe as a form of punishment. To keep him on the straight and narrow, alert.

His was not in a profession where you could afford to relax.

After breakfast, they walked along the banks of the river. She tried to hold his hand, but he shied from the gesture.

They ventured into the aquarium. Hopley had no interest in animals or sea creatures, but it was a way of killing time, he reckoned. He was trying to act like a normal man would, being pleasant, urbane, civilised, until it would be the right time to return to his room and undress her again and enjoy their lovemaking. He could have stayed there forever, watching the light pour across her body from the open window as she moved from bed to bathroom between embraces. He never tired of the beauty of women's bodies. He was assuredly a terrible voyeur at heart. And Ramona appeared to be a woman who was comfortable in the harbour of her nudity.

Hopley had something of a photographic memory, which naturally was useful in the context of his assignments. He stored a catalogue of women away at the back of his private movie screen, naked, clothed, still, in motion, in sexual action, in the languor of repose, dreaming, sleeping. A library of exquisite souvenirs he could access with ease if he closed his eyes and dredged the memories back. Sometimes these images proved more memorable than the receding instants when they were created.

Hopley. Contract killer. A man who preferred to look back than fully live and enjoy the present. He was aware of this terrible flaw in his character, but knew he had to endure it. It was the way he was built and it was much too late now to try and change it.

He sighed.

'Are you planning to join your friends later?'

'Not if I can avoid it. We're not particularly close. They appear to be more into all the touristy things, you know. And drinking. They're more friends of friends, if you see what I mean. I seldom see them, even back in New York.'

'Good. We can have lunch together, then.'

'I'd like that.'

'Oysters?'

'Absolutely.'

There was too much of a queue outside the famed Acme Oyster Bar on Iberville, so they continued on to the Desire on the corner of Bienville and Bourbon Street, attached to the Royal Sonesta Hotel. The maître d' placed them at a corner table which was right under one of the powerfully whirring ceiling fans and was much too cold for the two of them just in short sleeves and they asked to be moved to a table away from the fans.

They ordered the oysters.

The restaurant gradually filled up, making conversation more difficult over the rising hubbub.

After Hopley had settled the bill, they returned to his hotel room by common consent and fell into bed and made love. Slowly, sensuously, now at ease with each other's body, the way they fit together, engaged, synchronised their movement to maximum effect and mutual pleasure. But at the back of his mind, Hopley recalled the way Ramona at the Desire had squinted, peered at the credit card he had placed under the check, as if hoping to find out his real name. He feared her curiosity even as he understood it. Not that her rapid surreptitious glance would have uncovered much in the way of further personal information. He also owned a credit card in the name of the company he had set up for professional use, one he put to use when he was working, but would not take out in her presence. He was always wary. You never knew where a slip up might occur and, despite her perceived innocence and the fact she was unlikely to be anything else than a genuine supply teacher from Manhattan and would be accountant, who rented two rooms in a Brooklyn brownstone and purred like a cat when he touched her in the right places, she formed part of another world altogether which should never cross paths with his kingdom of pain and retribution.

It had always been a matter of survival to keep both worlds apart.

Which, on occasion, Hopley regretted. Bitterly so.

But it was the life he had chosen.

He allowed himself some fleeting thoughts of the way things could be different. Living with someone like Ramona. Loving her full-time, building a relationship. Not having to look back over his shoulders. But it was a dream. Ridiculous wish fulfilment.

Ramona was on her side, her eyes closed, breathing softly, her chest rising slowly with every inhalation, sleepy, soft, her skin a plain of beauty, her nipples still hard from his earlier kisses.

Hopley kept on dreaming. Of those roads he was not taking.

He sighed.

It was mid-afternoon already. The distant sounds of the crowds on nearby Bourbon drifted through the curtains of the bedroom; the windows were wide open to the street.

'Have a little sleep, if you want. It's OK with me,' he said.

Ramona shook her head.

'I should get back to the Marriott. At least get a change of clothes.'

'I understand.'

'Will you wait for me?' Ramona asked.

'Of course.'

He watched her dress, taking mental photographs of how the angles of her limbs formed a perfect geometry, how her hair dropped like silk down to her shoulders, how the curve of her breasts cast a shadow across the skin of her flank as she manoeuvred herself into her bra; smiling as, like so many other women he had known, she dressed her top half while her bottom half was impudently still fully exposed, the pale globes of her sumptuous arse, the dark delta of her pubes. A spectacle he had invariably always found beautifully obscene.

She gave Hopley a peck on the cheek, as she stepped towards the door.

'The Monteleone Bar at eight?' she suggested as she turned away. He had yesterday mentioned how famous the bar was and that she should not be allowed to leave New Orleans without visiting it.

Hopley nodded.

But his heart jumped a beat in the knowledge he was about to betray her.

Ramona had been gone half an hour, by which time he had packed his clothes into his cabin-size hold all, opened the hotel room's safe and pulled out the documents he had been working on before her phone call the previous day.

He carefully checked the contents of the folder. The photos he had taken of the warehouse in Métairie, every surveillance camera surrounding its perimeter ticked off, and the location of the nearby junction box he would have to break into to disable the building's electrics and negligible security system. The hand-drawn map he had sketched of the surrounding area highlighting all the points of entry but more importantly the best roads to escape should matters get complicated. There was also another hand-drawn outline of the geography of the bar in the Business District which his target owned and often spent time at, including the position of every window at the back of the building and a close-up photograph of the lock used on the fire door which was the only way out of the building apart from the front entrance into the bar. He'd read up on the man. Followed him for several hours and seen no sign of any bodyguards. He appeared mob-related and, no doubt, that's where the commission had come from. Misused funds, skimming off profits, drugs, alcohol; it mattered not to Hopley why the man happened to have a price on his head.

He unzipped the side pocket of his holdall and slipped the dossier down inside it.

He rang the airline and confirmed there were still some seats left on the next flight back to New York and booked one. Called reception and ordered a taxi to take him to the airport.

Walked out of the room with its crumpled sheets still no doubt retaining some of the heat of their mingling bodies, their smells, their sweat. He never looked back.

He settled his bill and minutes later the cab drew up outside on Conti Street.

Two hours later, he was at the gate waiting for his flight to be called. There was no woman reading an identical book this time around. Hopley didn't believe in coincidence. By now, he guessed, Ramona would have showered, changed her clothes and was readying to walk the short distance from her hotel on Canal to the Monteleone hoping to find him there.

He tried not to think of her any longer but her memory accompanied him all the way to La Guardia and beyond. She'd been different. If you had asked him, he wouldn't have quite managed to explain why, but somewhere deep inside Hopley was the kernel of a thought that she could have been significant to him. Not just a French Quarter beautiful fuck.

And then he forbade himself to think of Ramona again.

He knew it wouldn't prove easy. An insidious inner voice kept on telling him he had made a bad mistake.

He knew where she worked in Manhattan, even though they had not exchanged numbers or let alone addresses, but Hopley was also aware that what he had done was unforgivable and she was unlikely to accept any excuses if he reappeared on her doorstep out of the blue.

He'd fucked up.

8

The Killer Who Came in from the Cold

The rare book dealers' catalogues and listings kept on falling through her letter box, but it had been ages since Cornelia had identified a title she wanted to add to her growing collection of firsts.

There had been a Gollancz first of *The Spy Who Came in From the Cold*, but by the time she had enquired, it had already been snapped up. At any rate, it had appeared on eBay from a store in New Orleans she had never previously done business with and she doubted they would have agreed to set the book aside for her while she got round to raising the necessary cash, unlike two familiar dealers in California who were usually willing to do so and knew she was reliable.

Maybe she should volunteer to take on a couple of further jobs and build up something of a nest egg to circumvent this happening again?

She lived a frugal life. Money just went on rent, food, and the ever-changing outfits she wore (and quickly disrobed from) when she was stripping. Had it not been for the books she collected, she could live on very little and had no other extravagant needs. She wasn't even keen on travel or vacations. The assignments she took on usually were out of town, and even overseas on occasion and this was travel enough for Cornelia.

She'd built up a good reputation on both fronts.

For the club owners she was one of the more original dancers on the circuit. She was undeniably beautiful but managed to combine both a sense of danger with a contradictory homeliness that made her stand out but difficult to know and, as a result, even more desirable. Her body was lean and mean, her breasts small, her legs unending, her hair a Medusa-like tangle of natural blonde curls and the way she moved on stage was a combination of grace and filth that had most punters desperately hooked from the moment she appeared in the spotlight.

The only criticism her act attracted was the fact that she seldom smiled. But her dancing was undeniably in demand and she was in the privileged situation where she could negotiate jobs from a position of strength, never taking on long residencies and choosing her own preferred hours and slots, often to the displeasure of other dancers with whom she had just a distant relationship that moved between admiration and envy.

She was initially billed as just 'The Glamorous C'.

Following the Tallinn tattoo, she became 'C the Gun'.

Her name on the outside marquee or the neon sign overlooking a club's car park was a guarantee of regular punters, and good tippers at that.

It was a good life.

But her greatest pleasure was falling asleep every night in her duplex apartment on the outskirts of Pasadena and watching the two shelves of rare books on the opposite wall, knowing not just that she owned them, but that they had survived the years, had that undefinable smell of old paper that was almost like an aphrodisiac and the words on the pages would always remain the same, sacrosanct, things of beauty, lines that spoke to her like no human being ever could.

Cornelia had no close friends.

But she had her books.

On a Monday evening in a week where she had no engagements until the Thursday evening, Cornelia received a coded email. She duly acknowledged it and drove to a nearby mall and used a public phone.

'There is a job on offer. It's an urgent one.'

'I wasn't seeking one right now but I'm game.'

She had naturally never explained to her murderous patrons why she sometimes made herself available. They would have probably laughed in her face at reason for accepting hits.

'Thank you for that. But we're asking for a favour. It has to happen this week and we have no other operatives on the West Coast. You'd have to travel to Last Vegas. Not too far from where you're currently located.'

Cornelia was no fan of Vegas. Its vulgarity was contagious. She had been offered countless stripping opportunities there but had always turned them down with little hesitation. Not her sort of town, of sensibility.

'Hmmm …' she said.

'We'll pay double the rate for the short notice involved. Make it worth your while.'

'Can I ask you a question?' she said.

'That depends totally on its nature. This is a business where discretion is important.'

'I understand.'

'So?'

'Am I your only … how can I put it … contractor?' she asked.

'You're not. But our best operator lives on the East Coast and is currently away until further notice. Travelling. Rather inconvenient.'

'I see.'

Cornelia then remembered the fact that Bauman, one of the more exclusive and pricey New York book dealers also had a gallery in Las Vegas. It might offer an opportunity to visit.

Behind her, throngs of identikit shoppers raced between outlets and terrible muzak assaulted her eardrums. She hesitated. Then took a decision.

'I'll do it.'

'Good.'

The reason her employers had chosen her for the hit was her familiarity with the club circuit and the fact that the target had strong connections to it and was known to be a recruiter, although his activities had stretched well beyond and now included trafficking. Cornelia was aware this was not the reason he had been put on the elimination list, far from it, but at least it offered her some extra justification for rubbing him out.

However, she would have to be careful not to reveal her true identity. As she had worked on the circuit and established a strong connection that anyone in the target's inner circle might seize on and would draw their attention to her in the aftermath. It would make sense to have the killing resemble an accident of some sorts.

Cornelia was a good improviser.

A key to a luggage locker would be left for her at the Zanzibar tonight, which she could use at LAX and retrieve the necessary dossier about her target, alongside a credit card that would be used to book her flights to Nevada the following day. A room in a hotel on the strip would by then be booked to the name on the card. She was welcome to use the credit card for any necessary expenses related to the hit, as well as enjoy a generous per diem while she was on the job.

Vanessa, one of the baristas, was surprised to see her walk in to the club that evening.

'I didn't think you were working until Thursday.'

'I'm not. And there is a slight chance I might not be able to fulfil that slot either. I have to go out of town. Not sure how long for.'

She found the locker key wrapped in a well-sealed black plastic bag inside the cistern in the backstage women's toilet as arranged and returned home to pack a small bag. Her flight was early the next morning.

The flight was a short one and she reached the `Strip' by mid-morning, catching a cab with an annoyingly inquisitive and loquacious Filipino driver from the airport. As ever, the car glided into the city itself, like a projectile arriving from the desert and breaching a wall of light. She had visited once before and taken a profound dislike to the entrenched vulgarity of the place. Had even managed to spend a whole week there without gambling a single cent. They were still serving breakfast at her hotel, a monstrous amalgam of ersatz Chinese architecture with pagodas galore and a gallery of slot machines chink-chinking away between the reception area and the bank of elevators.

Dropping her bag in the room, Cornelia took a quick shower to refresh herself and then headed down to the hotel's giftshop. As she hoped, it was well stocked with all sorts of both gaming and glamour paraphernalia and she acquired a short wig; she would be a redhead with a Louise Brooks-styled bob. She also picked up the sort of make-up she would not normally use, even for her stage gigs. Brash colours with no subtlety, glittery eyeliner, and a pair of towering showgirl heels that she would normally not be seen dead in.

She returned to her room and rang the number she had been given of the target's office and, after a few begging attempts, pretending she was a poor visiting gal from Omaha, Nebraska, desperately in search of a gig, and pretending between muffled sobs he was her last-ditch chance and she was stone broke. If only he could grant her an interview, she assured him he would not be disappointed and she would be eternally grateful if he might be able to provide her a job as a waitress or a cigarette girl at one his establishments.

He relented and gave her an appointment early that evening at his penthouse hotel suite at the Luxor, which she had been warned in the dossier he was in the habit of using as a casting couch or more.

He was just a pornographer and had, she knew, no personal security.

Vegas was however a nightmare alley of CCTV cameras, particularly so inside the hotels and she spent much of the afternoon transforming herself, in an effort not to leave too much of an impression that might subsequently lead back to her.

The thin cotton skirt skimmed the lower cheek of her arse, the silk blouse was almost opaque and barely concealed the presence of the nipple studs she had acquired earlier and clipped on for the occasion. Had Cornelia known how much they would initially prove painful with every single movement she made she might have dispensed with them, but then it kept her on her toes and alert, she reckoned. She trimmed the wig so that just a quarter of her facial features could at most be captured by the intrusive lenses of the cameras in the lobby of the Luxor, and the elevator and the corridors she would have to gingerly make her way down on those impossible heels. The lipstick highlighting her lips was deep scarlet and aggressive, and she was careful to not follow the precise contour of her own mouth, muddying any likely attempt at later facial recognition. A trick she had picked up from a bad thriller book. She'd slathered dark blusher and foundation across her cheeks and almost looked exotic and not her usual pale waif persona. She topped matters off with a pair of super-sized sunglasses that Elton John in his glittery heyday would have been proud of. She knew she looked like a cheap whore, a provincial tramp with no sense of fashion or decorum, naively struggling to play a part she couldn't fit. Perfect.

She saw the man's eyes light up as he opened the door for her.

He was alone, as she had hoped.

'You look wonderful, darling,' he said.

'Thank you, Sir.'

'First of all, let me offer you a drink.'

'That would be nice.'

He sat her on a low couch where he had a close and uninterrupted view of her legs and more as he settled himself down in an armchair opposite her. Although she had not opted for the no underwear option. Not something even a desperate girl from Omaha would lower herself to do.

She explained her plight.

He nodded.

'I'd do anything. Well, almost …'

He smiled. Weighing her up, calculating the options no doubt, legal and otherwise.

'I'm sure we can find something in my organisation,' he finally said. 'There are quite a few possibilities I can think of,' he added.

'Oh, jeez, that would be so wonderful, Mr. Thomson.'

There was no way that was his real name. His voice had Eastern European intonations to it.

'So, tell me more about you, Carla?'

He refilled her glass. She'd kept a close eye on him throughout and was confident he hadn't slipped anything into the drink. That was actually more her scene!

'This is such a wonderful suite. Is it what they call a penthouse?'

'It is. Nothing but the best. Would you like a small tour? I'd be happy to show you the rest, Carla.'

She knew the bedroom would be an inevitable stop-over but delayed matters by asking him if they could move to the suite's balcony so she could see the lights of Las Vegas and the Strip in all their splendour as night was falling.

He readily agreed. Yes, it was sight to behold, he confirmed as he led her to the window and pulled the curtains apart so they could find a place on the balcony.

Five minutes later he had taken the fall, dropping to his death 30 floors below. So shocked was he at being forcibly pushed across the balcony railing that he didn't even think of screaming.

She hadn't even been forced to undress.

Cornelia exited through the service stairs and walked back to her own hotel where she promptly cleaned up, washing the gaudy warpaint away, changed into the simple combination of jeans and white T-shirt, and reverted to her natural appearance and colours before taking a cab to the airport.

By midnight she was home in Pasadena.

9

Edward Hopper Doesn't Live Here anymore

Hopley was getting itchy feet. He hadn't worked since the New Orleans job.

He rang Irish Ivan. Who was neither Russian nor Irish and actually had something of a Canadian accent.

'Long time.'

'I was away.'

'And now you're back.'

He was a man of few words.

'Been back for several months, in fact. But you've only given me a single assignment in six months or more. I like to keep my hand in. Not good to get rusty.'

'Welcome back, then.'

'You haven't made contact. No work around? What happened to the Paris job you had mentioned a while ago? You said it might wait until I returned.'

'It couldn't. Someone else took care of it.'

'Oh. Who?'

'None of your business.'

'Just curious.'

'And the job was done well?'

'Absolutely. You're not the only one around with the required skills, Hop.'

He hated when Irish Ivan called him Hop. Irish knew it. Did it deliberately.

He didn't rise to the bait.

'Don't call us, we'll call you.'

Hopley was curious. The following day he ambled over

to the New York Public Library and researched the newspapers for the months he had been away, looking out for unsolved deaths in Paris. There were a lot. He could have gone through the exercise on the Internet, but Hopley liked to research data the old-fashioned way and, anyway, computers sometimes left trails, history you couldn't erase.

It took him several hours, eliminating instances of deaths and murders through a process of intuitive guesswork.

'FRENCH HUMAN TRAFFICKER BUTCHERED IN SEX CLUB.'

This could be it.

Not the way Hopley would have done the job, but a curious one nonetheless.

The reports mentioned two unidentified women the Paris police were keen to speak to.

Hopley's interest was piqued. One of the women must have been the killer, and the other some sort of distraction or unfortunate witness. Killers didn't come in pairs. It doubled the risks.

So, the Bureau had a woman on the payroll. A rival, a fellow traveller in the dark arts. He was intrigued. On previous assignments he had often reflected on the fact that had he been of the fairer sex, the task at hand might have proved more straightforward on certain occasions.

A week later, he had a call and moved on to organise his next paid hit.

He was sitting on a high stall in a bar called Phillies with his back to the nocturnal street. Across to his left, a man and a woman silently stared straight ahead at the white-capped, blonde clerk busy cleaning dishes. The baseball cap-wearing man negligently nursed a cigarette while the woman, red-haired, in her late 30s he guessed, peered down at her well-manicured nails. There was no juke box. There was no noise except for the occasional gurgle of the twin coffee percolators on the nearby counter. It was a perfect three-in-the-morning silence, made for night hawks and lonely hearts. The woman in the couple was thin, even gaunt, the silky fabric of her red dress draped across her shoulders, opening up across a V of indifferent pale flesh. She sported aggressively red lipstick, just like Hopley imagined vamps did in black and white 40s noir movies. The couple hadn't spoken to each other since he walked into the joint. But their body movement betrayed the fact they were a couple, likely one of long standing. Only deep familiarity expressed itself this way, communicated in such a display of common silence.

Outside, it'd been ages since any car had driven by. They were enveloped in a sea of dead time, an urban *nature morte*, listening to the mute voice of the downtown Los Angeles night. Figueroa Boulevard was just a few blocks away, even more deserted than usual at this time of night. There was no game that night at the massive stadium by the nearby convention centre, so no stragglers were ambling aimlessly by or zigzagging their way past the flaming radiance of this old-fashioned street corner diner in search of a car parked forgetfully somewhere close some hours earlier.

Hopley sipped his second glass of cola. The ice cubes had long melted and diluted the syrupy sugar fix of the beverage. He kept on observing the couple, imagining their backstory, inventing a whole scenario to justify their presence here, to explain the way they once met and the curious reasons or apathy that seemingly still bound them together when they visibly had so little to say to each other. Surely, they had somewhere to return to? Hopley didn't. In a few more hours he would call for a cab and get it to drive him back to L.A. International for the first morning flight of the day to La Guardia or Newark and his apartment on Washington Square Park, with an unobstructed view of the arch and the wandering squirrels on the lawn. There he would while away the days until the next telephone call from Ivan Irish summoned him for yet another job. He would accept it, even though he didn't really need the money. Practice makes perfect and he never said no when offered a further hit. He had a reputation to protect, after all, now there was a hint of competition on the horizon. Anyway, he was no good at anything else.

He thought of Ramona.

Again.

But the memory was too painful. Hopley reasoned that life is just a shopping list of missed opportunities and roads not taken.

But it didn't help.

He quietly wondered whether the other insomniacs keeping him company in Phillies might also be speculating about his own presence here? He doubted it. He was anonymous. No one remembered his face. His hat was grey felt and his two-piece suit a boring anthracite blue, his hair was cut short and his shape was somewhat stocky. He could lose a few pounds. He guessed he looked like an insurance salesman. Which was good; because it was a suitable appearance, made him blend in. Forgettable. Indifferent. Safe. He should know, he was once a military cop, a run of the mill detective who happened to be too much of a loner to make the higher grade. Tradition dictated that cops should run in pairs, play the buddy game but he had always functioned better as a lone wolf. It just wasn't his style or inclination, and he had invariably alienated all his appointed partners. Nothing spectacular, no fights or endless arguments, caused the obligatory rift, but eventually all those he was paired with moved on of their own accord, leaving Hopley with a tainted reputation as a distant and uncooperative loner. Which was fine by him but didn't look too good on his record. So, one day, he had resigned his commission and moved across to the other side. It was easy to get connected after patrolling the dark side.

Once you've swum in one pool, it was easy to navigate in its counterpart. Hopley knew what to do and what not to do. He'd never much been encumbered by rules and regulations, or morality anyway.

So, there he was now, an anonymous man in a bar

whose face anyone would forget no more than an hour later, watching the world go by and wasting time until it was time to leave the city. Your average, ordinary contract killer.

Killing off what was left of the night.

The woman in the couple briefly glanced his way, but she visibly didn't truly note his presence, her gaze passing straight through him and likely alighting on some passer-by walking outside or a car drifting across the length of the boulevard, turning the corner on a slow journey towards Chinatown, just a mile or so away to the East. Her eyes were rimmed with too much kohl; didn't suit her, made her look older than she was. She glanced away, her indifference returning. Her silent partner lit another cigarette while the attendant refilled his cup of coffee. Night rituals.

Hopley couldn't help reminiscing. Maybe it was something about that time of night where the emptiness outside reflected the one that lay inside him.

Sometimes it was the ghosts of those he had killed that came back, not so much to haunt him – he wasn't that superstitious – but to chide him and remind him of all the many things that were missing in his life. And to wickedly point out how little there was for him to look forward to, if his life continued unfolding in the same manner, punctuated by jobs and with beaches of creeping dissatisfaction in between.

Was he always this way?

He was unsure.

Is it some form of guilt now assailing him?

He looked down at the black Tissot watch on his left wrist. The seconds tick off, slower than ever. Every minute felt like an hour. How much longer should he sit here and brood dangerously? *What's happening to me?* He'd always been a total cynic, dismissing all talk of mental health, believing it to be a sop for weaker souls, not something that could ever affect him.

For the first time in his life, he now had doubts.

'I am perfectly sane,' He muttered under his breath.

He blamed Ramona.

Why did he miss her so much?

He could park himself at the end of the school day outside the Friends Seminary, the Quaker school where she worked in midtown. Surprise her. But surely by now, she was no longer teaching and is juggling figures in ledgers or on screen as a fully qualified accountant, as she had hoped.

But what would he even say to her?

What excuses could he conjure up that would hit the right note and avoid her fully deserved scorn?

And even if he were to sway her and resume some form of relationship, what then?

How to explain his regular absences, the secrets he preciously concealed?

Hopley sighed.

It just wouldn't work.

10
Bruises on the Landscape

Hopley still sat on the same stall a full hour later. The sky outside would soon change its colours and beaches of grey will paint the sky.

Dawn. Another day.

With much effort, he had banished the spectre of Ramona from his mind. For now.

He tried to recall the eyes of the other woman, earlier in the evening. The younger one at the scene. What colour were they? He couldn't. He focused his attention on that minor detail. Much of what took place did so in part darkness, an oppressive penumbra, a stage in which he had played the leading murderous role. There had, he noted, been a haunting quality in those eyes when she had pleaded for her life. He had even briefly wavered. She had begged for his mercy. She was just in the wrong place at the wrong time. Damn!

'My name is Sarah,' she had declared frantically, looking towards Hopley with a sadness full of resignation, as if she already knew he could not be swayed and would make no exception to his principles for her. And even though Sarah was not a player in the untold game, she was instinctively aware of the fact.

He had not responded immediately.

'I will do anything you wish me to do,' she had continued. 'Or rather you can do anything to me you want. Anything.'

Maybe it was what she saw in Hopley's eyes that made her plead and say such pitiful things. He had heard people describe his own eyes as dark and the colour of night, steely and unfeeling. When he shaved in the mornings and examined his features in the bathroom mirror, he saw no such thing. He only saw sadness. But eyes are just eyes, he reckoned; they convey nothing.

'I'm just a bystander. I only see the guy on occasions, you know. Nothing permanent. Through an online network. I have nothing else to do with him. Don't even know his real name. He just rang me gave me the address and the room number. I'd only just arrived. I promise I won't tell. I'm just not involved in his life in any permanent way. Don't even know his name.'

The body of the man who had summoned her to this hotel room for sex was sprawled just a few feet away across the carpeted floor, stone cold dead. A single bullet had sufficed. It seldom took more; Hopley knew where to aim. Don't believe what you see in the movies. Killing a man with a gun is simplicity itself if you know where to strike and had a steady hand and the advantage of surprise. He had been supplied with a few, blurry photographs of his target when he had taken on the assignment and had stealthily followed him from his office as a realtor in Beverly Hills (no doubt a cover, but that wasn't Hopley's concern) to this rococo hotel downtown with a fascinating over-the-top décor that blended equal doses of terracotta Mexican colours with Indian artefacts and monstrously-sized potted plants strewn throughout its dark lobby area. The mark had parked his pastel-shaded Chevy in a lot at the back of the hotel, which didn't communicate with it directly, which had allowed Hopley time enough to move ahead and innocently share the elevator with him up to his floor. The man hadn't even given him a sideways glance. He had jumped him just as he was opening the door to his room with a key card. As the lock clicked Hopley had put the gun to his head and sharply shoved against the man's shoulders and forced him stumbling into the room.

It took Hopley a second or so to take it all in. The young woman, sitting on the bed adjusting her stocking, looked up with an air of surprise at Hopley and her client barging forcefully past the door. She was not expecting two men. Maybe a proposition she was particularly averse to, or that at any rate had not been mentioned to her and might require a considerable adjustment to her fee. The way her mouth formed an 'o' of surprise. The mark was just about to say something in protest when Hopley pressed the trigger, and the muffled sound of the weapon's silencer interrupted the *nature morte* of the scene that was so rapidly unfolding. The victim slumped to his knees, and then almost in slow motion to the hotel room floor, his limbs spreading incongruously across the shagpile carpet, his face three quarters burying itself into its lush texture.

Still frozen in shock, the escort's mouth returned to its normal thin-lipped shape; she was rooted to the spot on the sofa, a single stocking rolled halfway down, no doubt a million emotions, questions and fear spreading through her body.

The hit was clean. There wasn't even much blood, yet.

Hopley looked at her again.

Their eyes locked.

A torrent of silent communications and entreaties surging across the darkened, pastel-coloured room in the utter stillness of the late afternoon. All things unsaid but sadly clear in their respective minds.

Witnesses have no rights.

This was when she revealed her name to Hopley as he stood there, gun still in hand. In a forlorn bid to humanise herself. To make him revise his obvious resolve.

He didn't respond, just stood there, his legs now straddling the inert body of his designated victim.

'You can have me,' she continued. 'I won't say anything. I never saw anything. Let me go. PLEASE …'

She didn't at first glance look like a whore. She was more upmarket in appearance and speech. He speculated: maybe a girlfriend, or another man's wife the dead man was enjoying on the side? That's what hotel rooms were for, wasn't it? Her two-piece ensemble had a conservative cut, only spoiled by the fact that, on their abrupt arrival, the skirt had been hoisted up to mid-thigh as she had been adjusting the line of her stockings in expectation. The upper, uncovered half of her thigh was creamy, white, almost virginal in shade, above the darker, flesh-coloured fabric of the hold-up stocking.

No garter belt; Hopley couldn't help noticing.

As he kept on looking at her in silence, the echo of the gun's detonation now just a distant, muffled sigh, she continued to plead with him, a one-way dialogue born of desperation.

'Would you ever allow me to leave?' she asked quietly, as if she no longer believed it could happen.

'I fear not,' Hopley replied.

'Why?'

'Because.'

She lowered her eyes. Sighed.

Hopley felt sad. There was no enjoyment to be found in killing innocents. He was not a sadist.

She slumped, her shoulders sagging, her lips dry, the beat of her heart slowing in anticipation.

'Now?' she whispered, seemingly becoming resigned to her fate.

Hopley stepped nearer to the sofa where she was sitting.

Looked down at her. Juggling mental scenarios where her demise would fit in with the presence of a dead man now bleeding out on the floor.

'A waste, I know,' as if apologising.

'Yes,' she agreed, her voice a thin sliver escaping from her mouth, touching the very root of his heart, or was it just his stomach? Sometimes, deep emotions affected him in very curious physical ways.

A flash of Ramona's face invading his thoughts - he wanted to ask this young woman so many questions. Who she was, why she was here, the precise nature of her relationship with the dead man? Transactional, he guessed, but maybe not?

He wanted to know all about this woman he was automatically programmed to kill. But he knew it was impossible. He couldn't afford the time.

Her name was Sarah. That was all he would be allowed to know.

'Get up,' Hopley ordered.

She rose from the edge of the low-flung sofa and stood, her gloved hands by her side. She was shorter than he'd expected.

Sarah looked towards him, awaiting a further instruction, a veil of sadness drifting across her freckled face.

'Had he paid you in advance?' Hopley asked her.

She blushed. He was unsure whether the question embarrassed or angered her.

That sudden streak of emotion made her look quite beautiful, though, more alive, alert. Her cheeks an attenuated shade of pink that served to emphasise the sharp delineation of her cheekbones.

'With him,' she nodded towards the body, 'it wasn't just to do with money. Absolutely nothing.'

'Love?'

Hopley reconsidered. So not an escort? It unsettled him.

'No. Nor lust either,' Sarah answered.'

As Hopley seemed taken aback by her response, she brazenly straightened out her whole body, escaping her previous slump, almost growing by an inch as her back snapped into position.

'You just wouldn't understand,' Sarah defiantly stated. 'Not in a month of Sundays.'

No, he couldn't.

'Undress,' he ordered her.

She obeyed unconditionally, without a single word of complaint. He knew it wasn't out of fear. But, paradoxically, hostility.

Like so many women Hopley had known when they shed their clothing, she began by the bottom. She unzipped the invisible fastening on the right side of her skirt and the light fabric of the garment slid down to the floor where she elegantly stepped out of it. She wasn't wearing any undergarments and was shaven smooth, which just took his breath way, surprising him. She allowed him an interminable minute of oppressive silence to collect his thoughts and drink in the vision of her obscene, extreme nudity, just standing there in stockinged legs and nothing else.

Her sexual slit was a straight-line gash from which neither inner nor outer labia protruded, like a raw wound, a scar that hypnotised him. Hopley couldn't help but unashamedly stare at it.

The straightest of lines, like the work of a scalpel.

Then she rapidly shed the rest of her clothes., the suit jacket, the opaque black cotton blouse, and a small, and somewhat superfluous brassiere, which then revealed slight dark-nippled breasts he could have cupped in one hand, delicate hills in the olive- shaded landscape of her body.

Hopley couldn't help peering at her.

Once he had taken in her prominent sexual characteristics, he quickly noted that the whole geography of her flesh was dotted with small bruises. These blemishes travelled across a whole spectrum of colours from dark, almost blue to brown and pale-yellow areas where the skin had begun repairing itself.

These bruises had been created over a sustained period of time; there was no way they could all have been caused on the same occasion.

'Turn round.'

She did so, with elfin grace.

The checkerboard of bruises also generously populated her back, prominently spread across her thighs, with even redder, fiercer lines of impact, like the lingering remnants of whip lashes or continuous caning, crisscrossing her slightly androgynous buttocks.

In the small of her back, there was the tattoo of a Chinese ideogram, which Hopley was unable to recognise. He should have asked her but didn't.

He had a million questions for Sarah, but none could tunnel their way through the tortuous journey from his brain cells to his lips.

'Touch me.'

It was, evidently, her turn to give orders.

Hesitantly, Hopley moved an arm forward, brushed his fingers against one of her shoulders. Her skin felt damp. But electric. He slowly moved upwards, sliding his fingers through her short ash blonde hair. Like a journey through silk.

He made a mental note of some of the more prominent bruises on her body, a soiled few square inches of flesh between her navel and her cunt where the skin had almost broken and still waltzed between dark tones of black and a borderline crater of yellow. He approached and touched her there. The softness was divine. He perversely pressed harder.

'Does it hurt?' he asked.

'No,' she replied.

His fingers lingered over the flatness of her lower stomach, bathing in the nearby heat radiating in concentric circles from her sexual opening outwards. The pink gash of her intimacy was short and straight as a ruler, highlighted by her state of depilation. He'd seen shaven mounds in magazines and dubious movies, but this was actually the first Hopley had come across in real life.

'Did he beat you?'

'Not him,' Sarah said, nodding at the dead man on the floor. 'Others. He arranged it.'

'More than one?'

'Yes.'

'I see.' That was all he could prosaically find to say in the circumstance. Maybe an added reason for the victim to have deserved to die.

'I didn't mind,' she said.

'Really?'

'You can, too, if you want.'

'I'm not that sort of person.'

'How do you know?' Sarah responded. 'I'm available.

I'm here. I'm yours for the taking, anyway you wish. I won't scream. Pain Is sometimes good for the soul '

As she said that, all Hopley's imagination could conjure was the image of her being punched and whipped by other men, while she kept her silence and tears rolled down her cheeks.

How could she have enjoyed, accepted it, he wondered?

'You know I can't,' he said. Then added, 'But I like what I see. Without the bruises, the marks. Really.'

She sighed.

'Why did you ask me strip, then?'

'I have to make it look natural,' Hopley indicated.

'What is natural?'

'Two bodies, and what people, the police will think … Complicate the scenario; muddy the waters … Give them a jigsaw to assemble, one that both makes sense and no sense at all.'

A veil drifted across her eyes.

'Do it now, then.'

But he knew he couldn't shoot her point blank. Not like this. Not after witnessing the wonder and questions raised by the spectacle of her nude body and the complicated but fascinating tales it evoked. He could sense the strong tremor of life and softness coursing through her skin, the unknown history buried inside her soft Southern burr.

If he shot her, it would now be showing total disrespect, assimilating her to that piece of shit now draining dark blood over there by the door on the hotel room flooring.

A man who had repeatedly taken advantage of her submissiveness, her masochism.

She deserved better.

He'd reached a decision.

He nodded to Sarah, indicating the window that opened on South Figueroa Boulevard. Her eyes questioned him silently. Hopley blinked once and she understood.

That it would almost painless and instant.

She felt grateful for that.

The flight of her naked body through the air was not unlike the dance of a butterfly in the summer breeze, weightless and beautiful, as she swam downwards to the ground in slow motion, fluttering her invisible wings, her bare limbs caressed by the slight wind from the sea, her bruises like a kaleidoscope of colours indelibly inked across her white skin, floating, smiling.

Hopley looked away as he stood on the balcony watching her descent. She hit the ground.

Now he waited in Phillies for the long Californian night to end so he could catch the first flight out of town, wasting the remaining hours of darkness in an almost empty bar and inventing stories in his mind about the other souls present. The couple across from him were still communicating in total silence.

Not long to go.

He had a bit of cramp, a muscle giving him grief in his right shoulder, maybe caused by the recoil of the gun earlier. He must be getting older, he reckoned, no longer able to absorb the reverse shock wave in his gun arm. He shifted imperceptibly in the high stall, and across his shoulder, he caught sight of a man across the street, observing the café, sketching on a pad. For the unknown nocturnal artist, Hopley guessed, we and the other occupants of Phillies must be standing in an eerie pool of light and forming an image worth remembering or jotting down on paper. Anonymous shapes in a composition made of light and dark. The man looked quite tall and balding, an imposing Patrician-like man.

Hopley pivoted on the stall and had a closer look at the distant artist, watching as he drew a final line on his pad and, satisfied, closed it, and began to walk away, almost immediately melting into the night's surroundings.

Hopley adjusted his position and took another sip of now tepid and watered-down cola from his glass.

Nighthawks.

Who did the guy think he was? Edward Hopper?

11
Blondes and Redheads

Cornelia had been back in L.A. for a fortnight and had agreed to a week's residency at Razorblades, a club in Malibu that had delusions of grandeur but a safe clientele of mostly generous tippers. It was generally full of visitors to the city and the coast and just a few locals. She'd never worked there before and the gig had, exceptionally, come through an agent. She normally dealt with the clubs and their owners directly on a freelance basis, and had turned down numerous offers from this booking agency to join their fold of dancers. She was a free agent, and preferred it that way. Less questions to answer when she had to take off on a job in her other capacity. Accepting this job was something of an experiment.

To avoid travelling the busy highways surrounding the city, she had checked in to a small nearby motel for the duration, close to the beach and had not been in her apartment for several days and missed the messages.

She only worked the late evening shifts and spent most of her afternoons, after lazy mornings reading in bed, sprawling in the late spring sand, and had even contemplated taking surfing lessons, as she watched others dance around the waves on their colourful boards, but quickly concluded it wasn't her scene, and the dancing was exercise enough.

She was parking her rental Mazda outside the club, when Samuel Trimlin emerged from the surrounding penumbra, a heavy lumbering presence.

'Fancy seeing you here!'

'It's no accident. I've been searching for you all over the place. Checking out every single joint. I didn't think you worked this side of town.'

'It's a first. I wanted some sea breeze. Half vacation, half work …'

'I've been trying to reach you since last week.'

'What about? You know the procedure when it comes to assignments. And anyway, I normally like to take time off in between jobs and the Vegas gig is too recent.'

'That's what I needed to talk to you about.'

'Oh!'

'There is a potential problem …'

It had made the newspaper headlines. Not the front page, but well-featured on page three: MOB BOSS FALLS TO MYSTERIOUS DEATH ON THE STRIP.

'Tell me.'

Sunset was falling across the nearby sands, as they stood in the parking lot, in the shadow of her dimmed car lights. Trimlin wished to speak here and not inside the club, so they were not seen by too many others.

'Your Nevada target. His associates suspect it was not an accident.'

'So, what's the problem? It would come as no surprise that he wasn't a candidate for suicide.'

'They must have some informant in the local cop shop and were provided access to the hotel's CCTV records.'

'Damn it.'

'They're looking for a woman.'

'Is that all? Every Las Vegas hotel is crawling with women, whores, tourists, staff, and all that. We're thirteen to the dozen. I was careful.'

'I'm sure you were. She has red hair.'

'I wore a wig.'

But Cornelia was annoyed that they had managed to pinpoint her so precisely.

'I realise that.'

'So?'

'Somehow they've managed to narrow it down. Dangerous people have been asking around the clubs about tall dancers. With red hair, of course. But, no pun intended, anyone would guess it was a wig. Hair colour aside, the description they have does point to a tall, willowy girl who might be a showgirl or have a stage background.'

'There are thousands of us,' Cornelia protested, but deep inside she knew it was the way she moved that had probably betrayed her background. Once a dancer, always a dancer. Not something she could easily disguise. Unless she masqueraded in a wheelchair.

'What do you suggest I do?'

'The Bureau feels you should make yourself scarce for a time. Vanish from public view a while.'

'That bad?'

'We cannot run the risk of them locating you. We also believe they have connected you to the Anaheim hit you completed last year. It's our mistake, we only realised now that both men worked for the same group; they have evidently put one and one together, I fear …'

She remembered that night. She lusted for a Faulkner first edition and the target was a veritable pig, pawing all over her at the bar, almost slobbering at the prospect of guiding her to his bedroom upstairs later. Someone must have juxtaposed the CCTV coverage of that hotel with the footage from the Luxor, and noted the similarities in body shape and movement, even though she was always careful to muddy the waters with a different style of clothing and varying her make-up on each new occasion on the job. She no longer recalled with any precision how she had styled herself that particular night.

Just that she had used a scalpel. Repeatedly, as the guy just disgusted her to the core of her soul and the results had been particularly messy and it had taken her hours afterwards to clean herself properly in the shower, washing away every blood splatter coating the exposed part of her body in the action.

He had taken ages to die.

'What if I changed coasts? Make myself scarce for a prolonged period. I'm tiring of this place anyway.'

Trimlin pondered.

'That might work. They'll give up their enquiries if it all goes quiet, I expect.'

Cornelia had in fact been thinking for some time now that she should maybe move to New York. Or Boston.

Not a new life. She would still dance. And strip. But it was an environment that, she felt, would be more conducive to her book collecting and her peace of mind. The East Coast just felt more civilised than California.

Aside from Tallinn and Vegas all her kills had been local. Moving away would feel like starting again.

'You'll need a new handler,' Trimlin pointed out.

'Would that be a problem for you?'

'No. It's not a business where sentiment holds much of a place. But I would miss you.'

'Will you really?'

He grinned.

'A little.'

He knew she was not the sentimental sort.

'If you move away, will you keep on dancing? Stripping?'

'Absolutely.'

'Surely you don't need the money, do you?'

She was paid in the five figures for every hit.

'I don't do it for the money.'

'Ah.'

Cornelia pointed at the nearby building.

'Should I go in and fulfil my gig?'

'I suppose there is no harm in doing so. I might even come and watch … I've never had the pleasure.'

'You dirty old man.'

Trimlin didn't know if she was being serious. He had never been able to pinpoint if Cornelia had a sense of humour.

'You'd better tip good,' she added.

He did.

The following morning, she left the motel and returned home to her Pasadena apartment and set matters in motion.

She had settled for New York.

She might fit better.

She phoned a realtor and put her place up for sale.

Two weeks later, she was in Manhattan, temporarily staying in an Airbnb on Wooster Street in SoHo while she hunted for suitable accommodation.

Her book collection had to go into storage until she had a permanent place to live. That was the only immediate drawback. She was in no hurry, acclimating to the different rhythms of this new city, learning its ebb and flow, its scents and sounds, wandering aimlessly as her mood dictated. Spending hours in the Strand Rare Book Room, contemplating future acquisitions, wiping the dust off used volumes at the Mercer Street Bookshop, enjoying late morning coffee and Danish at the Union Square Barnes & Noble café or perusing the new title table at McNally Jackson on Prince Street in Nolita.

Just like a typical New Yorker, she felt.

A woman of leisure.

Prim and proper.

Then she remembered how she missed the lights, the exhilaration of being on a stage, the way men held their breath when she waltzed on to the dance floor, how she danced and teased and moved and provoked in turn, feeling as if she intimately controlled every one of them, puppets on an invisible string of desire, by their minds and parts as she flaunted her pallor and her soon to be unveiled secrets.

And knew it was time again at last to become whole.

She had been given some names and telephone numbers, and naturally came highly recommended.

She made appointments.

At each meeting she made it clear what she wasn't.

She would not do private lap dances.

She would only dance twice on any evening, even if other dancers were off and slots had to be filled in the line-up.

She retained all her tips, with the house not taking any percentage., nor would she place a percentage in a pot to be shared with the other performers.

She would not contribute a house fee to the club.

She could cancel any evening's work with no notice.

Only the taped music she brought along could be played when she danced.

Cornelia knew what she was worth and would not budge on any of these points.

Most club managers or owners agreed to her terms. Mostly those who had echoes of her reputation (and inflexibility) back in California.

Only one asked to peruse the 'goods' at their interview, and she promptly walked out on him and put the club on her personal blacklist.

She was Cornelia.

C the Gun.

She did not negotiate.

They knew, from word of mouth, she always delivered and would attract many new customers once the word got out on the streets.

But neither was she in any hurry to resume her dancing. A loft near Chinatown had come up on the property market and she had made an offer. Only once she had moved in, had shelved her precious book collection, and was properly settled in New York would she begin working again.

On stage, at any rate.

In the meantime, she needed extra money to complete the acquisition of her new home.

She emailed the address she had been given, expressing her immediate availability.

With the savings she had already squirrelled away, all it would take would be one more hit to have enough in hand, she estimated. East Coast kill rates were, for some reason, higher than the West Coast's, but then the risks were greater for a variety of reasons. Which was fortunate for Cornelia as there was of course no way she could apply for any kind of mortgage, considering both her professions, and the absence of any official credit rating.

Her timing was lucky.

They sent her to Paris.

She'd always wanted to visit the French capital.

'But I don't speak French.'

'It shouldn't prove a problem,' said the voice down the phone. 'Some skills don't require much of a vocabulary.'

There was another voice on the phone too.

Her newly-appointed New York handler or point of contact.

Unlike Trimlin who always preferred to use public payphones, he demanded she acquire a burner phone, to be strictly used only for their communications. Not enough public payphones in Manhattan worked properly.

His name was Irish and she quickly realised he was much tougher than his L.A. counterpart. He didn't sound Irish a single bit. Would tolerate no nonsense or delay. She would have no choice if a job came up. No opportunity to do it in her own time. If so required, she would make herself available immediately and never delay. No excuses. Anything going on in her private life would have to be dropped.

'That's the way it is. We do things differently here.'

He made clear their relationship as employer and employee.

This worried Cornelia.

She'd always been pretty ambiguous about authority.

'We' shall see about that,' she thought.

12
The Music, the Dance and the Trance

Darkness.

The stage.

A single spotlight threw a growing circle of light towards the raised stage.

At first, silence. Just the tremor of expectation in the air, as the customers twitched in their velvet-lined seats and, further back, in the calculated darkness of the circular room, on the banquettes.

Glasses clinked.

The shuffling of feet, as the punters nervously waited for the set to begin. Anticipating, licking their lips, holding their breath, their eyes wide open ready for a feast that would connect with every nerve in their body, trigger their goosepimples, tease their extremities.

The cash register back at the bar opened and closed like a clap of thunder, interrupting the silence. A waitress in tight black slacks, white cotton shirt and a bow tie circulated around the crowded tables depositing and collecting glasses, making her way through the night of the club like a blind woman with X-ray vision, secure in her knowledge of the territory, the geography of the floor she navigated.

A muffled sound drifted towards their ears as the PA system was switched back on.

A voice.

Suave, suggestive, an aural form of leer.

'Gentlemen, our star act for tonight.'

Someone at the back coughed. Another cleared his

throat.

'None other than the wonderful, the sexy, the dangerous … CARLA … '

There was a smattering of applause which soon cut off abruptly as those putting their hands together realised they were in a minority and ignorant of the right etiquette. Newcomers.

The announcer continued; his tone of voice clearly annoyed by the interruption of his shtick.

'… the wonderful, the unique … CARLA THE GUN …'

Breaths were held.

A whisper here 'Why the gun?'

A furtive answer 'Just wait and see …'

The auditorium was full. An upper-class club just a block from the SoHo Grand called The Walkabouts. Regulars, visitors from all over had flocked to it. Her first East Coast appearance. Her reputation preceded her.

The spotlight faded to dark.

The music began.

Moby's *Porcelain*.

Under the cover of darkness, Cornelia glided onto the stage as if springing out of nowhere, just an evanescent shape for the spectators in the back rows or a fuzz of a cloud for those nearer the actual proscenium.

The lights came on. Suddenly, with violent visual impact, flooding the stage with white fire and pinpointing the slim young woman motionless like a statue standing at its very centre. The onlookers blinked at the ferociousness of the spotlights in the gantry as they assaulted the stage and Cornelia.

The music was serene, like the way the sea sounded as wave crashed calmly against and over wave, fluid geometry in motion caressing the shape of water, like a sheer desert of sand in motion, if it happened to be a melody.

Still Cornelia remained motionless.

She was wearing very little.

Her satin G-string was virgin white and adhered to her

skin like a shroud pulled tight around her intimacy. Her legs appeared to stretch on forever. The camisole covering the top of her body was made of the same shimmering material, equally white, and fell loosely from her shoulders to her waist, its straight flow barely interrupted by the gentle rise of her nipples behind the material. Her blonde Medusa-like curls had been teased and shaped into what almost appeared to be a Greek goddess's helmet, lacquered, shining like a golden halo.

She wore no make-up on her face whatsoever.

Her eyes stared into the distance like blue steel, her nose pert, her cheekbones straight as razor blades.

A synth rumbled below the song's melody, underpinning its flow while Cornelia matched her body to its rhythm and slowly raised her left arm, extending her fingers with agonising slowness, then her left leg set in motion, forming a demi circle like a ballerina flexing her muscles at the bar.

She was not wearing shoes. Her toe nails were painted gold.

Finally, the rest of her body was activated as if by remote control and she pirouetted in slow motion, one full circle, so that all her curves are seen in action, presented to her admirers out in the club's pit.

Every movement was synchronised to the music, adhering to its tune like clockwork, subtle, languorous, sultry, studied.

It was not quite classical ballet. It was not strictly speaking dance. It was just Cornelia.

It was graceful, hypnotising, compelling, displayed none of the inevitable vulgarity that most burlesque dancers can't avoid manifesting in their haste to titillate as they tease and provoke. It was as if she was indifferent to her public, unbothered by the fact they are feasting on the sight of her pale body, that their hands moved to their crotches as if they had no control over their actions. As if she was declaring 'I am my own masterpiece and for this brief moment I take note of your pity and allow your eyes to feast on me'

Every single man watching had almost ceased breathing, captured by the hypnotic nature of the way she blended with the music. She had still not barely moved. Just sketched an arabesque, had not inched away from the very centre of the stage, pinned there at the heart of the white fire shining down from the gantry lights.

She had not yet broken sweat and every man in the audience already desired her.

She allowed herself a thin smile. Secure in the knowledge each male onlooker present believed it was addressed to him and him only.

Halfway through the song, the ferociousness of the light shining onto the stage reduced just as the Moby song embarked on a slow fade to be succeeded by strains of Kristin Hersh's version of Cat Stevens' *Trouble*, its jagged rhythms and changes in tone allowed Cornelia to imperceptibly accelerate her movements and finally move sideways from her fixed spot at the centre of the stage. Now she was dancing properly. Not quite a waltz, not quite a one-step, a halfway repeated twirl that showed off her agility while retaining her outer grace.

The male audience was truly captivated as she inclined the top half of her body forward and back, then in concentric circles, flaunting herself, displaying herself, never quite the way they expected, quirky, both impudent and restrained, fanning their pent-up desire.

Halfway through she pulled on the Velcro tabs holding her white satin camisole against her chest and it drifted to the ground, leaving her breasts fully on display. They were small, modest but perky, not overtly sexual in their timidity, but firm, high and her rouged nipples acted like a magnet for the men's eyes. The more perverse among them were already imagining ahead and speculating whether she has rouged other parts of her anatomy, still to be uncovered. Their hearts beat faster.

Cornelia paraded leisurely. Topless below the warm glow of the spotlight that now followed her as she traversed her domain, while providing generous hints of more fleshly revelations as she executed dainty ballet figures and her long legs danced the light fantastic, carried by an invisible wind, scissored her limbs, flexed them in lazy harmony.

Soon, the next track surged through the speakers dotted at regular intervals around the circular low-ceilinged room in which she performed. Her private territory.

It was a faster one. A Neil Young and Crazy Horse tune with raging, duelling guitars playing off each other against a metronomic beat and she moved quickly over to a couple of chairs a stagehand slid onto the battle ground of the dance floor, and thrashed around and above them often in perilous equilibrium. She threaded her fingers through the G-string, along the perceived line of her slit, her crotch hurled forward as she defied gravity above the chairs and the chasm separating them, dividing her arse-cheeks and allowing fleeting glimpses of the smoothness of her intimacy in captured seconds of sheer indecency, until with the last power chord still resonating she unhooked the final piece of apparel and the thin material of the G-string fell to the floor, allowing their eyes full access to her most private country, her delta of heat and the apex of their lust.

The final chord of the music still echoed and, then she was pinned motionless again under the glare of a single spotlight. She stood, regally, her legs apart, naked as the day she was born, not so much Venus on a seashell, but more Eve by the fateful tree, tempting but out of reach, insolent, dangerous.

This is me. Take me if you can. Watch but do not touch, the stance said. *Eagerly drink in every square inch of my pale body.*

Her final tune was a Nick Cave and Warren Ellis song, with a repetitive chorus that skewed her heart: one of the few things that had ever moved Cornelia's cold heart. She now danced like a dervish, in a daze, alternating between frenzy and beaches of slow motion like a ghost at the end of a hanging rope. Her limbs twitched. The flatness of her stomach vibrated like the sands of a desert buffeted by an invisible sirocco wind.

She stretched in lazy abandon, ever flashing the hint of pinkness between her legs while the staring men watched open-mouthed and squinted in a desperate hope to see more, or retain the fleeting flash of intimate colour, but she was constantly in motion and no eyes could settle on this brief vision of her displayed innards before she moved again and all that was left was the memory of her inner lips, the taboo of her privacy that they have been privileged to capture just the once, never to see again tonight, as her body turned on itself, rolled, feinted, sketched the most teasing of dances so that every inch of her skin had become a kaleidoscope of shimmering pallor.

Finally, she moved towards the pole standing at the centre of the stage which had earlier been lowered down on her signal, gripped its steel, and flew around like an epileptic butterfly, a spinning top of flesh that left onlookers dizzy and unsteady on their feet. Then she tiptoed away from the pole and went through her floor routine, with sleepy moves that left nothing to the imagination, a final reward when they least expected it, displaying her secrets one final time, her agile fingers flew across her sex, almost caressing herself and opened herself fully to the gaze of all those envious eyes out there in the surrounding darkness of the male Walkabouts audience.

The chorus of the song faded graciously.

'… this morning is amazing and so are you … this morning is amazing and so are you …'

And there she ended her set, immobile again. Bathed in the lone spotlight, fully nude and exposed, fragile, imperious, unattainable, eyes closed, like a broken doll crucified across the dance floor, almost sleeping, not quite dead, a staked out captive prey, ripe and ready to be plundered.

Then the light went off.

They all held their breath.

There was just a smattering of applause as she faded into the darkness and, unseen, departed the floor for backstage. But soon the banknotes began to float across the stage, a shower of tips, even some flowers, which the stagehand soon gathered up.

There was no encore.

It was an act she had taken a few years to perfect. Some rival dancers and club managers had often remarked that she exposed too much, or didn't tease or flaunt herself around enough, but Cornelia had a sense of pride in her difference. She abhorred vulgarity. If they didn't like her act, she could always work elsewhere, move on to another establishment. She was confident the customers would follow her. If she danced, stripped, it would always be on her own terms. There would always be a demand for a striking, ice blonde willing to open her legs and display her wares. She didn't fool herself and believe it was art.

And if there wasn't, she could always go on killing.

13
The Things We Do For Love

Maxwell Donleavy had fallen in love with Sarah Sparks back in high school.

Although he was always aware that it would lead nowhere. He was gay. He loved her more like a sister. Maybe the way she mirrored his own uncertainties was what brought them together. There was both a beauty and a meekness about Sarah. She had victim written all over her even from that young age. She was also pretty in an unassuming sort of way, straight straw-coloured hair, diminutive in stature and lacking in feminine curves.

Because of their respective submissive nature they had both, step by incautious step, ventured into their small town's demi-monde of BDSM as they grew older, finding themselves at dubious private parties, where Sarah's innate masochism manifested itself to his dismay, and he had to witness her being caned, whipped and used publicly, while out of the corner of one eye she blushed heavily watching Maxwell being mounted by party stallions until tears flowed from his eyes and down his flushed cheeks.

The fracture lines in their psyche brought them together and even later when they drifted apart, Sarah moving to the city and Maxwell staying back while he perfected his computer hacking skills in the privacy of his parents' basement, they remained in touch, sharing confidences, secrets that others would have run miles away from. Speaking to each other about their needs and cravings, they could be honest with each other, knowing there would be no disapproval or scorn. Distance made no difference to their closeness. But Maxwell felt a sense of suffocation where he was stuck in small town boring mediocrity and ached to move out into the larger world.

Maxwell was also a talented piano player and one day caught sight of an advertisement for a pianist to work on a cruise ship and, to his surprise, got the job, a six-months contract on a vessel cruising the Caribbean out of Fort Lauderdale.

He had three shifts a day, playing in the Raffles Lounge to an audience of retirees, peroxided widows and a procession of Zimmer frames, mobility scooters and walkers. His brief was to play easy listening versions of classic showtunes, but after a few weeks, the stultifying routine, as well as the lack of appreciation, got to him and he would, halfway through his set, begin to improvise his own tunes, ethereal and rambling Keith Jarrett-like solos, which the attending baristas soon reported to the entertainment boss running the ship's activities. After three warnings, into his third month onboard, he was dismissed and disembarked in Key West and had to make his own way back to California and the Valley.

He had been unable to call Sarah whilst on the ship, as the free wi-fi was not available to staff, and when on land there had been no privacy in the zones where crew and passengers rushed to connect.

Her phone was not responding. He would leave messages but saw she was not picking them up. After a fortnight of unsuccessful attempts at making contact, he reluctantly called her parents. He knew they disliked him, either homophobic or blaming him for the bad company their daughter had kept, before she had moved to Los Angeles, where she worked as a paralegal and had confessed to Maxwell she was still prey to her inner demons, having acquired a protector. Maxwell shuddered at the thought of the nature of the protection, remembering the patchwork quilt of marks on her body at the private parties where he had witnessed her being willingly abused and led triumphantly by collar and leash by her users.

Sarah's mother picked up.

'Hullo, Mrs Sparks. This is Maxwell Donleavy. A friend

of Sarah's. I've been trying to get in touch with Sarah in the city, but she isn't responding.'

She tried to speak but the sound struggled to make it past her lips. There was a long pause, as Maxwell had a terrible premonition.

'Oh, Maxwell ...'

'Yes?'

'Sarah has passed ...'

'What?'

'She's dead.'

'How?' His heart froze.

'The news hadn't reached you?'

'I was away.'

'It's awful.'

'I didn't know she was suffering from ill health.' It was his initial, obvious thought.

'No,' her mother said, fighting back the tears.

'I'm so sorry, Mrs Sparks,' he tried to recall her first name; he'd known it once.

Forgetting her past antagonism to him, she explained how the accident had occurred. She had fallen to her death from the balcony of a hotel room, two months previously. The police had concluded it was an accident, but the circumstances were murky. There was also an unexplained dead man involved.

Maxwell was stunned, asked for further details but Sarah's mother had put the phone down and he knew it would be unadvisable to persist with more questions. The woman was, from the sound of it, still in shock.

He felt totally deflated.

Sarah was so tiny. How could she have stumbled over a balcony which must surely have reached her waist or more likely higher?

And what about a dead man? Maxwell was puzzled. There was no way, he was utterly convinced, that Sarah would have committed suicide. Despite her sexual inclinations and cravings for degradation, she was not depressive in any way. She fully embraced her faults, assumed her identity. The last time they had spoken, before he had gone off to sea, she had confessed the man she was seeing, her dominant as she put it, a realtor, was keen to cement a more permanent sort of relationship. At the time, this news had made Maxwell jealous, not that there was any way he could have presented himself as any form of alternative, unable to service her sexually, or with the slightest inclination to inflict the pain she fed on.

His sleep that night in his basement nook was full of terrible dreams, in which Sarah invariably took the front of stage, in all her vulnerability and loneliness. As if she was calling to him from beyond the grave. For what? Revenge? Punishment? Help?

He knew they had been misfits. But this didn't mean she deserved what had happened to her.

He determined to find out more and, the following day, began scouring the internet for more details about her so-called accident.

The man found dead in the room at the hotel Figueroa, close to the Staples Centre, was a local realtor and without a doubt the person Sarah had mentioned she was seeing. He had been found shot, and the gun used was still in the room but did not have any prints, whether of the victim, of Sarah or anyone else. It was reported Sarah might have been his mistress, where she had worked, and the praise her erstwhile colleagues lavished on her post-mortem as a lovely person and certainly not someone who had any shady associations.

The whole farrago made no sense to Maxwell, and the fact the police had closed the file and somehow concluded it was a double suicide sat uncomfortably with him, as the facts did not, to his mind, point in that direction.

A day later, he travelled into the city and located the hotel. He had no idea which window she had fallen from, and any impact her fall might have left on the sidewalk had by now been thoroughly cleaned away by human hands or the weather.

He walked into the hotel, which had Mexican exotica written all over it, large terracotta vases full of cacti littering the narrow corridor leading to the reception area and, beyond, a small swimming pool area. The hotel felt like a throwback to the mid-20th century and was unlike the glittering edifices of steel, light and modernity most other hotels he had visited evoked. The lobby was badly-lit. He knew there would be no point asking any of the staff about the event and the night it had taken place. Would have proved suspicious and it was unlikely anyone would provide any information they hadn't already given to the police investigation a few months back.

He looked up at the low, brown ceilings and noted there were no visible CCTV cameras. Nor had there been by the entrance to the hotel.

Back on the Boulevard, he peered around, circling on himself to observe all the vantage points with a view of the hotel and its entrance. Noted a camera over the door of a night club on the other side of the wide road, some fifty or so yards away. And another over the nearby junction, installed there to monitor the traffic.

A couple of days later, after conferring online with several fellow hackers with a better knowledge of surveillance apparatus and how it was networked throughout the city and after acquiring some pirate software that allowed him both access to the dark web and possible infiltration into official systems, Maxwell sat down at his computer and began his own investigation.

His first shocking discovery after he had gained sight of the official police report was that when Sarah's body had hit the ground and been found, she had been naked.

What the hell?

No one decides to kill themselves and strips first, surely?

The post-mortem was also inconclusive.

Her body had been badly bruised, and the coroner had determined many of the more superficial blemishes were not from the impact, but had existed before, some up to weeks prior to her death.

The saving grace, for Maxwell, was to learn her head had suffered the brunt of the impact with the pavement and her death had been instantaneous and she had not suffered any pain.

But, why oh why had she been found naked?

He couldn't put the pieces together.

And the thought of her pale, marked body hurtling through the night sky in the seconds before she hit the ground became an obscene obsession in his mind, a puppet of flesh flying down, limbs akimbo, having lost all dignity, exposed, probably crucified in flight.

Maxwell felt sick to the core.

He continued to scroll through the rest of the police report. Noted the dead realtor was killed by a single bullet. Maxwell wrote down the details of calibre and speculation about the weapon's make in his notebook. He knew nothing about guns.

There was also an interesting footnote, where in a different set of handwriting, someone associated with the LAPD had indicated the deceased had on a previous occasion come to the federal authorities' notice suspected of trafficking women, but that sufficient proof had never been gathered to make a case against him. Connections with foreign operators in the skin trade was inferred, involving women from Eastern Europe.

Maxwell sighed.

It was a puzzle, although he had not expected to have all his initial questions answered so readily.

Over the following weeks, he attempted to hack into the club's camera only to find it had been out of action, and just acted as a deterrent. One avenue closed.

It took repeated efforts to infiltrate the city's traffic camera network. And to wind back the gigabytes of film to the night of the event. He was lucky the system erased itself automatically after eight weeks, and the day in question was still 48 hours away from being wiped clean.

He sat himself down and meticulously watched through the five hours of film prior to the time of death, a parade of blurry images of occasional passers-by, cars whizzing past on the Boulevard but, most importantly, a view of the hotel's sheltered entrance.

His heart seized when he saw the diminutive silhouette of Sarah entering the Figueroa at 8.05 pm. He even recognised the skirt she was wearing. Her features were at peace, unknowing of the fact that she was just a lamb marching to the slaughter. Maxwell felt an uneasy tension grip his stomach.

Various others walked in and out of the hotel and, in his notebook, he noted down every single one of them, giving each an alias so he could tick off their time of arrival and should he spot them again later on the screen, their time of departure.

At 8.57, a man walked in who looked like the dead realtor from the photo that had been published in the initial newspaper report of the strange deaths at the Figueroa. Another man, wearing an old-fashioned fedora, stepped into the hotel, just a few yards behind him.

Maxwell leaned over to the screen. He knew, from to the police report, the brief interval of time during which Sarah had fallen. Or been pushed?

He waited. Glued to the screen. The report had listed the number of the room in which the body had been found and from the balcony of which Sarah had fallen, but he had not managed to determine the hotel's own room plan and identify which window he should be watching.

At 9.26, here was a blur of a movement at the last window on the left-hand side of the image, a room situated right at the edge of the screen. Almost like a bird flying by. There was little to see, but Maxwell knew he was witnessing the final seconds of Sarah's life. He held his breath but the body hitting the ground was off camera.

He now concentrated on the hotel's entrance, eager to catch any departures.

He was rewarded by the sudden appearance of the man with the fedora leaving the premises within a couple of minutes of Sarah's death. He froze the screen, tried to enhance the image but the man's features remained in shadow, his left hand raised to pull the brim of his hat down further across his forehead. He was quite anonymous, ordinary in stature and silhouette.

But, right there and then, Maxwell knew.

14
The Book Thief

The first book in Cornelia's collection was a stolen one.

By some quirk the parents of her best friend Lucy in fourth grade had managed to get a copy of an early Wimpy Kid volume signed by the author and it formed part of their daughter's birthday stash of presents.

Cornelia was not even a fan of the series but she coveted the book because it was signed.

She stole it.

Lucy never even noticed it had gone missing.

It was a first step towards a life of crime.

She was never a cuddler as a child, but neither was she ever emotional. She was distant. Obedient and never subject to tantrums. An amused observer of the comic tragedy of life.

When retribution didn't manifest itself, Cornelia persisted.

She lifted books from travel concessions in airports, when she travelled with family, although concealed the fact and it was assumed she had diligently spent her pocket money on something useful or educational. Giving the appearance of a studious child. She didn't get any particular thrill from stealing books. Nor shame. But never did so from actual bookstores. Already a skewed version of right and wrong was embedding itself inside of her thoughts.

She was a bright child, from a wealthy family. She was also an only child. Her parents were often away for long periods and she was left to her own devices, albeit supervised by relatives. No one knew quite what to make of her.

As a teenager, she would always volunteer to babysit for close neighbours and friends, always in the hope she might find a book to steal in their house while she did so. This was often a disappointment, as so many of the houses she visited on these occasions were devoid of books altogether, splendidly decorated houses with expensive furniture and fittings but no soul whatsoever.

She was a loner at Vassar, keeping to herself., never inclined to join any of the sororities or social clubs. She studied literature and during that time, bloomed. She had been ordinary in appearance but the new environment, the freedom, helped her blossom and her beauty became apparent to all. But also, her remoteness, and the fact that she didn't belong.

A brilliant student, she left university garlanded with honours but had no wish to begin a career of any kind. She was allowed a year to find her feet by her parents. Cornelia travelled extensively during this time, only to see the year interrupted by her fathers' death in a car accident. And her mother being diagnosed with early onset dementia. To her surprise she was left with very little. Her father's business ventures were in a sorry state and he was crippled with debt. She soon realised she would have to make a living for herself on her own terms.

Boys, men, younger and older had always coveted her. She had always sensed this and realised she could monetise her body, her looks. It felt preferable to any kind of 9 to 5 job and she had no taste for waitressing. She had been told she could model, she had the looks, the exoticism what with her striking pallor and ranginess, but she had no wish to see her face splattered across magazines, advertisements, catalogues.

Neither did she ever consider prostituting herself, or allowing herself to be subsidised by men, although several did offer.

Things happen, life happens.

Just like a year later once she had established a reputation as a dancer, the need for additional money had manifested itself when the care home costs came knocking at the door, and various coveted first editions came up for sale. She added contract killer to her résumé. A natural development.

Cornelia knew she was good at it. She suffered no guilt.

Considered herself a professional, both on the dance floor and in the execution of target.

By now she had been directly involved in just over a handful of messy deaths,

Some years went by. Her book collection was now well past a hundred titles, and she had, by her own count, killed 18 men. She had watched blood spreading out of control from diverse wounds to the body, seeping, dripping, regurgitating; there had been dirty deaths with desperate pleas, vomit, bladders, and entrails emptying themselves of liquid and odorous substances; her pulse had frantically raced at heart attack speed during clumsy struggles with heavier men, uneven fights but she had survived them all.

Her last job had somehow felt like it was straight out of a book. Had disturbed her in subtle ways. Her target was seemingly aware of who she was and why she had been sent to eliminate him and had offered no resistance or protest. As if he welcomed death.

This had never happened to Cornelia before.

Had the guy read Hemingway's story *The Killers*?

It had forced Cornelia to re-evaluate her secondary job, her life.

By coincidence, at the very same time, just a mile or so away from her in Manhattan, Hopley was experiencing a similar dilemma.

She decided she needed time off. Not a good thing. Maybe somewhere in the sun? She realised she had not taken a real vacation in ages.

Cornelia arranged for an expensive security system to be installed in her apartment, even though she knew that any break-ins in her absence would be of a more opportunistic nature. Targeting her hi-fi and TV which would be in more peril than her book collection. Then she planned her stolen time in an exotic place. Yes, it would have to be in the sun. Although her pale complexion would need the protection of much suncream.

She had never been to the Caribbean and, after much hesitation, selected the Playa Dorada area in the Dominican

Republic. She landed at Puerto Plata airport with a single small suitcase full of T-shirts and an assortment of skimpy bathing outfits she'd swooped on while on a rapid shopping trip at Century 21 and Daffy's. Her bulging tote bag was full of paperback editions of books she already owned in first printings but had never found the time to read until now. Whilst in transit at Miami International, she picked a few more volumes in one of the airport's shops, including a Woolrich short story collection she'd recently seen reviewed in Book Forum.

Non-essential items she could find locally, she guessed. Toiletries, make-up, condoms, a hat, or baseball cap to protect her vulnerable skin. She also deliberately left her laptop at home in her East Village apartment. She intended to distance herself from the world and go back in time by some strange quirk of thought. To the days before she had unwittingly taken up her killing trade, to the days when still unknowingly swam in a sea of relative innocence, if such halcyon days had ever existed.

The hotel dining room overlooked a bay where Cornelia could enjoy watching the sun set first across the mountains to the east and then across the varying shades of blue of the warm sea. Daytime, she lay on one of the beaches, listening to the wavelets lapping the beach or crashing gently against the breakers of the stone jetty, reading lazily, or sipping cold drinks from the nearby 24-hour bar that serviced the beach. It was slightly out of season, so the resort wasn't crowded. She relaxed by going to bed most evenings at ten or even earlier, deliberately ignoring the conducted festivities organised daily around the large swimming pool, blissfully falling asleep with her book still open in her hands, her long and lanky nude body stretched out beneath the thin white sheet while the air-conditioning buzzed away with metronomic regularity, drifting away into untroubled dreamland. She would awaken early in the morning and take long, solitary walks across the still deserted beaches that lay miles beyond the borders of the resorts, refreshing her body as the sun began to emerge over the distant line of the horizon by shedding her shorts and T-shirt and dipping naked into the warm ocean. It was a sensation like no other. Playa Dorada was perfect, but it would have been better, she thought, if she had been able to sunbathe nude all day, in isolation, without the pesky onlookers it would attract as the day moved on. Nudity gave her a wonderful sense of freedom, as well as exacerbating her dormant sexual senses. It was a different sort of nakedness to what she had grown accustomed to on stage.

Following a week of routine relaxation, Cornelia began feeling the need for some stimulation and allowed herself to pick amongst the occasional single men who would nod in her direction during meals or even accost her at the bar. Truly, whatever they said was of no interest whatsoever to her and the words and needless sentences of their pathetic rituals of seduction went straight in one ear and out through the other, while she checked up on them, their looks, their size. She bedded a few, never the same again twice, much to their dismay, treating each new lover as if he was only there to scratch her lackadaisical urges. Some would happen to be good lovers, filled her well, even made her come, while others proved mediocre, hasty or unfulfilling, but it made little difference to Cornelia. One day later, she could no longer even remember their faces, let alone the girth or hue of their cock, or the position they took her in. It was just a matter of selfish holiday sex, as far as she was concerned. Utilitarian.

Soon, the sand and sea and the meaningless embraces began to take their toll, and boredom set in. She'd changed hotels twice along the length of the resort, seeking new culinary experiences and bed partners as well as avoiding previous fuckers who couldn't take no for an answer, and the fun of being in the Caribbean was beginning to fade by the hour. She was also running out of books to read and the hotels' gift shops reading fare was unappetising. After all, she realised, she was a city gal through and through, and she came to the conclusion that she preferred her solitude at the heart of bustling crowds. She settled her bill and flew home at the next opportunity.

Even after several weeks away, there were barely a

handful of messages on her answer phone mostly from club managers in search of her services, although her computer mail box was full to the brim, mostly with commercial spam. No, she didn't require unlimited supplies of counterfeit Viagra or weight loss programmes that came with ironclad guarantees. Let alone discounted solo cabins on a cruise to the damn Caribbean.

She hoped the punters would not comment on her tan lines when she stripped on stage or disapprove.

She felt she was at some form of crossroads.

She was about to throw away a bunch of copies of the Village Voice, which had piled up in her absence, but then decided she would just check out the book pages before she did so. Some reviews often brought unknown titles to her attention.

Out of idle curiosity she then moved on the personals, mostly sex for sale, escorts, and every combination of sexual activity under the sun and more she would rather not know about were liberally on offer through here, with and without euphemisms. It was believed these advertisements were what kept the publication financially afloat.

One headlined 'Books for Sale' caught her attention.

Cornelia jotted down the telephone number listed.

She would ring it tomorrow.

She had often been curious about the line illustrations in the Dos Passos trilogy reprint edition. The books were not advertised as firsts, and the price sought was reasonable. She had seen a similar set listed at the Strand Rare Book Room before her beach break, but it had already sold when she had contacted them.

'I'm calling about your ad.'

She liked the voice on the other end of the line.

15
Books and Dust

Ramona.

The Figueroa mess.

The previous ten years of his life as a conveyor of pain.

Hopley was feeling old, beginning to feel aches in parts of his body he never knew he had.

Understanding with some element of fatalism that things were catching up with him and there might soon be a bitter price to pay.

He never thought of himself as a bad person but the face that confronted him in the mirror of the bathroom every morning was now a repository of untold sins, he realised.

But an insidious form of lassitude had burrowed deep into his mind and body, and he was uncertain whether anything could now change.

He had felt its onset months ago, which is why he had taken the sabbatical. In search of a reboot. Something that would re-energize him, renew his sense of purpose.

He thought it had worked.

Until New Orleans.

He had returned there just a fortnight following his amorous encounter with Ramona, and executed the job he had been researching on the previous visit.

Just another bloated body floating in the Mississippi that surfaced close to the levees.

A clean job.

Another spring morning in Manhattan and Hopley was still in the grip of his dark night of the soul.

Life had been quiet on the work front, not that it bothered him. He drank some fruit juice from the fridge and bit into a piece of soft cheese. He picked up the mail from the line of letter boxes scattered across the building's lobby. A utility bill, a bank statement for one of the varied accounts where he dispersed his ill-earned funds, coupons from nearby supermarkets, the latest issue of *Publishers Weekly*, which he subscribed to and leafed negligently through. His homework for his sometimes cover as a book trade executive. The landline rang. Not many people knew his number. He didn't know many people.

He reached for the phone on the window ledge.

Picked it up but remained silent, waiting for whoever is on the other end to break the silence.

Inwardly, he felt a veil of hopelessness. He didn't feel ready for yet another job. But he was also aware that there are only so many times he can turn assignments down.

'Mr Hopley?'

It's not Ivan Irish.

'Yes.' A voice he didn't recognize.

'Mr Silas Hopley?'

'In the flesh.'

'I'm Ronald Wintsch, an attorney at law, from Cedar Rapids ...'

Hopley has never set foot in Cedar Rapids. Can't even remember in which state it is.

'How can I help you?'

'We represent the estate of the late Jonathan Quentin.'

Hopley was nonplussed.

'It doesn't ring any bells, I must confess.'

It turned out the said Quentin was a long-forgotten distant cousin on his mother's side. It had been ages since Hopley had had any contact with his family. He was an orphan of sorts anyway; his parents had died in a car crash when he was still only five and he had mostly been brought by an aunt, who had herself passed away when he was in the army. The late Quentin had, it appeared, bounced Hopley on his knees when he was still a child and taken a liking to him and left him something in his will.

'I'll be damned. I can barely remember the man, let alone what he used to look like.'

'No matter, Mr Hopley. But it's taken us much time and effort to track you down.'

'I travel a lot.'

'I see.'

'The majority of the deceased's estate has been divided, as per the will's instructions, between his children and grandchildren, mainly consisting of his property and cash liquidity, but he made a few bequests to more distant relatives such as yourself and others we haven't been able to locate yet. He wanted you to inherit his books. Explained in his will that as a child you were a precocious reader and best placed to appreciate the gift.'

Hopley chuckled.

Poetic justice coming back to slap him gently in the face; the reward for pretending to be a publisher when he had to equivocate about his profession?

The lawyer misinterpreted his laughter.

'Not many book lovers around these days. I hope you still are.'

'Oh, I am,' Hopley replied.

He was no book person by any stretch of the imagination. Mostly read when he was travelling and restricted himself to mystery thrillers. Making his meeting at La Guardia with Ramona quite serendipitous. Abandoned books in hotel rooms or airport lounges once he had read them; barely kept more than half a dozen paperbacks in his Manhattan apartment.

He was tempted to ask the lawyer to donate the books he had inadvertently come into to a charity of their choice, but had second thoughts. It would appear as if he was ungrateful. If only he could recall what Quentin actually looked like. He asked for the books to be despatched to a storage facility he kept in the Bronx.

Three weeks later, by which time he had almost forgotten about the curious inheritance, he had another call, this time on his cell phone, that the bulky carton had reached its destination and was now stored in his locker.

On his next visit to the storage facility, Hopley finally opened the box. He was expecting a mass of well-thumbed, broken-spined paperback titles and was surprised to find all the volumes packed tight together were hardcover books, almost all with dustjackets, going back to the 1930s and 1940s.

They smelled as if they had been stored in an attic for decades, but showed no sign of water damage.

He looked through the two dusty piles he had pulled out of the carton. Recognised the names of many of the authors represented: Hemingway, Faulkner, Dos Passos, Dreiser, Mailer, F. Scott Fitzgerald, Anaïs Nin …

He repacked all the books and brought them back to Manhattan.

He realised they were probably quite valuable and pondered what he should do. Were he to keep them, they would just sit decoratively on his shelves – he would actually have to build a shelf for them. And he guessed they were too precious to read without possibly damaging in the process. The paper was often thin and yellowing, the books fragile and susceptible, he knew, to temperature and humidity.

On the other hand, he had no need for further cash and was reluctant to get them appraised by a specialist dealer who would no doubt make an obscene profit out of re-selling them should Hopley offer the collection in bulk.

No, what they deserved were owners who would covet and cherish them and enjoy their ownership more than Hopley. True lovers of Modern Firsts.

He resolved to sell them individually and investigated the ways and means of doing so. Amazon? eBay? AbeBooks? Personal ads in the *Village Voice*, the *New York Times* or even *Publishers Weekly*?

It would give him something to do to pass the time, he reckoned. Until his burner phone inevitably rang again.

It turned out that many of the titles were, he eventually discovered, not proper firsts but book club editions where the price had been clipped off or much later printings that did not attract anywhere as high a value. Cousin Quentin had not been as astute or proficient in his book collecting!

No matter.

As Hopley discovered, there were still book lovers out there who wanted these titles, irrespective of their reduced market value.

People he would feel safe communicating with on his landline, keeping his private life, or the little there was of it, from his business activities on the wrong side of the law.

'I'm calling about your ad.'

A woman's voice. He estimated she was in her late 20s or early 30s. A game he liked to play when hearing people talk for the first time and not being able to see their faces.

'Are you a dealer?'

'No.'

'Good. It's just that I try and avoid selling to professional dealers. I'm seeking good homes for the books. Not speculators.'

'That's most admirable. I am definitely a private collector.'

'Excellent. I haven't come across many female dealers, anyway, so you have the benefit of the doubt!'

'Hand on heart, I'm kosher.'

'Which ad are you responding to?'

'The *Voice.*'

'Which volume?'

'Volumes with an S. The *USA Trilogy* by Dos Passos in the facsimile book club edition.'

He quoted a reasonable price in line with a listing he had recently seen from the Strand Rare Book Room for the same set of volumes.

'That's fair. The Strand had a set a few weeks back, but I missed out on it. Was out of town when they listed it, and it had been sold by the time I returned.'

It pleased Hopley the volumes would find a good home, although it was uncommon for young women to focus on these sort of books, he'd found.

'But I'd like to see them first,' she added. 'Check on the condition. I'm sure you understand?'

'Absolutely. Makes total sense.'

'Maybe we might meet for a coffee and you could bring the books along?'

'I'd be happy to do so. I'm free whenever you are?'

'Let's do that.'

'And your name is?'

'Cornelia.'

'I'm Hopley,' he reciprocated. He was grateful she didn't ask for his first name in return. He liked her already.

16
When Hopley Met Cornelia

They agreed to meet up in a quaint coffee house with a hidden interior back garden which Hopley had visited on many occasions, close to St Mark's.

But the place no longer existed. One of the many victims of Covid. He swore at himself for not checking first. He waited in front and soon saw Cornelia approaching in the distance. She took long strides, her elongated silhouette crossing 3rd Avenue at the lights, her hair a crown of wheat in the afternoon greyness. He knew instantly it was her although he had no idea what the woman he had spoken to on the phone looked like. It was gut feeling. Immediate.

She made her way to the location of the defunct café, where Hopley stood.

'It appears to have gone out of business,' he said as she gave him a quizzical look. 'I've made something of a fool of myself.'

'It happens.'

'There is that ice-cream parlour over there, unless you have any suggestion of another place to go?'

'I'm sure it will be fine. I actually would prefer an ice-cream to a coffee. Shall we?'

The establishment was cavernous and almost empty with as many staff on duty as customers. Hopley was also not much of a coffee drinker, but found himself stymied when the drinks cooler displayed lonely health drinks in various dubious colours, all pastel variations. They had no cans of Coke or Sprite, just fruit flavoured mineral waters. He selected a lemonade for himself, while Cornelia opted for chocolate ice cream. He paid and they made their way to a table towards he back.

The drink was tasteless and hadn't been close to a real lemon for ages, he reckoned.

The woman was striking, and he felt somewhat tongue-tied. Not at all what he had expected.

'If I might be impertinent, you just don't look like a book collector ...'

She smiled.

'Should there be a type?'

'Spectacles, grey hair, tweed ...'

'Well, I'll be impertinent: you appear to have some grey hairs,' she chuckled.

'Touché!'

She brought a mouthful of ice cream to her lips.

'Are you in the book trade?' she asked.

He was about to come up with his usual book trade alibi, but held back. She would see right through him, and looked like the sort of person who would paradoxically know all about the publishing business and he would betray his ignorance rather foolishly.

'No. Just someone who has come in to a cache of books, and is hoping to find good homes for them.'

'You have others? Not just the Dos Passos titles?'

'Yes. I've only just begun searching for the right customers for them. I'm doing it piecemeal; the ad you saw in the Voice was one of my first.'

There was a smudge of ice cream above her upper lip. Hopley had the urge to raise his hand and wipe it away for her but refrained from doing so.

Her tongue washed the brown streak of the chocolate away as if she guessed his thoughts. A rapid, imperceptible movement that took him by surprise.

'Then you interest me a lot, Mr Hopley. Very.'

'No need to call me Mr, Hopley will do.'

'My apologies. Not the talented Mr Hopley, then ...'

It was his turn to sketch a wry smile. He had caught the Highsmith reference. He liked he could verbally spar with her.

It had been a long time since he'd enjoyed a little challenge of this kind.

'So ...' He pulled up the tote bag and emptied its contents on the table, at a safe distance from his drink and her ice cream. A large brown Jiffy bag in which he had stuffed the three books she was interested in, each individually wrapped in its own yellow envelope.

'Let's clear the table top first,' she intervened. 'Don't want any unfortunate spills, do we?'

He agreed.

She liked the condition of the three-book set he had brought along and they sealed the deal. She paid cash.

'Now, what about the other stuff you have. Do you recall some of the specific titles?'

'Not in detail. I could make a list?'

'How did you come in possession of the books in the first place?'

Hopley explained the circumstances of the curious inheritance and how much of a surprise it had been to him. And the fact that he did read books but never held on to them.

'But tell me a little about you?'

She retreated.

'Not much to say. I make a living. And I collect books but others would no doubt say I hoard them.'

'A question of perception, eh?'

'Indeed.'

The spring sun was setting over Manhattan. Hopley didn't want to let her go just now, he realised, even though he knew he would see her again as he had agreed to let her peruse the other titles he'd come into. He was deadly keen to learn more about her and could feel she was holding back and he didn't want to push too hard. He would give her time. She went to the washroom and he considered how both similar and radically different she was from Ramona, with whom it had also begun with a book in an airport lounge.

He determined to not let her go as easily.

'Getting dark outside,' he stated. 'So, what are your

evening plans?'

Cornelia had no bookings that week.

She considered at length.

'Nothing much.'

'Can I invest some of my ill-earned lucre by offering to take you to dinner? Or am I being too forward?'

Once again, that enigmatic smile lit up her face as she visibly weighed up her options. Was he some old pervert? Was he harmless? He seemed different, as if living in another dimension to most of the men she frequented.

Her curiosity got the better of her and she agreed.

Hopley suggested Veselka, a nearby Ukrainian restaurant on 2nd Avenue. Cornelia had heard of it on various occasions but never been. Ukrainian fare it would be.

How do you communicate, keep a conversation going when both parties are holding back so many terrible secrets and have to maintain almost military-like cover?

Somehow they managed. It even seemed to come naturally. Which was encouraging.

Cornelia quickly guessed that beyond his polite and affable exterior, Hopley was a repository of small mysteries. His age was indeterminate, could have been anything from mid-30s to 50s, she guessed; it was the greying, unkempt hair slightly parted to the left that marked him as someone who wasn't overly bothered by his appearance, although on the other hand his clothes were casual but visibly expensive. He wore a black open-necked shirt, black slacks and loafers, his cream-coloured and well-cut jacket tailor-made to fit his stocky top half. He had narrow hips and was a few pounds overweight, and wore glasses. He could be anything in between an academic and a businessman with a sense of restrained style. He was well-spoken, with no trace of any regional accent, with a softness in his voice that somehow didn't fit along with his face.

It was that furtive hint of delicacy in his tone that

clinched it for Cornelia.

If he made a pass, as she hoped he would, she would give in and sleep with him. It had nothing to do with coveting the books he had amassed.

She knew in her heart it would be different from the experiences she had had with other men. He seemed a one-off.

The way he smiled at her, as they ate and assessed each other in part silence between mouthfuls, was both sardonic and inquisitive as if he knew already they were destined to fuck, but was also shy and would not be the one to make the first direct approach.

Maybe she should open up to him and reveal her profession, the more harmless one as a stripper. If only to see how he would react. Whether he would distance himself after the revelation or whether if it would fan his curiosity and make him desire her even more? She couldn't in truth predict how he would react to such a revelation.

He had settled the check and they sat in silence, waiting, as the crowds milled around them in the busy restaurant, a constant buzz of voices surrounding them.

They eyed each other, almost daring the other to speak first, to break this silence that was so full of underlined, pent-up expectation. Neither blinking. Provoking each other into some form of positive action.

Cornelia was the one to falter.

'That was a lovely meal. I'm sorry I hadn't tried eating at Veselka before. The recommendations were absolutely right.'

'I was worried for a moment that after seeing the menu, you would inform me you were maybe vegetarian or something. I'd forgotten that so many young women are these days.'

'I'm not. I wouldn't eat here every day, though; it's earthy food, not for the faint at heart.'

She looked so fit and slim.

'Afraid of putting weight on?' Hopley remarked. 'I gave up the ghost some time ago. As you may have noticed.'

Cornelia chuckled. 'You're not fat …'

'I know, but neither am I thin.'

'Nothing a bit of exercise would remedy.'

'Do you?'

'What?'

'Exercise. I jog a little, sometimes attend a gym.'

'I lack the motivation.'

'So, what motivates you?'

He didn't answer, unsure how to, without confessing to his desire to sleep with her.

They exchanged meaningful glances. She pulled her thin denim jacket from the back of the chair. Hopley pushed his own back. He wasn't wearing a coat.

'I will,' Cornelia said.

'You will … what?'

A strange, deep vibration was racing through his stomach, as he knew the answer all too well. But would never admit to doing so.

This was her way of allowing herself to be seduced.

'Where do you live? I assume it's close as we arranged to meet here?'

He told her.

'Let's go, then.'

'You're certain?'

'Absolutely.'

They became lovers at first sight. Just like in a book.

Cornelia had slept with more handsome men, had exchanged pillow talk with wittier men, had allowed more skilful men to enjoy her body. But Hopley instantly connected with her most private of wavelengths.

Hopley, for the most part, restricted himself to sex with women of his own age in the years leading to their affair, and Cornelia was a good decade and a half younger than him, which made him feel self-conscious and on trial as he undressed her in the darkness of his apartment's living room before taking her by the hand and leading her to the bedroom, tiptoeing between the clothes they had shed, her body pearlescent in the thin light racing past his windows. A beautiful ghost he led by the hand towards the bed in which they would fuck as if tomorrow would never come.

It wasn't just the two of them making love, but also their respective share of darkness coming to grips with each other, of terrible secrets colliding as their bodies met in unholy communion.

They vigorously fucked in total silence, neither of them vocal. Not their style to be noisy.

Afterwards, they remained similarly laconic. Both simultaneously fearful the other would express the desire for a post-coital cigarette, but neither of them smoked and they giggled like children realising they had shared the same thought.

Nor did they ask each other any questions about the quality of the sex or each other's personal enjoyment.

They spooned. Then slept.

In the morning in the light of day as she pulled the crisp white sheet away from her body, he noted the SIG Sauer tattoo close to her pudenda.

'Why a gun?'

'I thought a rose or a flower would appear too sentimental.'

He turned round and she saw the crimson scars crisscrossing his back and the deep indentation in the crook of his shoulder a bullet had left a decade earlier.

'And those?' she pointed at the permanent marks on his body.

'Sort of war trophies,' Hopley said, with similar discretion and a marked reluctance to allow the past to undermine their coming together.

Neither of them asked again. The ground rules of their relationship were being established and they would in future have to live with pockets of silence.

They understood each other.

17
His First Kill

Even with sophisticated facial recognition software, which he didn't own or could likely obtain, Maxwell knew it was unlikely he would shed much light on the identity of the man wearing the fedora.

Neither did he think he was capable of tracking his movements from the moment he had left the Figueroa Hotel through the city's network of CCTV cameras mostly installed at junctions on main roads. It had been arduous enough to access the camera facing the hotel, and it would take all his computing capacity and more to delve any further down this avenue of investigation.

He felt he was at a dead end and every question still had to be answered.

But he resolved he would one day get to the bottom of the circumstances behind Sarah's violent ending.

However long it might take.

But first he needed to earn some money.

He'd heard of a network of shady clubs and watering holes scattered along the periphery of the airport. And which ones were also gay meeting points. He quickly found work in one of them, mostly as a waiter, but also allowed to sometimes tinkle the ivories, his piano-playing skills coming in useful and his patchy repertoire not being questioned the way it had been on the cruise ship. This paid for the basics but, as he had hoped, the extras were readily available if he were willing to whore himself to older men. A profession he took to like a duck to water. He liked cock anyway, so why not get paid for doing something you enjoyed?

Six months later he had moved out of his basement

room at his grandparents' house and found an apartment in an old refurbished motel situated inland between Marina Del Rey and Venice Beach, which he shared with a fellow hustler with whom he would occasionally do threesomes with local dads on the prowl for younger meat, who would always pay well, desperate as they were for discretion.

But Sarah's fate was never far from his thoughts.

Midnight. The time when male Cinderellas, or more precisely errant husbands with a taste for young men, pulled up their trousers after washing all traces of forbidden lips from their genitalia before taking the fast road home to unsuspecting wives and family.

His client had come quickly inside Maxwell's mouth, and was now gathering the garments scattered across the motel room floor. He hadn't been able to sustain an erection long enough to fuck Maxwell.

He'd left two fifty-dollar notes on the bedside table.

'That was great, boy. You have talented lips ...'

'Only happy to please.'

'So do you do this a lot?'

Maxwell had no shame about his new profession.

'Yes.'

'Can I ask you a question?'

'Go ahead.'

'Do you only go with men? For the money? Do you also have a girlfriend?'

'I did,' Maxwell lied. 'She died. In an accident. Fell off a balcony.'

'Oh, I'm sorry.'

'In downtown. Almost a year ago. Fell out of a hotel room window.'

'I think I might have read about it on the news or the newspapers,' his client said.

'They don't know whether it was an accident or something else.'

'Yes. But didn't I hear the room she'd been in also had a dead guy? A shooting?'

'That's the one.'

'You just never know,' the man said. 'How can people fall off balconies. Unless they're very drunk, of course ...'

'She didn't drink.'

'Like all those Russian oligarchs who were hostile to Putin. In Russia, falling off balconies seems to be a fact of life,' he chuckled.

'I read about another similar death, round about the same time. Some guy was pushed off a balcony in Vegas. Some mobster probably. There was speculation a mysterious woman had been seen with him, but she was never identified.'

Maxwell's curiosity had been fired up.

Later, he did a deep internet search and found out about the incident his client had mentioned.

There were certainly similarities.

But a tall, lanky woman was alleged to have been involved. There was no way it could be the same person in the Figueroa screen shot. He was medium height and definitely male.

But there was evidence of a similar modus operandi, as if it might be some trademark for a fellowship of contract killers. And Sarah had inadvertently become caught up in their activities.

It sounded like far-fetched fiction but could explain a lot.

Now a mainstay of the queer underworld, Maxwell had come across a variety of acolytes who he knew had mob connections. He began discreetly asking around. Few people would agree to answer his questions, even when he pretexted it was just research for something he was planning to write. Others shunned him, or warned him not to seek that kind of information so publicly.

He knew from other hustlers he ran around with that a certain Italian-American club owner with obligatory mob connections also had a taste for young men, but most of Maxwell's rent boy acolytes avoided him, as he had a reputation for playing rough.

Maxwell did not hesitate and put himself on the line.

He was rough, very rough. And verbal. Enjoying his dominance, both verbally and physically. The guy was showering and Maxwell was nursing his body and mental wounds, for which he had been extremely well paid.

'I know you are connected …' he said. The guy was dressing with his back to him, his hairy back a jungle of unruly webs and strands.

'So what?'

'It's common knowledge.'

'Good.'

'I'm curious, have some questions?'

'Ask.'

'Maybe I've read too many books, or seen movies, you know. But do the mob use freelance hitmen, or women?'

The guy burst out laughing.

'Damn it, you are too much …'

Maxwell stood firm, trying to look like a genuine figure of innocence.

'Why? Are you looking for an extra job? Isn't opening your legs on demand enough for you?'

Maxwell retreated. 'Not at all. Just curiosity. Sometimes you have these sorts of crazy thoughts and you wonder how things work.'

'Well,' the man kept on laughing, 'Not that I would know, but I don't think we'd ever recruit out of house, if you know what I mean. We have all the talent we need. We don't outsource. Keep thing in the family, I guess. Makes sense, no?'

'I guess so.'

'Answer your question?'

'Not entirely.'

'You have a certain cheek, you know. If I wanted to rid myself of you, I wouldn't need to use outside help. These would suffice,' he indicated his large hands, and Maxwell wondered if they had previously strangled or choked anyone. They looked right for the part.

'I realise.'

'And any more questions and you give me a discount the next time I want to pound the shit out of you, boy …'

Maxwell agreed to a full 100% discount and over the course of the following fortnight he learned there was an external organisation, a shadowy corporation with whom the mob never interfered, had a wary status quo with, known as the Bureau, who would take on any freelance tasks with a modicum of discretion and a money back guarantee in the event of failure. It might even have strong political connections and was available to whoever paid, no questions asked. There were whispers they had also acquired a redoubtable female operative in the past few years. It was also made clear to Maxwell that any further discussion of the matter was strictly off the table.

By then, Maxwell was sore and aching all over and in strategically intimate places. The information had cost him too much of his dignity already. But he felt he was making some progress with his enquiries. The possibility was tenuous but he would now have to puzzle out what the next step to take might be.

Maxwell was patient. And determined.

He might not have been the best lounge room pianist but he was an assiduous sex worker and continued to navigate the muddy waters of the twilight world in which you invariably came across all sorts of characters. He kept on asking questions. Until someone made a note of his enquiries.

'Have you ever heard of the movie *Shoot the Piano Player*?'

'It rings a bell. French, no?'

'But actually inspired by an American novel.'

'You learn new things every day.'

He'd been accosted by the cloakroom of the club he'd been playing at by a man he'd vaguely recognised, a character often seen around the club circuit. He was tall, sported a three-day growth of greyish beard and wore a grey suit that had not been dry-cleaned in a month of Sundays.

'You've been asking questions, young man. Don't think it hasn't been noticed.'

'So what?'

'The sort of questions a young punk like you shouldn't been seen asking. Why?'

'It's a personal matter.'

'The personal becomes public when you make waves.'

'Glad to know I am.'

'I wouldn't if I were you. You're out your league, boy. We know who you are. Just a cheap hustler who is visibly too curious about matters that shouldn't concern him.'

'Is that a warning?'

'It most definitely is. If I were you, I'd take note of it.'

The guy was a regular presence on the scene and it was easy for Maxwell to find out his name over the following days. It was Samuel Trimlin. No one knew what he did for a living but he was frequently seen around. He was rumoured to be some sort of go-between.

One night, after noticing him in the late hours in a tiki bar in Santa Monica by the pier, Maxwell followed him from the parking lot to a building in Century City where he appeared to be residing. How could a minor hood afford to live there? Trimlin had left his car, an early model Lexus, in the underground car park of the towering apartment block. Anyone could access the car park, he noted.

Two days later, he entered the basement in early morning and located Trimlin's car, parked in one corner and concealed himself in a dark corner of the concrete maze. He'd brought a gun along; it had once belonged to his father. It was loaded. He was wearing a balaclava over his face.

When the guy emerged from the elevator and made his way to his vehicle, Maxwell pounced, shoving the weapon between Trimlin's shoulder blades, and enjoining him to follow his orders., open the car and sit in the driver's seat. He then handcuffed him to his own steering wheel and installed himself beside him in the passenger seat.

He asked him about the Figueroa job.

Trimlin refused to answer.

He slugged him in the face, breaking his nose.

'I don't know anything about it. It had nothing to do with me. I can only assume the instructions came from New York. I'm just a West Coast point of contact,' he pleaded.

'How do I connect with your New York centre?'

'Even I have no idea. They keep us compartmentalised.'

It looked as if was another dead end. Maxwell's frustration was brewing.

He had an idea.

'What about the guy from the Luxor in Vegas?'

'I can't tell you that. If the organisation finds out I've provided the information, I'll be the next one to end up dead. And they'll probably use her for the job.'

'Her?' So, it was the woman that the police report had cast suspicion on.

Trimlin clammed up.

'I want a name?'

'Carla. But it's not her real name.'

'How can I get to her?'

'You can't. She no longer works the West Coast. Moved away.'

Maxwell tried to extract more information but by now Trimlin had said all he was willing to, albeit under duress.

The plan had been to get the man squealing and leave him handcuffed inside his own car, but Trimlin then signed his own death warrant when he taunted Maxwell.

'I know who you are, punk. That mask doesn't do shit. You're the queer piano player. You won't get away with this. After they hear what you've done to me, they'll come looking. Be certain of that.'

He had feared it might come to this and was prepared. He injected his captive in the neck with some tainted heroin he had got a hold of. Ten minutes later, his eyes had glazed and he had slumped forward over the steering wheel. He unlocked the handcuffs. Hopefully, it would look like an overdose.

Who needs contract killers when you can do it yourself?

Now to find the lovely Carla.

Maybe she would know who the man in the fedora was? After all, didn't they appear to be working for the same organisation?

18
The Legend of the Ice Queen

He now had a name. Carla.

Although he had no evidence it was the woman's real name, nor whether she would have a connection to the man in the fedora. He guessed that whoever controlled the suspected hit people ensured they had no likely knowledge of each other.

Then a kernel of memory came flooding back.

The illuminated marquee of a burlesque club in Oxnard.

Previewing a new dancer. Carla. Yes, that was it.

Carla the Gun. How could he have not remembered this?

That gut feeling, the adrenaline coursing through his veins as the revelation crystallised. As if the solution had been staring him in the face all along.

The lanky silhouette of the woman on the Vegas screen capture. The way she moved. Like a dancer hovering an inch above the ground as she stepped ahead and departed the Luxor and blended into the neon night of the Strip. Pieces of the puzzle coming together in Maxwell's mind.

He travelled all the way to Oxnard.

Carla had not performed there in well over a year and no, she didn't have a booking agency through which she could be reached.

He hung around the club until all the dancers on duty that day had arrived for their evening sets. Most had no recall of Carla. Hadn't been working in L.A. at the time. Only one had a vague recollection. 'A cold bitch, she was. Never had the time of day for the other performers. Kept to herself as if she was superior. To us all. But she a had great act. A sexy lass, she looked innocent on the outside, however much you can achieve that in the buff, but there was a hint of sheer filth on the inside. I wish I could project the way she did. Made a fortune in tips, she did. You remember her, Callie? The ice queen.'

'Sure do,' Callie, a tiny Latina with striking red hair – or was it a wig? – said. 'I heard somewhere she'd moved to the East Coast.'

'Oh yes, there's something else …'

'What?'

'She was always reading a book between sets, at her dressing table. And ignoring the rest of us. Too much of a loner if you ask me. Can't even remember hearing her speak.'

For once, the Internet was of no use to Maxwell, and neither was its more sinister mirror image on the dark web: there was no register or listing for burlesque or exotic dancers he could consult in his search for the suspicious woman departing the Luxor. In the screenshot he'd saved.

But there were fanatical online discussion groups devoted to every subject under the sun and the dubious art of striptease was certainly one of them. He joined several in the hope of narrowing his research, both as a participant and an eavesdropper. He labelled himself 'Sarah's Avenger' for this purpose, which was no more a quirky moniker than those used by other visitors to the sites.

He quickly established that she was now likely based on the East Coast, and had been known to perform regularly at some of the more upmarket clubs in Manhattan, Brooklyn, and the nearer perimeters of New York State, but there was no news of dancing over the past six months.

But she was no longer known as Carla, let alone Carla the Gun.

Her working name was now Cornelia.

She was a minor celebrity on the circuit, renowned for the fact she sported a small tattoo of a gun in a most strategic area on her body. Which made a crazy sort of sense, if Maxwell's speculations were correct. Cornelia attracted rave reviews for her art, if you could call it that, but it seemed made only parsimonious appearances on the circuit. Maybe by making herself scarce, she increased her desirability?

The more Maxwell investigated her, the more she intrigued him. She was allegedly beautiful in some fearsome way all the participants on the sites who had actually witnessed her perform found both daunting and particularly erotic. Something of a cult. Maxwell had not seen many stripper acts and found the comments contradictory, but then he was not attracted to women. In his mind, exotic dancing was vulgar and loud and unlikely to demonstrate much in the way of subtlety; it was just women undressing to music, wasn't it? And offering up lap dances and other sexual favours, no doubt.

He tried contacting every booking agency in New York that claimed to represent dancers, but none had heard of Cornelia or Carla. He guessed she didn't work through an agent.

Being miles and hours away was proving something of an obstacle, slowing any progress he was making in his very personal investigation. Maybe it was fate's way of telling him it was time to give up?

But then the memory of Sarah and the mental image he had of her naked body hitting the sidewalk and her life leaking away acted as a jolt and, invariably, strengthened his resolve. He had killed a man already to reach this point in his quest and it was too late to turn back. He had lost his innocence a long time ago and confusingly this might be the only way to regain it, by avenging his friend and justifying the cold-blooded murder he had himself committed.

He had to travel to New York. It was the only way forward. He had to hunt his prey down in the heart of the jungle where he now thought she lived. To monitor the half dozen establishments where she paraded her wares and wait for the moment she finally reappeared on the scene.

But first he would have to earn enough cash to finance the venture.

And it wasn't the piano-playing that was going to help steady his finances. He'd just put his arse on the line yet again, he concluded. Although with a degree of irony, considering how he was mentally so dismissive of Cornelia's version of sex work. Anything you can do, I can do better, Maxwell reckoned. And anyway, he liked going with men, although it would now also mean he would have to be less selective and agree to some indignities he would normally have shied away from, limits having to be stretched and all that!

He was young, maybe no Adonis but older men liked him, particularly the bears, the hairy ones who slobbered over him as they mounted him like a mare, even though they were nowhere near nature's version of true stallions!

It took a few months of liberally whoring himself for Maxwell to finally get a small nest egg together and make arrangements to travel to New York. He had friends there who had agreed to put him up on their sofa for a few weeks and he was hoping that, in that time, he could get closer to the elusive Cornelia.

By now, he had educated himself and become an expert on New York and its network of strip clubs and kept his eyes and ears open hoping Cornelia might manifest herself and resume working on the circuit again. All the dancers and baristas he would arrange to meet agreed they would get in touch with him should she surface, but all warned Maxwell she was anything but a creature of habits, and often disappeared for months on end before making a spectacular return to the circuit, with customers hungry for a sight of her in action. Other strippers would not have been tolerated had they adopted her lifestyle and habits, but she was worth every cent and the owners and bookers on the scene readily agreed to her idiosyncratic terms.

Eventually, his money ran out as did the number of sofas he could move between and he regretfully went back on the game. Yet again. Piano playing was never enough. He had hoped the final months hustling in Los Angeles might have been his last hurrah as a sex worker, but it was not to be. How long could he last doing this, he wondered, before it broke his spirit altogether? Sarah's ghost whispered to him in the dead of night and kept the flame of vengeance alive, although he was by now despairing he would ever obtain justice for her.

Even if he did locate Cornelia, what were the odds she might connect him with the mysterious man with the fedora?

It was unlikely.

It was winter, cold and miserable, the weather as bleak as his mood. He knew his looks were fading; already the men who picked him up were not willing to pay what they once were willing to. He was soiled goods. He wasn't even sure he could even find the energy to play piano again; his fingers frozen through the tattered woollen gloves he wore as he roamed the streets looking for a warm place to shelter or a bar where he could kill time long enough for his body to unfreeze over a cup of coffee that might last forever, or look into the eye of a possible punter and recognise the gaydar signs that this would be someone willing to pay for his sexual services.

Soon, even his cell phone would no longer be working as he couldn't afford to keep up the payment plan.

And then, it rang.

Esmerelda. She, like him had been pulling cheap trips back in California and they had kept in touch. She danced, she was also a hooker, she survived like carrion in the twilight world, both a user and someone accustomed to being used.

'Your girl?'

'Yes?'

'That stripping bitch who thinks she is an artist. She's surfaced.'

His stomach lurched.

'She's signed up for a week at Sapphire in a fortnight.'

'The Sapphire?' It was an establishment he had previously been unaware of; a private gentlemen's club.

'You owe me.'

It was up on the East Side. The classiest of joints. They

even had butlers to greet the customers. Just up Cornelia's street, judging from past experience.

Two weeks still. It would feel like eternity, Maxwell knew.

But he would be there, in waiting. Maybe the hour of reckoning would come.

Now he had to plan accordingly.

How to approach her. Deceive her. How to get her to talk. On a voluntary basis or otherwise. He relished the prospect.

19
The Life and Times of the Bureau

Underworld lore had it that the Bureau's origins dated back to the eighteenth century. Amongst the decaying splendour of Santiago de Cuba, on the southern coast of the Caribbean Island, and once a vital hub for the real-life pirates who had engaged in countless battles in the vicinity both against the reigning powers and between themselves.

There had been a bitter rivalry between two local warlords allegedly over a woman, which logic dictated could not be assuaged by a naval battle which would fatally harm both parties and encourage their peers to revolt against their respective commands. The English buccaneer had found another way to rid himself of his Spanish rival and had solicited the services of a local miscreant who, one night, took advantage of the dark and inebriated state of his target to spear him through the neck with a rapier, thus bringing the dispute to an inevitable conclusion.

The remaining pirate would die in 1748 a few years later when he allied himself to the British Royal Navy in the 2nd battle of Santiago and their combined forces were destroyed by the batteries of Morro Castle, protecting the city's harbour.

But, by then he had recruited further freelance locals who were willing to hire their swords or knives for monetary reward, and with the officer of a warship who had managed to escape the battle and retreat to sea soon after, was running a thriving business in well-renumerated assassinations. The clients were rival smugglers, jealous husbands, wives or lovers, but all trade was welcome.

The British officer who survived, and whose name posterity has not recorded, returned to Britain where he continued the business, no doubt finding it as easy back home to recruit willing criminals with the talent to kill on demand.

The threadbare organisation he had created must have survived him and, through family or acolytes, remained active across the next two centuries, such is the ever-constant demand for practiced assassins in all walks of life and internationally.

It was only in the late 20th century that the loose grouping acquired a name: the Bureau, when it moved to the USA and, if the rumour was correct, was taken over and given a more modern slant by a variety of retired CIA operatives, some of whom had used its services during the course of their own respective shadow careers.

By then, the organisation was being run as a dedicated business venture and with ruthless efficiency, all its operations carefully compartmentalised, and divided into operations, resources, information retrieval, computer services and communication, with few involved having precise knowledge of what occurred in adjoining sections. There was a thriving business in killing and the Bureau was the ultimate machine dedicated to its furtherance outside of the rules of law and national borders.

But now alarm bells were ringing. A lower cog in their American West Coast operation had been found dead in a club parking lot. He was insignificant in the greater order of things and had possessed little knowledge of anything beyond his own sphere of work but had in the weeks prior to his unfortunate demise flagged the fact that a stranger was asking uncommon questions pertaining to the Bureau had come to his notice. He duly reported the fact and had been asked to investigate the matter further. The news came as a troubling coincidence; one that couldn't be left unexamined.

The Bureau Head of Operations and his deputy had become involved.

'The police report we've accessed indicates the fact it

was a drug overdose.'

'And they've conveniently closed the case accordingly '

'Sounds wrong. We would never have employed the man if he had been a druggie. He was carefully monitored; we'd been using him to cover L.A. for over five years and there was never any sign of it, or any other infractions to the rules.'

'What do you think?'

'We have to go back to his reports. See if we can locate this man who was asking questions.'

'I agree.'

An operative was despatched from San Diego.

He reported two weeks later.

The individual who had been asking too many questions was a minor hustler with a side-line as a piano player, but he had completely disappeared from the local scene a few days earlier and a visit to his last place of residence had determined he had moved away, leaving no belongings, or forwarding address.

A nationwide alert was put out.

A month later, he was reported to be in New York, still hustling, still asking unwelcome questions but this time he appeared not be enquiring about the Bureau itself but one of its freelance, East Coast-based operatives. One of their best assets. A woman, one of the few they had on their books.

'What do we do?'

'Warn her?'

'Who is her handler?'

'Ivan.'

'Seeing as it was his West Coast counterpart who met a sticky ending, maybe not. Don't wish to alarm the troops too much.'

The Bureau executive in charge of oversight pondered for a moment.

'We'll use an independent contractor to act as liaison instead.'

'As you wish.'

'In the meantime, track this guy down and set up a hit dossier. Maybe it would be poetic justice to ask her to do the job? She might even, prior to the *Coup de grace* be able to find out why he's proving such a nuisance.'

'She's only known for her termination skills. She's not a trained interrogator.'

'Let's wait and see how she feels about it once the information retrieval team have compiled a case dossier.'

The Bureau machine slowly moved into gear. A momentum that once initiated could seldom be stopped in its tracks. In their marine graves, maybe the erstwhile pirates of the Caribbean were smiling through their empty sockets and skulls garlanded with weeds and melding into the coral reefs?

20
The Ballad of Cornelia and Hopley

Every love story is different.

Every love story is the same.

Although both Cornelia and Hopley would have strongly denied that what was happening to them was actually a love story. Or a meeting of minds. Or even a meeting of bodies. No, it was just a happy accident.

For the initial two weeks of their affair, she never suggested they go to hers. She was content to camp at Hopley's apartment, making occasional forays outside to pick up essential groceries and drinks, and walk the quarter of an hour to her own apartment to change clothes and refresh her underwear – although she soon became accustomed to not wearing much with him around. Which Hopley initially found disconcerting, unfamiliar with Cornelia's unashamed level of comfort with her own nudity. He had never come across someone so at ease with her body.

Although no rules were formally established, it soon became apparent to both of them that neither welcomed personal questions about their past or present life or appeared in the least interested in asking any back. As if they wished to just remain strangers outside of the bed and of any particular piece of furniture over which they had lustily fucked.

One of her initial requests was to view the other volumes he had inherited and expressed interest in several of the books.

'Just because we've been to bed together doesn't mean I'm granting you a discount,' Hopley joked.

The blank look on her face betrayed her lack of humour.

'Of course not, I wouldn't expect any. We should keep our private lives separate from any form of business arrangement.'

'Very formal, but fine with me.'

They even haggled a bit once he had priced the volumes she wanted, after checking their value on eBay. But they quickly reached a satisfying middle-ground.

She was wearing skin-tight jeans and a shirt she had borrowed from his closet and kept unbuttoned and was vigorously brushing her hair in front of the bathroom mirror. She had taken a shower and washed it and then was briefly taken aback not finding a hairdryer. He'd never found the need for one.

Her curls were an unholy mess of embedded small reptiles as she tried to untangle them.

'Your conditioner's not doing a great job …'

'Next time you go home, why don't you bring your own back … Or just tell me which brand I should buy?'

'I'll be going over later.'

'Can I come with you? I'd like to see your place. The rest of your library. Just curious.'

'Some of the more valuable ones are still in storage. But if you want; it's just a small studio. Not much space.'

Hopley felt he was making progress and was glad he had asked. He was curious about her home environment.

'For your business, don't you ever go out? Have an office somewhere?'

'No. I just work from my laptop. Easier that way. Don't like to be tied down. What about you, you never talk about your life. Are you studying or something like it? I was wondering.'

Cornelia turned to face him.

'I work. But I am my own boss. Choose when and where. Freelance, you could call it.'

'Oh.'

'I hope that us having come together has not affected

it?'

'No. As it happens, I'm taking a lengthy break. As long as I can afford to do so.'

'I did that last year. Like a reboot.'

'You could call it that.'

'To do with books? Although I recall you saying you were not a professional dealer when we chatted first on the phone.'

She looked him straight in the eyes as she buttoned up the shirt, stealing away the spectacle of her slight breasts from his greedy gaze.

'I strip.'

Hopley gulped. It was the last answer he had expected.

She continued, 'but I don't do lap dances or have sex with customers. I just dance; I'm not an escort. Never have been.'

Hopley was digesting this new information.

'Are you disappointed?'

'No.'

'I'm a good dancer. I see it as an art. A minor one, true, but a skill nonetheless. Call it a craft, if you will.'

'OK.'

He wasn't sure what to quite say next.

Cornelia was now concerned at having said, revealed so much. She was enjoying being with Hopley. Didn't want things to change, or at any rate not yet. Had she said too much?

'I'm not ashamed of it,' she said.

'I'm sure.'

'Does it make you uncomfortable?'

'Not at all.'

'If you wish to keep on seeing me, you have to accept it. I will not change for you, or any man.'

'Why would I have a problem with it?'

'Some men would. Knowing others have full access to my body...'

'Not quite full access, though, right? The way you

explain it, it's a look but don't touch situation.'

'Exactly.'

'You're not the jealous type.'

'I don't think so.'

'Think or know?'

Hopley hesitated.

'You must never come to see me when I perform, though,' she asked him.

He reluctantly agreed.

'In that case, you may visit my place and see for yourself.'

The moment they passed the door to her apartment, she grabbed Hopley by the hand and pulled him to her bedroom. The bed was unmade, smelled of her. She hurriedly undressed him in silence as he held his breath, then enjoined him to sit on its edge and she stripped and danced for him to invisible music. The lovemaking that followed was rough and savage, with a degree of obscene intimacy neither of them had ever experienced before.

The nightmares began after they had been dating for about three months, although Hopley told her he had suffered from bad dreams his whole life.

On half or more of the nights they spent together he would wake her during the early hours twitching and kicking and groaning in his sleep like a man possessed. He left the pillow wet with sweat and sometimes damp with tears. Cornelia could do nothing to keep the images that haunted him at bay, nothing but wrap her arms around him and pull his head into her lap and rock him like a baby until he fell asleep again with his face in her lap while she stroked his hair. In the morning, he would have no memories of the episode.

Other times she would wake to find his side of the bed empty, and Hopley pacing up and down by the window, naked, his strong thighs and narrow rear end a tantalising reminder of how she loved to hold onto his stocky body as he straddled her. Or, he might not be in the apartment at all, and she would lay awake and fret until he returned, sweaty from an early morning run around Washington Square Park or soaking wet from a sudden downpour in which he had been caught.

'Do you ever think about death?' he asked her on one of these occasions, when neither of them could find solace in sleep and they repaired to his kitchen where Cornelia wrapped herself up in his heavy navy and gold-striped towelling robe and made a pot of strong coffee.

'Is that what you always dream about?' she asked him.

'Sometimes, yes.'

'I think everybody thinks about death. It's one thing we all have in common.'

She briefly regretted her words. Too much information.

He didn't say anything further after that. They ate their early breakfast, went back to bed, and she took him into her mouth and helped him forget his fears.

Hopley was surprisingly the first person who made her feel truly needed. His nightmares had woken in her a strong protective urge and the desire to take care of him, which was something she had never felt for anyone before, and she enjoyed it. Nursing his vulnerable streak gave her a skewed sense of purpose.

They fell rapidly into a routine. Weekdays at his and weekends at hers. Hopley was a minimalist by nature, and his apartment was one of those modern developments with all the cupboards built in and the carpets and walls in shades of taupe, cream and grey. Soon some of her slacks and dresses hung on the rails of his walk-in closet alongside his business suits, her shoes and trainers piled up on the rack below, a half dozen packets of her flavoured teas were deposited in the kitchen (popcorn, and mint chocolate were her favourites), but once all the cupboard doors had been slid shut her presence was barely noticeable, except in the bathroom, where a mountain of hair care, bodywash products and cosmetics filled the mirrored cabinet and overflowed to the corners of the bathtub, vanity unit and along the windowsill.

It was only when their clothes were sometimes drying together on the small fold-out laundry rack in the living room that it occurred to her his life had practically absorbed hers. The brightly coloured underwear and silky blouses that she had hand washed and set out to drip dry looked out of place and almost crowded off the rack hanging alongside his T-shirts and other monochrome items of clothing. She thought of bringing over a carton of her books along, but she never read when they were together, always finding better things to do whether in or out of bed and she didn't want to come off like a cartoon possessive girlfriend, marking her territory, and besides which, there were in fact no shelves in Hopley's place.

Neither had yet been presented with the conundrum of a call from Bureau acolytes and a job assignment, although both dreaded the inevitable day. And, despite a few offers, Cornelia had turned down any further dancing engagements for the foreseeable future.

Small doubts would surface but this was natural, they both reckoned; there would inevitably be shifts in their relationship, seasons. Cornelia forgot her fears and worries soon enough when Hopley would out of the blue and wordlessly hold her in his arms, and they fucked on the sofa, and the floor of the living room. They were comfortable together.

But occasionally they would exchange concerned glances. They both knew it couldn't last forever this way. Life always has a way of allowing shit to happen.

21
The Drinks Waitress

Sladjana was born in Belgrade and, from an early age, had starry dreams of travelling. Her family had come unscathed through the civil war and she was, to a certain extent, a child of privilege. But the unravelling of the old Yugoslavia took a toll on her father, a dentist, his loyalties torn in conflicting directions, his long-standing friendships with other communities questioned, as was her mother's different ethnic origins and he had turned to drink. He was a bad alcoholic and quickly frittered away their savings, lost his practice and became an emotional and physical wreck which soon saw him turn against his family in violent ways. She was an only child.

She was unable or unwilling to complete her university studies in anthropology and took a secretarial job in a local health cooperative who had taken pity on her family's fall from grace and reduced circumstances. But the job was boring and had little prospects of advancement and the possibility of earning enough to afford her own flat, or even to be able to share with someone, not that she had any acquaintances with similar ambitions with either the same desire for independence or the means.

Since abandoning her studies, Sladjana had seen a couple of boyfriends come and go. The sex was disappointing, their manners clumsy and selfish, and it hurt her to hear them complain she wasn't even a good fuck, was too passive, and quiet. What did they want her to do? Scream like a bitch in heat as they thrust between her legs and pretend she was enjoying it? She would look at herself in the mirror on the inside of her cupboard's door and all she could see was a small girl, looking so much younger than her 22 years, weak-chinned, flat-chested and with mousy hair that even the blonde streaks she applied on a regular basis did little to enhance.

Even her rare girlfriends from back in secondary school probably laughed at her behind her back, no doubt in possession of all the intimate details her erstwhile boyfriends had liberally revealed about her lack of aptitude at sex. The mouse who fucked, she'd heard whisper.

What she enjoyed most were all the travel documentaries she'd overdose on whenever they were screened on the TV. Exotic places, beaches, rivers, monuments, skies that were bluer than blue, bridges, forests, islands, all so distant and unattainable.

She fell into an affair with an older man who had known her father, who was in management at the Ministry of Health. He was rumoured to have played a significant role in the paramilitaries during the troubles. She was almost grateful he would take her to his bed. He was coarse too, but there was a subtle degree of cruelty in the way he manipulated her, both physically and mentally.

She tried to be compliant, hoping that her subservience would encourage him to deepen the relationship, maybe even make her his official mistress, dreaming that one day he would be satisfied enough with her that he might even take her travelling to some of those places she fantasised about. A fair exchange for opening her legs and other openings for him at will and often at short notice when he felt like rutting and ordered her to drop all else and present herself for use.

To the extent she lost her typing job, following too many absences or sudden desertions of her office desk due to alleged illnesses. When she confronted him with the fact, blaming him for her loss of employment, he just shrugged his shoulders, arguing that the sex they had was just transactional, that surely they both profited from it and he had no further responsibility for her. Sladjana cried. Out of fear for her future, out of shame. Her older lover suggested she whore herself. Could even offer advice as to how to proceed, help her with contacts. But Sladjana no longer trusted him. She had read too many accounts of naïve Eastern European or Slavic girls not much different from her who had been trafficked to terrible places and labours overseas. If sex had to become a currency, a last resort, she decided, it would be on her own terms. She didn't need a pimp.

She began waitressing. First in a local restaurant much frequented by foreign tourists who were good tippers, but the other women she worked with felt she wasn't attractive enough, conveyed the right sexy image, to be part of their fraternity and lowered the place's tone and, inevitably, the tips they were granted and pooling together.

Sladjana found a job at a café, on the outskirts of the city centre, where the standards were not as cynically demanding, and she was allowed to dress more properly and not display as much skin and wear shorter skirts that barely covered her arse. Maybe the customers here were less sophisticated or had lower standards as she had had regular offers to meet outside of her place of work, some of which she agreed to if she felt the man was safe. And now she no longer had any qualms about asking for gifts or money in exchange.

Boris had just handed her a fifty Euros note for her services. He was staying in a classy hotel. He dressed well. Not like any local man. He now lived overseas but was very reluctant to tell anyone what he was doing or precisely where. Sladjana wouldn't have been surprised if he was connected to some criminal outfit. He was the type. But he treated her well on his occasional visits to Belgrade.

'Thank you.'

'No problem.'

'So, tell me, big spender, how does a poor girl get to go abroad?'

'You ask me every time, Sladjana. Overseas is no land of milk and honey, be aware.'

'But at least it's not here. I want to escape.'

'Well …'

'But on my own terms, Ivan. I don't want to be doing this all my life. It's just to make ends meet, you know.'

'I understand.' He was always economical with words.

'I'm a good waitress. Maybe I could be one abroad?'

'They have their own. You're one in a million.'

Sladjana sighed as she zipped up her skirt and slipped on her low-heeled work shoes. She had a final shift to complete today and had no wish to be late.

'But …'

'Yes?'

'Have you ever thought of cruise ships?'

'What are they?'

'It's becoming an increasingly popular tourist activity. You have these huge ships which can take thousands of passengers. They have multiple bars and restaurants, pools, Jacuzzis, shops. Like small cities on the water. And they just travel around the world and places. They need tons of staff, workers. Employ people from all over the world; used to be a big way out for Ukrainian girls, but of course that's off the menu now. A chance to work in the West with few strings attached. You might have a chance.'

'So where do I apply?'

'I think they recruit through specialist agencies. There might be some in Serbia. You should try and find out.'

'I will …'

'And a word of advice: don't be so meek. Be more assertive. Sladjana, you're a good girl, but it's so evident you're too submissive. If you're not careful they will take advantage of you.'

'They do already.' His smile was enigmatic, as if there was so much more to his words and he had left the subject hanging in the air, for her to reflect on further.

The conversation stuck in her mind for weeks as she hunted down possible employment agencies who might have contracts with or worked for foreign cruise companies. Most of the ship owners appeared to be American or Norwegian, countries with whom Serbia had limited business contacts.

His words about her submissiveness had also stuck and she began to haunt the internet and an assortment of sites the word led her to, in an attempt to see where she might fit in the world of BDSM. Hopping from link to link she once spent a feverish night in a chatroom, where the conversations both shocked and excited her more than she thought was healthy, touching herself repeatedly throughout, her face flushed, her mind is a state of sheer panic. The participants all had screen names: Zelda, The Pianist, The Master of Pain, Stallion, Bookcock, Aida, The Author, Vina, Réage, London Fuckmeat, Roquelaure, Jasmine Tea … Sladjana remained just an onlooker that night and the many following ones, logged on as merely a guest, too scared to reveal her eavesdropping presence there and knowing her written English was still too weak for her to be able to participate fully in the ongoing conversations on the screen. Should she try and participate? Ask questions? Find herself a suitable name? Shy Sladjana? Sub Slad?

She was aware her fascination for this new scene was unhealthy and that her resolve would falter if she remained online too long or kept on returning to these sites but couldn't find it in herself to leave the night screen which captured her attention and sexual imagination after returning home to her small room following her final waitressing shift.

She was saved in extremis.

She had received an answer to one of her cruise online employment enquiries and was being offered an interview in the very same Belgrade hotel where she'd been with Ivan. Poetic alignment! A company was seeking engineers, electricians, cleaners and bar staff. On 6-to-9-month contracts. Was she interested in applying?

Sladjana promptly deleted her web history, although she remained morbidly curious about the play date the Pianist, Zelda and the Master of Pain had arranged in a basement on the Bowery; an area of New York she had only heard of because of its past music connections. Would Zelda go through with it? She'd never know. Would she have been tempted had she lived in the mirage that was New York? She deliberated for days on end what to wear for the interview. Prim and proper? Elegant? What was normal anyway? The agency was from Bremerhaven in Germany and was touring capitals in Serbia, Croatia, Bosnia and Montenegro on the outlook for potential suitable staff for several cruise ship companies. Previous experience useful but not necessary.

To Sladjana's great surprise, the interview went swimmingly. The German woman who asked her questions was a grey-haired lady, square-jawed and with a steely composure, wearing a pinstriped tailored trouser suit and initially scared the heck out of her. But she was professional and attentive, perusing Sladjana's meagre CV and the food trade references she'd managed to collect in silence, as Sladjana sat uncomfortably across from her, with just the desk, and its open HP laptop and a notebook astride it, separating them.

The German woman, who'd introduced herself as Claudia, explained all about the contract, the hours involved, the renumeration, the restrictions, the fact she would have to share a cabin with someone else and how different cruise companies organised their schedules. Sladjana just nodded approvingly, already mulling over the places she might visit: the Fjords, the Amazon, the Caribbean, around the British Isles. seven months away at sea sounded like a golden opportunity to recalibrate her life.

Two days later she had a phone call offering her a position on a ship owned by a British company although registered in Nassau. She had to look Nassau up. She had to arrange various health certificates, including Covid, had no need for actual visas and a month from now would be flown to London where a coach would await to transport her and the other new crew members to the port of Tilbury. The agency couldn't yet provide the specific itineraries the ship would be going on during her contract but she was assured it would be far and wide. She joyfully agreed to the terms.

Six months later, and with just a Scandinavian cruise left on her contract, she had reached the stage where she would have to decide after a necessary break back home, whether she wanted to agree to a further contract later in the year. It had not been all she expected and there had been a strong measure of disappointment. Most of the other women working on board alongside her appeared to be from India or the Philippines, and she found she had little in common with them and feared they found her snooty and uncommunicative, but she had liked the customers who sailed on the ship. Not rich people as she had initially expected, but amiable pensioners with an abundance of canes, wheelchairs, motorised scooters, hearing aids and Zimmer frames who were making the best of their final years and were always surprisingly cheerful, especially the English who formed most of those sailing on this particular vessel.

On the other hand, she had barely seen all the wonders of the world she was expecting. The hours were long and she was only allowed a few hours to walk offboard with other staff when they docked, and then not at every single destination, depending on her rotas. The Caribbean ports were mostly tourist traps with shops and stalls selling T-shirts, Hawaiian shirts, fridge magnets and duty-free diamonds and there was never the opportunity to venture further into the interior of the islands or countries before it was time to return to duty on the ship. But the sea was beautiful, a landscape in constant motion she would never tire of and always remember, an awesome vision waltzing her senses as she peered through the windows of the Botanical Lounge to which she had been assigned to serve drinks. But she was also terribly lonely. And had begun smoking again, a promise she had made to herself and broken within days of the initial cruise's departure, puffing away like a witch between shifts and after dark, buffeted by the night sea winds, huddled in the corners of the deck where she could remain mostly unseen.

She reckoned it could have been worse. If the cruise ship job had not come up, she could well have turned into Zelda and succumbed to her base instincts. It still gave her an obscene, shameful thrill to think of herself violated in a New York basement. At sea, it was the only thrill available.

22
Angels of Death
at the Angelika

Inevitably, the calls came.

By a stroke of luck, both Cornelia and Hopley were apart when it happened. She had gone on an errand to the Strand Rare Book Room to check the condition of a new arrival, when her cell phone rang. She was summoned to meet up with a representative from the Bureau in the lobby of the Angelika Film Center, on the corner of Mercer and Houston two days later at 8pm. It was not her usual handler and she was wary of the fact that the cinema would be particularly crowded at that time on a Saturday night but had no choice but to agree to the instructions. She immediately tried to think up a suitable excuse to explain her absence to Hopley on the weekend, not that they had made any specific plans for the evening.

Hopley's call came the following morning, when Cornelia was in the shower. He would be needed in Boston the following day. When he advised her he had to take an urgent trip for business to Philadelphia and wasn't certain how long he would have to be absent, she was secretly relieved, the circumstances combining to avoid her having to lie to him. He was to pick up his hit dossier from a locker at La Guardia.

It was the first occasion they had been forced to conceal facts from each other. It didn't quite feel the same as deliberately not providing answers to questions.

'While you're away, I think I'll stay at mine.'

'Good idea.' He didn't feel comfortable about Cornelia

remaining in his apartment while he was on a job. Hopley didn't think there was anything incriminating about, or that would point to his illegal activities – he was a very tidy and cautious person – but it was a case of being better safe than sorry, he reckoned. He also expressed a silent vote of thanks for not being despatched to L.A. again; the whole unfortunate episode with the girl, Sarah, had left an indelible stain on his conscience. Or for that, New Orleans and the inevitable echoes it would summon of Ramona. It was strange how some cities were now forever associated for him with certain women. As Manhattan now was inseparable from Cornelia. Who would have thought him, just a few years ago, he would be so sentimental?

Meanwhile, Cornelia was already puzzling hard as to how she might justify her own absence to him should the upcoming job also take her out of the city, for however long it would take. But it did not come to that. Once inside the movie house's foyer, she spotted a man with an Anomaly.com tote bag draped across his corner table by the ticket machine, bought herself a coffee and joined him. She was wearing old grey track suit bottoms, a Handsome Family tour T-shirt and a baseball cap. He looked like an anonymous office nerd in a cheap, creased suit.

'Thank you for coming.'

He had the sort of face she knew she would forget within instants of leaving the place.

'You're not my customary contact? Any reason for that? Changes to the routine do make me a tad nervous.' Although she had never been a great fan of Ivan's, whose demeanour was always rather intimidating at the best of times.

'There is a good reason for this. This is not your usual customary sort of assignment. Hence my presence. I'm management, not operations.'

'Tell me more.'

'There is someone who has been asking questions. In California. We don't know why but by unfortunate coincidence your erstwhile local handler has come to a sticky ending and we suspect there might, I fear, be a connection.'

Cornelia recalled the affable Trimlin. She was sorry to hear he was gone. He was the one who had introduced her to her shadow life. He was also the one who had suggested she move coasts. Was this coincidental?

'He'd recommended I leave the West Coast. Is the matter mob-related and connected to one of my past jobs?'

'We're uncertain. The questions initially being asked were in fact not about you but concerned another operative. As you well know, we prefer moving contractors around so that their connection to hits is geographically random. However, lately the man has been enquiring about you too.'

'That's worrying.'

'Yes, he is presently in New York.'

'Damn.'

'But he is working in the dark. Been bothering people around the strip club circuit. Your patch.'

'I haven't performed for ages.'

'We know. But should you resume your dancing activities, there is a strong likelihood, the man will surface.'

'I'm unsure if I will ever go back. My personal situation is undergoing changes.'

'Be that as it may, the man is a nuisance; something has to be done before he becomes a bona fide problem for the Bureau.'

'You want him taken out.'

'Indeed. But we have to find out what or who is behind him, why he is enquiring about us, you, our other player. We're currently shadowing him but he moves around, has no place of his own. A minor hustler.'

'I'm not an interrogator.'

'But you're the one he appears to be seeking, the honeytrap, and we strongly believe he would tell you what his motivations are.'

'And how do I do that?'

'You have built a solid reputation. You are professional. You will find a way.' He could have reminded her that declining the job was not an option, but he didn't have to. Cornelia knew the rules of the game

'I'm not a torturer. Neither a professional interrogator; nor would I wish to be one. Not my skill-set.'

'That's not the point. It's a job and you are the one we are assigning to deal with the matter. It's not a matter for negotiation.'

Cornelia sighed.

'Usual fee?'

'On satisfactory completion. And a substantial bonus if you can get him to talk before doing the deed. We've leaked the fact you might be found at a given club at a future date, if it helps putting the two of you in contact.'

'I'd rather you hadn't done that. I try and keep both sides of my life separate.'

Cornelia shrugged. She was in no need of money anyway, but knew they'd expect her to ask. The rules of the game. Which he didn't feel obliged to play any longer.

He took a sip of his now cold coffee and handed over a thin folder with the information the Bureau had collated about the mark.

Maxwell. Male prostitute. Gay. No fixed abode. Originally from California. Occasional piano player.

He was a nobody. How could he present a threat to the Bureau? To her?

Sure, she could find a way to eliminate him. That wasn't the problem. What bothered Cornelia was the fact it had somehow become a personal matter. Why was he so keen to find her? For what purpose? As a stripper, she naturally attracted undue attention and the occasional minor league stalkers, but she had quickly put them all in their place and discouraged their unwanted attentions. Without having to resort to killing them. What made this guy so different? Anyway, he was gay so that couldn't be the reason he was seeking her out. And querying her connection to the Bureau.

'Is there a time frame?'

'As soon as possible.'

'Normally I am given an indication where to locate the mark. According to your dossier, he moves between places on an almost weekly basis. I'm not a detective. How do I find him?'

'He's sniffing around the clubs. As I mentioned, in anticipation we've leaked the news you are about to resume your glittering career. He might come running. '

'Fuck.' This was the last thing Cornelia wanted to do. And she was concerned it might unduly complicate matters with Hopley.

'You're an intelligent girl. Think of something. It's important you do so. Time is of the essence.'

'OK.'

He rose to his feet, then reminded her 'There is a contact number on the final page; we need you to report progress by the end of next week.' He moved away, making his way through the crowd of now queueing moviegoers eager to see the new David Lynch restoration.

It was dusk as she walked out moments later onto Houston; there was a thin curtain of rain and people were scrambling for umbrellas. She tucked her unruly hair into her baseball cap. Her brain was running on overdrive. Ways to ambush Maxwell, get him on her side, gain his confidence. However, not knowing the true motives for his seeking her out meant she was not in possession of half the equation. Too much could go wrong. It was like a jigsaw puzzle with pieces still missing.

Although the opportunities had certainly presented themselves, she realised she knew very little about the business of sex work, and even less when it came to gay men.

She was walking down Wooster Street, just about to reach the junction with Prince where all the designer stores were taking over the neighbourhood when she called the number she had been given.

'It's me.'

'Already? That's quick work,' he ironized at the other end.

'Just a question.'

'Shoot ...'

'Does this guy Maxwell actually know what I look like?'

'We don't think he does. He has a screen grab off a street camera he's been showing around, but it could be anyone. He just knows the milieu in which you navigate, which is why he's been buzzing around the stripping circuit.'

'Good. That helps,' she disconnected.

Hopley arrived at his Boston hotel by the Seaport late in the afternoon and resolved to eat locally. He walked at a leisurely pace down the Waterfront in search of somewhere to sample a clam chowder. It had been over a decade since he had initially visited the city for the first time and had retained the taste of that chowder ever since in his palate. The restaurant was noisy but an ideal place to disappear in, not attracting attention to himself. He'd changed into what he termed his work clothes, an off the rack grey three-piece suit, a white button-down collar shirt and the fedora he never wore in New York and which proved an invaluable foil to the inquisitive gaze of CCTV cameras. The only item of attire he would also wear back home in Manhattan were his comfortable black shoes. It felt like a uniform, a combination of clothing he would only wear when on assignments.

Target: Benjamin X. A minor league drug dealer who was trying to elbow his way into territory controlled by more powerful interests. He had an office in Mystic, a front as a financial adviser, which fooled no one.

Hopley was waiting for him in early morning as the guy pulled up in his Lexus and walked up the brownstone's steps. The Bureau had arranged for a formal appointment. Introducing Hopley to Benjamin X as a possible new source of product. Insisting they had to meet alone with no others present.

'You're early, man.'

'I prefer it to being late. I'm not familiar with your city

so thought it would be advisable should I lose my way coming to you.'

'Great.'

'Shall we go in?'

Benjamin X unlocked the door. He had three keys for three different locks. He probably kept his stock inside, not that this concerned Hopley who looked up and down the street a few times to check on onlookers as he followed the dealer into the two-storeyed building. He slipped his leather gloves on as he stepped in behind Benjamin X.

He was out ten minutes later, similarly scouting the empty street for possible passers-by.

He had done the deed just as the door slammed behind him. Piano wire. Invariably did the job fast. Clean and noiseless. Hopley only used guns as a last resort. The last time he had done so was on the unfortunate Figueroa job.

Benjamin X never saw him coming and slumped silently to the ground.

Five blocks away, Hopley called an Uber on a pre-programmed burner phone he would later flush down the toilet at the airport and was boarding his return flight by midday.

He hoped Cornelia would be glad to see him back so fast.

23
Down in Sordid City

She rang Hopley.

'Something has come up. I might be away for a few weeks. I'm sorry.'

He knew not to ask, but he did.

'Book stuff?'

She was honest with him, within reason, 'No, something else. But I will be in touch as soon as I'm back. Promise.'

'And when you do, we might take a serious look at that long vacation we've idly been talking about for ages?'

'Why not?'

They had discussed it. A way for both of them to turn a possible new page. Now on hold for reasons beyond their respective control.

Cornelia then called a few acquaintances from the dancing circuit in California who, she was aware, had more experience than her of the BDSM world, gay hustling and its mores. She was confident this would provide a path to establishing contact with Maxwell and hopefully, initially engaging with him in some unsuspecting manner. Apart from bibliographical matters, she hadn't indulged in research since university and recalled how much she enjoyed the meticulous digging through archives and slowly mining obscure websites. Now it had become more than a hobby but a necessity.

Little did she know where it would lead her.

She was lying on her stomach, her arms extended forward, handcuffed to Maxwell, fully stripped, stretched out on a mattress of dubious cleanliness, and listening to him moan while a bear-shaped and hirsute dominant mounted the piano player just a few inches away from her wide-open eyes. She also knew she might be fucked next. The room smelt of beer and stale tobacco; they were in a basement in Alphabet City, and there were total strangers in the darkness at the periphery of the room watching in all impunity as the play developed. Cornelia hoped no others would wish to participate and join the sexual fray. Or bring out for use or display further accoutrements of the BDSM scene like whips, canes, paddles or worse. The sex she could tolerate. It was a means to an end. But she had a phobia of being marked. Aside from the fact that what with the natural pallor of her body the resulting contrast would make an uncomfortable canvas to behold.

The stallion to Maxwell's mare kept on pumping him with a terrible energy born of lust and anger and the young, gay hustler closed his eyes as the filling brought tears to them, and he rode the wave of sensations she assumed were by now racing through his body from his anus to his brain.

Sadly, she knew how it felt. A sensation she initially rebelled against, angry at the fact her body and senses sometimes made her such a slave to sexual desire. But also, one she welcomed with a deep sigh of frustration and craving when she was in need and lost part control of her actions and surrendered in to the lust. She'd heard say that men were guided by their cock, but in counterpart she also knew that some women, or at least the woman she had become, were also as much in the grip of sexual dependency. It just translated differently according to gender; erotic zones at genital and anal level as well as in the cortex and, also, the heart when the conditions, and person, were right. When it clicked.

Cornelia reasoned that this was also work and that what Hopley wouldn't know wouldn't hurt him, although she would rather he not learn of this somewhat extreme episode. She liked him, he fucked her well. But there was also the curiosity, particularly now as she witnessed Maxwell being ruthlessly used, of finding out how it would be with this redoubtable stranger.

She had made some form of contact with Maxwell on a gay dating site which flirted heavily with the dark site of sexual matters. He listed himself as 'The Pianist'. On his profile, he indicated he was partial to heavy dominance, group use and bears. He also advertised for a female partner in crime, with similar cravings to form a pair of submissive for joint play.

It was the opening she needed. She had responded.

Calling herself 'Zelda'. She'd always had a soft spot for F. Scott Fitzgerald, his books and his life.

When he reacted, he was eager to advise her that should they 'click', he had no interest at all in seeking sex of any nature with her. But he had been invited by several doms to find a fellow female submissive who could be present when he was playing, as a form of humiliation and degradation, to witness how low he could stoop in subservience to superior men. 'Masters', he called them. He emphasised that no money was involved, from either party. It was all consensual.

Cornelia was tickled by the idea but asked for certain reassurances, so as not to appear too eager. They then agreed to meet.

With a muffled roar, the dom gave a final thrust and moaned aloud as he came. Maxwell's body was almost convulsing and she could feel every single vibration as their hands touched each other through the handcuffs that connected them.

The hairy colossus remained inside Maxwell, still breathing hard, a smug smile of satisfaction spreading across his lips. Cornelia's heart waltzed the light fantastic as she both feared and craved what might now happen next.

There was a ripple of applause from the back of the small rectangular room, as if an artistic performance had reached its climax and the spectating voyeurs were pleased by the show that had taken place in their honour.

Behind her, Cornelia heard feet shuffle. A hand grazed her left arse cheek. Then moved to the other, as if weighing the merchandise, assessing her worth, or her fuckability. It moved to her hair, combing its way through her morass of blonde curls. She could feel a dozen of eyes gazing at her, at the intimacy she had no choice but to display to the massed onlookers hidden in the darkness of the room's depth.

The man who had fucked Maxwell shouted out.

'No. She's mine.'

There was a murmur of disapproval; the animals being deprived of their exposed prey.

'But this boy bitch has drained me,' he said, nodding at Maxwell's prone body. 'Next time, I will take her for myself before she's allowed to become public property.'

Cornelia sighed in relief, although part of her knew would keep wondering how it might have been had the dom been able to recover his strength and get erect again faster.

'Anyone want sloppy seconds with the boy,' he called out. There were no takers. She heard the spare audience shuffle away; the door to the room opening and closing. The hairy hulk moved away from Maxwell, circling the mattress. His penis was still at half-mast as he stood himself next to Cornelia's face. Visibly damp from his own and Maxwell's secretions. It was wonderfully large and obscene even in this rapidly detumescent state. Cornelia couldn't keep staring at it, her mind in a frenzy of abominable thoughts. Prior to Hopley, when sex was for her a pleasant way to free her libido, leaving all feelings excluded, just something her health demanded, she had never been properly attracted to any man, his face, voice or personality. They were just objects, and only good to her for their cocks. She remembered the latter, never the faces. Had she really changed, she wondered?

Maxwell came out of his post-coital trance and whispered weakly 'Thank you, Sir.'

Their handcuffs were unlocked and they were allowed to rise from the mattress that had been lain on the wooden basement floor. Cornelia stood and noticed that all the spectators had now filed away in silence, leaving just the three protagonists of the play in place.

The brute had slipped on a pair of tight leather trousers through which his impressive junk was still clearly outlined and ordered them to dress. Their clothes were piled up by the door where they had summarily been ordered to strip bare on their arrival. They hurriedly did so.

'Tomorrow, same time,' the man demanded. 'And little girl, see that your shithole is properly douched and clean, OK?'

Cornelia meekly nodded, although she bristled at both the peremptory injunction and how he presumed she was willing to get fucked in the arse, as Maxwell had been. She kept her silence.

Once dressed, they were shown the door, and exited onto the Lower East Side. There was a thin drizzle of rain shadowing the nearby buildings and the lights of a nearby bodega shone through the haze.

Maxwell was still silent, as if part of his mind had been annihilated by the violence of his treatment, let alone the fact that Cornelia had witnessed his sexual destruction at such close quarters and what it said about him as a man.

The rain was now heavier. Maxwell almost slipped on a metal grate. Cornelia had neither umbrella nor baseball cap to shield them, having come to the assignment with no handbag or tote and almost nothing in her pockets that might have betrayed who she was. She was particular about her anonymity.

24
Killing Maxwell

'So why do you do it?'

They were sheltering from the rain that was now pelting down, isolating Manhattan in a wet, wintery shroud, in a nearby coffee house.

'What? Get fucked by men? I'm passive, not top.'

'Not just the sex. The way you allow them to own you, degrade you?' she asked.

'Why did you agree to come along? Wanted a thrill watching gay sex?'

'I must admit I was curious. Initially liked the idea of being coupled with a sub. But I never realised it would become so extreme.'

'Are you having cold feet about tomorrow, then?'

'I don't know.'

'Did it turn you on?'

'A little. But I'm also a bit of an exhibitionist, so that was possibly another motivation …'

Cornelia was mentally navigating through murky waters and, almost as a way of justifying her rationale, she was about to reveal she stripped for a living but thought better of it. Maxwell might make the connection. It was too early for that. She was not here to chat about their respective twisted psyches, but to get answers and then complete the job, as she always did.

'But don't you get a thrill, too, from obeying orders, sometimes not knowing how far it will go, where it will take you?'

'I don't. I'm not good at taking orders.'

'But you said online you were submissive.'

'I'm not sure we're speaking the same language. What is submission for you, young piano player?'

'It's a long story.'

'That rain outside is not going to stop any time soon, so indulge me.'

A veil of memories drifted across Maxwell's eyes. He took another sip of coffee from the paper cup. She held his gaze. She seemed a different person to the one who had willingly accompanied him to the play. Determined, steely, remote.

He told her the story of how he had been friends with this girl, Sarah, back in high school on the West Coast. Familiar story: outsiders coming together. How she had confessed her terrible attraction to submission to him. He revealed he was probably gay, only attracted to men. As they grew up, Sarah was always the braver, slowly giving in to her hidden cravings. Telling him. About both the constant shame and the compulsion to always take a step too far in this descent into madness. It was her courage to accept the nature of her desires that encouraged Maxwell to assume his queerness and eventually, clumsily, to embark on sex with other men, although never boys of his own age. How Sarah had moved away and had died in unclear circumstances. Which he now was still attempting to uncover the facts about but had reached a point where he had almost given up when, just the previous week, he had heard a rumour that someone implicated in her death might be reappearing following a lengthy absence. He confessed to Cornelia that even though it was unconnected, he could not help blaming himself for having let her go and her eventual, tragic fate. And by delving deeper into his own submission, he knew all too lucidly that he was not indulging in a death wish, but acting almost in homage to her, moving further into the mental depths she had lived through.

'Does it all sound crazy to you?' he asked Cornelia.

'No, it makes sense, in a twisted sort of way.' She needed a thinking pause to absorb the new information. She deflected the subject. 'Did it hurt when he fucked you? He looked ... big. And rough.'

'It did, just part of being a sub, I suppose. I think it's supposed to hurt.'

'Does it?' Cornelia was being quite sincere asking that. She'd never equated sexual pleasure with pain. Men who had tried in the throes of passion to twist her nipples or spank her gently had all earned a rapid and robust rebuke.

'You'll see tomorrow, I expect ... He won't be gentle with you either.'

'Hmmm ...'

She had no intention of repeating the encounter, even more so with herself as the main course. It had proven useful in helping her establish the initial contact with Maxwell and nurture some form of rapport. She had to move on from there before the opportunity vanished.

'So, what is this story of yours? Your friend who died. Can you tell me?'

It was as if she'd pulled an invisible trigger. Maxwell took a deep breath and explained how Sarah had come to a bad end, and how he was convinced it was not an accident. About a man in a fedora leaving the hotel, and the uncanny similarity between that case and what he had read in the paper about a similar murder or accident at the Luxor in Vegas and the mysterious woman seen departing the hotel and how he thought she was a dancer and now happened to be in the New York area. He was still trying to puzzle out the connection between the two murders; he was convinced Sarah's death had been a crime, and not an accident.

Cornelia was all solicitous. 'You said you had screen grabs of both scenes which you hacked from the central traffic databases?'

'I do.'

'Can you show me?'

He had both, carefully folded in a section of his wallet.

Her heart skipped a beat when she took note of the familiar silhouette of the man departing the Figueroa Hotel.

162

The fedora, which hung in his parlour, which she had never seen Hopley wear in Manhattan, the shape of him. It was unmistakably Hopley. She held her breath, her mind zigzagging into a hundred different directions. She glanced at the other photo and, naturally, was confronted by her old self. Her face was well concealed but anyone who knew her would have put one and one together. Maxwell visibly hadn't. Yet.

She returned the photographs to him, with no further comment.

'Fascinating. Don't you think it's a mighty coincidence? True, the deaths are similar, but these are two different individuals. And you said the Los Angeles cops found a man's body in the room from the balcony of which Sarah had fallen?'

'I know she couldn't have shot him and then jumped to her death. I knew her well. It makes no sense. The answer lies with the woman.'

'Does it?'

'I'm hoping to locate her soon.'

'Here, in New York?'

'Yes, she's a dancer, a stripper, and she is booked to perform here in a few weeks.'

He'd swallowed the bait.

'So, what will you do. Confront her?'

'Yes.'

'And then?'

'I'll get to the truth. By hook or by crook. I owe it to Sarah.'

Planning for the encounter, Cornelia had temporarily moved out of her apartment and rented a small Airbnb in Gramercy with cash under an assumed name as her base for the week. She asked Maxwell to come and fetch her there a couple of hours prior to the following day's assignment in the Alphabet City basement. She'd reported her findings to the Bureau overnight and explained that Maxwell's investigation was a purely personal one and appeared to have stumbled across two operatives using a similar method of despatch quite fortuitously and that in her opinion he was not a threat to them. She was however asked to complete the job; loose ends could not be tolerated. The material she requested for the job at hand would be despatched over by early morning.

He arrived at the apartment and she opened the front door for him and greeted him, inviting him in to the hallway.

'Wow, this is quite a swanky place. What do you do for a living, Zelda?'

'It's not mine, I just stay here,' she answered truthfully. 'I do this and that.'

'You hustle? Escort? You have the looks.'

'Not quite.'

'It's OK, you don't have to tell me.'

They walked over to the kitchen table, and she offered him coffee. Maxwell had to wait several minutes before he could begin drinking it. It was initially too hot for his tongue.

'Freshly made,' she remarked.

'You're not having any?' She was sipping a glass of water as she stood there, tall and languid, her tangled hair and curls shot through by arrows of light piercing the blinds that hung against the kitchen window.

'I never have coffee later than midday. Makes me too nervous and agitated if I have too much.'

Maxwell sniggered. 'Well, you'll need to stay awake for the play …'

Cornelia was smiling. Suddenly Maxwell felt uncertain, puzzled by the situation he was in, as if various memory strands were slowly coming together inside his brain. Something about the woman's glacial silence. He tried the coffee. Didn't scald himself and took a first sip. Then another. She had brewed it strong. Time slowed to a freezing halt as they faced each other. Then it all came together in an enlightening flash. The way her lean, graceful silhouette was outlined against the halo of light invading the room through the blinds. Like in the Luxor screen grab. Then, that brief vision he'd caught of that small tattoo next to her sex when they had undressed in the Alphabet City basement. But which he hadn't had the time to process, quivering inside as he was in the knowledge he was about to be mounted by the dom who'd summoned him there. A gun. A tattoo of a gun. The sort a stripper might display. C the Gun … He felt dizzy. Looked up at her, his knees unsteady.

'It was … you … in the photo?'

She held his unsteady gaze.

'Yes.'

'You …'

'But I had nothing to do with your friend Sarah's death. That was just a bad coincidence, Maxwell.'

He wanted to say something more but his whole body froze, and then seized up and he dropped to the floor, realising the coffee had been spiked. Then his heart stopped.

Cornelia checked for vital signs and satisfied the job was done, picked up her burner cell phone and called the Bureau number she had been given.

'It's done. You can send a cleaner for the body.'

She searched his jeans pocket for his wallet and pulled out the two photos. Of Hopley and herself departing separate hotels and avoiding the gaze of the CCTV cameras. She would tear the screen grabs into pieces later and dispose of them in various refuse bins along the road to Washington Square. Together with the miniscule, now empty vial that had contained the poison she had been supplied with to spike his coffee.

She left the key to the Airbnb under the mat and walked away.

She hadn't shot the piano player; she had just poisoned him. An act of mercy, she reckoned; knowing he hadn't had time to suffer.

She would now return to Hopley.

And that incongruous fedora.

Apprehensive though; and with a much-troubled mind.

Unsure whether she should ask him anything. Or was it a coincidence they had ended up together? She was the one who had answered to the *Voice* ad about the Dos Passos trilogy set; she had initiated their first encounter.

Maybe she should keep silent?

Wait and see.

The only thing she knew right now as she stepped into the buzzing commute rush hour Broadway traffic to make her way to the Village was that she didn't want to know how the Bureau would dispose of Maxwell's body. Too much information.

25
Killers in Paradise

Cornelia had left all the travel arrangements to Hopley. He was more of a planner than she was, with attention to detail and the type of patience she found it difficult to build up in civilian life. He'd assured her he knew the Caribbean well and asked to trust him. Which she did when it came to the actual plans, but the seeds of doubt had now been planted in her mind and she was wary of possibly hidden motives.

She just hoped he wouldn't be packing the damn fedora. Fortunately, it wasn't on his checklist.

On the evening preceding their flight, they had both slept apart in their own apartments. The call came at midnight. She recognised the voice at 'hello'. The man she had first met in the Angelika foyer.

'I'm about to leave for a vacation. Maybe you could find someone else?'

'We know where you're going.'

How the hell could he be aware of their plans? Neither of them had confided in anyone. More to the point, neither even had close friends with whom to share the news of their growing relationship.

'So, assign whatever the job is to another operative. I can't cancel my plans at this late stage.'

'That won't prove necessary, my dear.'

'How come?'

'The person we require you to eliminate is the man you know as Hopley.'

Her heart seized.

Words failed her.

Her stomach felt as if it was in freefall, an avalanche

rushing towards the ground and breaking through until it reached the other side of the world at the antipodes.

'I'm sure this comes as a shock to you, but …'

'The hell it does,' she was shouting at the phone.

'But it has proven necessary.'

'I …'

'You're a professional, my dear, you will go along with it.'

'And if I don't?'

'We have the fullest confidence you will come to your senses when you think it through.'

'Why?'

'You did good work with the piano player. Now we know Hopley is the weak link. He's been connected to the Figueroa Hotel job. He's become a loose end.'

'He's also a man I'm currently involved with and this has no connection with our respective activities on your behalf.'

'We are sadly aware of the fact.'

Were they being watched? By who? Since when?

She fell silent.

The Bureau representative continued, 'He's become a loose end. It is an unacceptable risk.'

'No one else knows or is ever likely to find out,' Cornelia pleaded.

'Be that as it may.'

The fog clouding her brain began to clear. A shroud of sadness held her in its grip, squeezing her heart, her guts.

'Naturally, there is no dossier this time around as you know all there is to know about your target. And neither will you require any equipment this time; we're confident you will find a way without when the opportunity arises as it will inevitably do. If it's any consolation, there is no timetable. All in your own time. We're cognisant of the fact that you may have feelings for each other. But I fear emotions have no place in our kind of work. I'm confident you can understand that.'

He'd been off the line for several minutes before Cornelia could bear to disconnect from her end.

What with all the non-stop rush of the final day prior to the trip, spent packing, repacking and packing again, preoccupied by the task ahead and the looming end of her time with Hopley and whether she could actually go through with it, Cornelia joined her lover at the airport without having properly slept. Still hoping her feelings would not betray her. In addition, there was a niggling thought at the back of her mind that maybe Hopley had received a similar call and was himself right now battling identical doubts and steeling his resolve in preparation. A cohort of thoughts that she had never imagined she could fit inside her skull, like electrons bouncing around in a frightful dance of death. Next to her, calm and collected, her lover appeared unruffled, reading a book, listening to music on his earphones. As she'd effortlessly drifted away into sleep, her mind had idly recognised some of the tunes he was listening to, buried under waves of ambient aircraft noise and the buzz of ever fading layers of somnolence. It was as if she were both here and elsewhere, conscious of dozing but also calmly registering the distant, almost alien sounds of the on-board announcements, the chatter from nearby seats and the gentle, irregular rattle of the drinks trolley wheeled by at irregular intervals. Sometimes her eyes would briefly open only to note his reassuring presence at her side, the solid bulk of his arm and shoulders, or his hand lingering, almost weightless, on her knee.

So, this was how the adventure began.

In that welcoming state between sleep and consciousness, floating, lingering lazily, Cornelia swam, reminiscing over the past few months in an attempt to clumsily recall what she knew of the tropics, the Caribbean, from books, movies, features in travel supplements of disposable magazines and, further back in her past, lessons in school she had automatically not given much attention to.

It was like a dream through which she drifted, abandoning herself to the sheer pleasure of idleness. Until the fatal moment would become inevitable.

Rising from the deep, several hours into the flight, came the announcement of some turbulence and a request to secure the seat belts. She felt his warm breath against her cheek as he leaned over and tightened her belt. Dizzy, slightly unsure of herself, Cornelia muttered 'Are we almost there?'

'No, it's only halfway to our destination. Don't worry. Sleep.'

There was a temptation to follow his advice and fall deeper into the well of torpor seductively beckoning her, but another part of her resisted, realising she was wasting all this remaining time spent with him. She struggled to open her eyes, shake herself awake.

'I think I need a drink,' she said. 'My mouth is dry.'

'No problem,' he extended his arm upwards and pressed the call button above their seats. 'What do you want?'

'Water will be just fine.'

The flight attendant came and took their order, returning rapidly with a cool bottle of mineral water and the can of Seven-Up he had requested for himself.

She handed over their drinks, and disposed the glasses full of ice, napkins and floats on their tables.

Cornelia brought her lips to the glass, savouring the cold flow of the liquid down her throat. She dropped her head on his shoulders and closed her eyes again.

'Should I wake you when the food arrives?' he asked her.

Cornelia didn't answer, keeping her eyes shut, still pondering about what Hopley might be thinking right there and now, if he was experiencing the same feelings. If he had taken a decision yet.

Walking down the gangway, she was enveloped by a blanket of warmth. The tropics. A humid form of heat that seeped right through her clothes all the way to her skin. And then the distant smell of spices, or was it rotting vegetation maybe? No, definitely spices, caressing the back of her nose, both sharp and tentative but quite pleasant, she decided. The sun caressing the uncovered nape of her neck as they ambled towards the single-storeyed terminal building which looked so resolutely old-fashioned, even primitive, like a building from the 1950s, its architecture and lines so straight and simple.

'Warm, eh?'

She nodded. Looked around her; green hills stood tall behind the parallel lines of parked aircraft, the nearest of which they had just disembarked from, as the file of weary, pale-looking passengers snaked towards the airport buildings.

They entered the terminal and joined the queue at passport control. They were close to the front. She'd handed her travel documents and passport to Hopley back at JFK so he could negotiate their passage to the plane, taking the burden away from her. Just like a normal couple. It felt good not to have any immediate responsibilities, just follow, hold on to his hands, trust him this far, Cornelia felt. But then, that was what she essentially liked about him: how he calmly took charge of matters.

The formalities were soon over, their luggage picked up from the creaking carousel and they stepped out of the building into a cacophony of sights and sounds. Courtesy coaches, buses and mostly dilapidated cars pretending to be taxis surrounded by a noisy throng of locals or travel company staff respectively soliciting for business or trying to orientate the arriving hordes of tourists towards their appointed transport. For a moment, Cornelia was overwhelmed by the sheer amount of movement and colours, her mind faltering, but Hopley was winding his way through the bustling crowd, holding her hand firmly in his while, with his other, he guided their trolley piled with suitcases along. He wore a cream-coloured Panama hat. Not his fedora, which she now associated with his past kills.

A white mini-coach with a crisp-uniformed attendant holding a sign with the name of their resort was parked by the kerb. With a wide, welcoming smile he greeted them, ticked their names off his list and ushered them onto the vehicle while a scrawny T-shirted helper accepted their luggage and placed it in the vehicle's hold. They were each handed a bottle of cold mineral water that must just have come straight from a nearby freezer and climbed into the ten-seater bus, where the air-conditioning was switched on to the full and made her shiver briefly as her body negotiated the abrupt transition from the heat outside.

'Almost there,' Hopley said. Her lover, her target; notions she still had to pinch herself to believe. Let alone this holiday trip. But it was happening, for real. She was here, on a Caribbean Island in the blazing, sultry sun, with a man she had once loved in her own, remote and idiosyncratic way, but now doubted, feared even. Something caught in her throat. There was something untrue about the whole situation.

The coach soon filled up with other passengers, although Cornelia gathered they were not all going to the same resort and they would be dropped off in turn after the hour-long drive through the island.

He had assured her that the hotel they would be staying at was one of the best, a veritable paradise. She'd wanted to ask him whether he'd stayed there before and then, with whom, but had quickly reckoned that would have been the wrong thing to do and hadn't. His past was the past and she would rather not know too much about it.

Ten minutes out of the local airport, away from an industrial zone full of warehouses and single-storey squat factories, they emerged onto a straight road that headed into the hills, joining the local traffic. Cornelia peered out of the windows, watching the landscape pass by, a litter of roadside bars, crumbling villas and vast empty plains of red dirt and dust all the way to walls of trees. There was so much free open space. You could lose yourself here, she thought. Then, the vehicle took a sharp turn along a small rise and the sea appeared below. Turquoise blue and endless. The view was just so striking that Cornelia just sat there, her fingers digging hard into Hopley's arms. 'Wow,' she muttered. 'This is beautiful.' Waves lapped against a rocky shore, cresting, throwing spume in indistinct patterns flying above its surface, but it was the colour that moved her so intensely. As if all the infinitesimal variations between blue and green were contained within it, glittering, shining, every single, magical shade of an azure rainbow. She recalled the sea by the coast of Maine, on a distant past vacation, how grey it was, so flat, so boring. This was quite a different incarnation of the sea altogether!

'It's even more beautiful where we are headed,' he said soothingly into her ear.

'Really?'

'It's on the other side of the island, towards the North. We'll soon be turning into the interior,' he continued.

'I can't wait.'

The resort was all he had promised.

The hotel's principal building was nested in the hollow of a cove, facing the ocean and a maze of paths threaded their way through the resort, leading to rows of cabanas lost in a labyrinth of gardens where every single plant appeared at first glance to belong to a different species, as if paradise had indeed been recreated here. The tallest tree she had ever seen sat behind the principal building where the dining room was situated, facing the sea, its trunk a thick, burnished mass of wood and its branches a serpentine thread of leaves and bifurcations thrown to the non-existent winds. The whole resort had been designed, built around the immemorial tree. She was informed by the porter pulling their luggage along how old it was, but soon forgot the date. Amongst the gardens, three separate swimming pools were scattered, and a man-made stream meandered in zigzag motions through the vegetation, at times a hidden river, at other time a series of paddling pools bordered by sturdy wooden deckchairs and miniature wicker pergolas. Staff patrolled the area non-stop, serving cool drinks like clockwork to the prone tourists who were sunbathing in the splendour.

That first night in their room –walls aquamarine, mirrors reflecting the sweat of their nude bodies, the contents of their luggage still strewn across the floor among the damp white towels they had shed following the shower they had taken together – he made love to her.

It was different.

Of course, they had already fucked many times by then, in New York, furtively, tentatively, wildly, amorously, but this felt to Cornelia like the first time all over again. As if every act of lovemaking she had indulged in with him – or others - had merely been a prelude to this night on St Lucia.

It was tender, it was rough, it was rapid, it was slow, it was him and her grasping at each other to celebrate their togetherness, cement their sensual affection, exploring not so much new positions but a new way of communicating, of fitting their parts into each other, stretching boundaries in both obscene and innocent ways.

Lost in a whirlwind of thoughts and sensations, wandering like in a daydream in some zone that was part of her and outside of her, Cornelia perceived a new dimension that she had previously been unaware of. A new world. Full of joy and possibilities. As if the unknowing as to who would kill the other one first added another dimension to their coupling, a danger, a poisonous delight.

They were both wet with sweat, panting, their feet tangled in the sheets, catching their breath in unison, and Cornelia opened her mouth, words ready to pour out in an unwieldy stream, full of questions and feelings but his hand slowly rose and cupped her lips.

'Don't say anything,' he said, a spark of tenderness illuminating his eyes in the room's unsteady penumbra.

'But …'

'Shhh … No need.'

And the look on his face was worth a thousand words.

He turned onto his side, moved his hand to her hips and

adjusted the way she lay and deftly entered her again.

Cornelia gasped. Never had he filled her so much, so well. But it didn't hurt. On the contrary, it made her content and complete.

The week that followed was like time out of time. Had she not already been madly in lust with him before, she would have become even more so, without pretence or reservation as he made every minute of every day a memory she knew she would forever recall, in the certain knowledge that their days together were now counted. Attentive, gracious, funny in his sardonic way, his eyes twinkling with untold, benevolent mischief, clever in bed, elegant in the way he dressed for lunch and dinner on the marble terrace facing the sea or even when they rambled up and down on the beach in shorts and T-shirts and flip flops, caringly devoted to her as he affectionately slathered her body with suntan cream or helped her shampoo her hair, playful, sexy… Was he the perfect imperfect man? At times she wondered what the other guests at the resort, with whom they had limited contact, just a hello, a nod and a goodnight on occasion, wrapped as they were in each other, might be thinking of them. Illicit lovers (which they were …), married couple, ideally matched? Who cared?

If only those bastards at the Bureau had been around to witness her happiness. Or maybe not quite right now, it occurred to her, as she sprawled naked and spent at her lover's side, her face a satisfied portrait of unfettered lust and sensual greed and his fingers lingering still between her thighs as he suggested they shower together and maybe take a dip in the secret river pool a few steps away from their terrace.

'Both my swimsuits are still drying,' she told him.

'Come as you are,' he suggested, the back of his left-hand grazing slowly over her still hard, excitable nipples.

'Naked?'

'Absolutely. It's almost midnight. There's no one around. And what if they do anyway. You're accustomed to stripping; surely you have no qualms about being seen naked?'

They drew the window open and, hand in hand, tiptoed out across the grass, making their way through the narrow gap between the bushes and emerged onto the meandering, artificial stream. She dipped her foot in the water. It was still blissfully warm even at this late hour of day. He followed her in. Cornelia looked up to the starry sky. It was a full moon. Its light shone against her wet body, highlighting her modest curves. She bent her knees and immersed herself in the pool up to her neck and just sat there for a moment, absorbing the silence, the distant sounds of the nearby sea. Hopley remained silent. Immobile. She turned to find where he was: he was standing a yard away looking at her, his gaze fixed, his eyes sharp circles of darkness against his tanned skin.

'What is it?' Cornelia asked. 'A penny for your thoughts?'

'Nothing,' Hopley said. 'Just looking at you and savouring the view.'

For a mere second, Cornelia felt a pang of disappointment, as if she had hoped he would say something else. Like 'I love you' maybe?

But his eyes kept on observing her, a thin smile drawn across his full lips.

'You're nothing but a peeping Tom!' she chuckled as she deliberately turned her back away from him and paddled the few meters to the next communicating pool which was deeper but narrower, enjoying the joyous sensation of the tepid water all over bare skin.

Would he ever say that he loved her? Before it was too late? Even if it was untrue. *Jesus*, Cornelia swore under her breath, *what is happening to me?*

26
Save the Last Dance for Me

Almost daily, Cornelia grappled with the quandary: should she inform Hopley that the Bureau had ordered his elimination? By her hands. How would he react? Might they be able to collaborate, compromise, make any suggestions to their puppet masters to get the order rescinded? Escape together? But where to?

Her sleep was interrupted by too many conflicting thoughts. Should they plead with the Bureau, argue that neither of them presented a risk? That their contacts had been mostly limited to their direct handlers and they had little insight into the rest of the organisation? And what then? Both of them setting up in business as a freelance hit couple. Just like Angelina Jolie and Brad Pitt in that old movie she'd once seen on a flight to Miami. But had the fashionable couple not been secret service or something of that ilk? Living in the real world, she and Hopley would only become a second division Brangelina, without the karate skills.

They were lounging on deck chairs in the sun by the Spa Pool. The area was encircled by an explosion of shrubbery, with the pagoda-like building where the spa itself was situated roasting in the late afternoon daylight, its slanted roof fighting off the dying rays of the Caribbean sun. The jacuzzi bubbled away on the edge of the pool, where the day's stray leaves were beginning to accumulate in one corner like harmless squatters on the peaceful surface of the warm water. Most of the other tourists had already returned to their rooms, defeated by the torpor of the heat, or dressing for dinner. A barman was wandering around the pool's stone-slabbed perimeter picking up empty glasses and towels left lying abandoned by the chairs by the deserters.

Cornelia lifted her own glass and the barman asked her if she wanted a refill. She nodded lazily. On one hand she felt a bit ashamed to be waited on so obsequiously, while on the other she secretly enjoyed the sheer luxury of the experience. It was something she would never have thought she could have enjoyed just a year ago. Unaccustomed to being part of a couple and doing the ordinary things of life. Was this what normal life could be?

Hopley was still swimming laps in the pool below her. The rhythm of his movements steady, his strong arms cutting into the water with what appeared to be minimal effort, his face half-submerged, wading through the stream with all the precision of a dolphin.

The sun finally disappeared behind the slanted tiles of the pagoda's roof and a few moments later Cornelia shivered and pulled one of the still damp towels hanging by her side across her legs. Today was Spanish night, and the waiters at the dining room on the terrace that faced the sea would be decorating the tables and the rooms accordingly. She began to wonder what she would wear. She had not expected every night at the resort to have a theme, and felt she was running out of clothes. It was easier for him, all it required was a different shirt and a sports jacket. She had packed her best summer clothes, but best wasn't saying much, compared to the variety of outfits some of the other guests paraded every evening.

She had mentioned this to him the previous day and he had joked that, if this was the case, maybe he should have taken her to a more hedonistic sort of resort, where she could have sat naked in all impunity at the dinner table in the restaurant. His smile had been at its most mischievous.

'Have you ever been to a resort like that?' she asked him.

His eyes glinted. 'I'm not saying.'

Cornelia already dreaded the trip home. He had suggested at the planning stages of the vacation that they could connect with a cruise ship which would be docking in the port of Castries the following week and which would take them back across the north Atlantic with a couple of stops in Bermuda and Key West, rather than flying home the way they had travelled to St Lucia. She had never been on a cruise before. Maybe it was the childhood memories of the small coastal ferries she had often been obliged to take with her parents and all those occasions she had been violently sick aboard, and decided in her foolishness that once she was an adult she would never voluntarily set foot on a boat again.

In addition, she had never been a keen swimmer and always much preferred beach life and its lazy rituals of sun worship.

She had been apprehensive that she would not have sea legs and would suffer from sea sickness, and disgrace herself abominably during the journey, and had stocked up on pills to counter it.

She was also nervous about dining etiquette on-board a ship, being invited to the captain's table and all that, or having to make polite conversation with so many well-bred strangers who could afford such a cruise. She would feel so much more out of place than even here at the resort where, at least, she only had to share a table every evening with Hopley. The solitary life of books, dancing and hit work had turned her into a very anti-social animal.

But Hopley had reassured her, convinced Cornelia not to worry about the seemingly indigent state of her garde-robe and warned her not to be self-conscious. She'd always been a big city woman and leisure wear far from her thoughts.

He had an answer to every question, it appeared.

Hopley hired a jeep and they drove to the Pitons.

They left the resort in early morning before the sun was at its fiercest. As soon as the road led out of Castries, it rose steadily as they drove into the hills towards the leafy interior of the island. Sharp turns, vertiginous drops on either side of the sometimes crumbling tarmac of the road, the slope rising up sharply further up the road until Cornelia was concerned that the straining sounds of the vehicle's engine would sputter to an untimely death and it would stand still on the spot before careening backwards at accelerated speed to their doom. But Hopley's feet switched across the SUV's pedals with relaxed ease and they passed every small summit and hairpin turn before dipping again and rising yet again all the way to their destination an hour and a half away.

The panoramas were astounding. They were now above the canopy of a limitless kingdom of dark green forests, forming a solid sky below the real sky of blue and raging sun. During the drive here, it had felt as if they were the only travellers around but here small groups of visitors were scattered across the parking areas, coaches and open-roofed trucks stationed artfully along the ledges of the valley that overlooked he dead volcano.

Cornelia noticed a small group of tourists of approximately their same age, communicating in a mix of languages. Some spoke English and the others she thought were Dutch from their accents and she suggested to Hopley that they join them.

'It might be fun?' she said. She was trying to be more of a social animal. Fitting in better.

But he didn't wish to mix with others, he insisted. It was odd how insular he had been throughout this holiday, she noticed, unless they were in bed. Always wanting them to be on their own, often turning down the opportunity to converse with others around the bar, the pool, as if unwilling to share her with anyone or be seen around with her. Was it a plan? Like the damn fedora, part of a larger plan. It nagged her to think he might have received a similar call from the Bureau to hers and might quietly be planning her demise.

'Just you and me, darling.'

How could she complain? They had long looked forward to a vacation just for two.

Wandering down a narrow path, holding on to his hand, sweat pearling down her forehead even though she'd tied her hair back with an elastic band to keep her face and neck clear, moving down towards a ledge where the view, he had been assured by a local guide, was allegedly even more spectacular.

They'd left their backpacks with drinks and fruit bars behind.

Cornelia felt the faint buzz of a mosquito close to her ear.

'Isn't this a little dangerous?'

'Not really. Trust me.'

'It's a bit far to venture to take yet another photograph, I reckon.'

He was always snapping away on his iPhone. Although she'd often noticed it was always landscapes and places he was taking pictures of, seldom, if ever, her. Future evidence? Compromising images that would lead back to her following her possible disappearance?

They continued down the narrow path, compacted earth and small stones crumbling beneath their trainers. His hand held hers tightly as he ventured ahead towards the ledge, he assured her they would soon reach. Tugging slightly as she stepped hesitantly behind him, far from confident in her movements, her heart beating ever so much faster as the path narrowed to almost nothing and it felt as if they were clinging on to the bare wall of the hill. She didn't want to look down, but the reflex was inevitable. Yes, this would be the ideal place. A body flying through the air. The past repeating itself. But whose? Which of the two of them would be taking the initiative?

Cornelia shuddered. Her body tensed. Readying herself for any sudden, untoward movement by Hopley while also estimating their respective positions and how she could either counter his possible approach or take over the initiative.

The drop below their feet was sheer and hellishly scary. Had she the courage to extend her head just an inch further she would, she knew, witness an abyss, a dark hole of a cavern of trees and emptiness, a hole with no end. She'd never had a head for heights.

Her nails bit into his grip. She tried to pull back. But he held on to her tightly. Even pulled her further towards him.

Negating her resistance. So, this was not to be the day. Neither did Cornelia feel in any hurry herself and spurned the opportunity.

'I don't think I can go any further,' she protested.

She could see in his eyes that he was surprised by her perceived cowardice. Or was it disappointment? A thin cloud of reproach swam over his gaze.

But all Cornelia could think of was the terrible fall that might beckon her should they advance down the perilous dirt path just one step further.

'Please ...'

'Oh well ...'

He agreed to halt their progress. Swivelling their bodies round to turn and climb back up proved as uncertain as if they had continued their halting route down the ledge, but she managed it somehow and soon they were at the top again, where they walked in silence to the parked Jeep.

'I'm sorry,' she pleaded on the drive back to Castries, by way of explanation.

'I didn't realise you were uncomfortable with heights. A chink in your armour,' her lover explained. 'Had I known, we could have remained around the pool.'

Cornelia was unsure whether this constituted an apology or not.

There had been a major terrorist incident in Europe and most of the tourists at the resort were preoccupied about it. The atmosphere in the open-air dining room was gloomy that night.

After they had returned to their cabana, he had taken out his laptop and spent a half hour looking up the latest news. Cornelia had peered over his shoulder as he skipped from website to website. Fortunately, the US had been spared any of the atrocities. This time.

The information was still patchy and, after a while, there were no further up to date bulletins to be gleaned, just repetitive comments by countless politicians hoping to reassure the general public. He asked her if she minded if he spent just a quarter of an hour or so, while he was connected to the wi fi, catching up with some pressing work and personal matters. Of course, she didn't and moved over to the bed where she undressed, slipped between the crisp, faintly perfumed, white Egyptian cotton sheets, picked up one of the mystery paperbacks from the bedside table and began to read, while he typed away sitting with his back to her.

'I'm done,' he finally said.

Cornelia had been dozing, her book still open at the same page she had begun, the words barely making any sense, floating relaxedly between alternate states of sleep and semi-consciousness.

He rose from the chair. Stretched.

'All OK?' she asked, dreamily, almost yawning.

'Yes,' he answered. 'But I feel a bit restless. What about you?'

Cornelia shook her head.

'No. Just sleepy.'

'I think I need some fresh air. Would you mind if I popped out for a few minutes, clear my head, walk around the gardens, maybe have a final drink at the bar?'

'Not at all.' She didn't feel like getting dressed again. 'I'll wait for you.'

But once he had left the room, she realised she had somehow woken up fully and her gaze kept on alighting on the weak pulsing light at the front of the thin laptop he had abandoned on the dressing table, which he had forgotten to switch off. It was like a pale beacon. Calling her, attracting her attention. Distracting.

She resolved to switch the laptop off and got out of bed.

Her finger grazed the mousepad and the screen lip up. He had forgotten to log out and the sharp landscape of dazzling constellations he used as a screen saver appeared, interrupted on the right-hand side of the image by three orderly columns of small boxes, the documents or files he normally worked or consulted often, she guessed.

Most of the content of the various folders consisted of a jumble of numbers and abbreviations she couldn't decipher, but down in the far-right hand corner of the large laptop screen was one that caught her instant attention.

B.

As in B for the Bureau?

None of the other files he stored in the computer appeared in any way so cryptic.

She leaned over, brought her eyes closer to the screen, as if peering into it would explain what the file was about, her curiosity primed.

A gentle tropical breeze animated the curtains by the window. There was no sign of him outside. He must still be at the bar in the main building, just a five-minute walk away.

She pondered briefly until she could resist no more.

Lowered a finger to the mousepad. Moved towards the icon and clicked.

The file opened.

She recognised the first page instantly.

Her stomach tightened.

Just a list of initials, places, dates and sums. She instantly realised its significance.

His kills. Where they had taken place. The fee for each.

So, her instinct had been right all along. This was final absolute proof they both worked for the Bureau and that, dangerously bending the rules, he had kept a record. Confirming why he was now a liability. Why had he done it? Was it a death wish?

She had never written anything down pertaining to her assignments. Never would. It was unprofessional.

She promptly closed he document, pulled the lid down and, again, the weak pulsing light began its regular on and off rhythm.

When he returned to their room soon after, a faint sound of singing cicadas filtering through the bay window into the cabana as he walked in, he stripped in the semi-darkness of the bedroom and joined her in the bed where she lay awake, eyes wide open and mood febrile. His lips and tongue tasted of whiskey, flavoursome, pungent, and Cornelia quickly jettisoned her worries and surrendered herself to the indulgent pleasure of being with him again. She now knew to enjoy every single moment. Because it couldn't last.

The vessel felt like a veritable mammoth of the seas, standing ten storeys tall above the dock, with layers and layers of windows and portholes puncturing its side, like an overgrown jumbo jet caught in an optical illusion, its straight lines repeating almost to infinity.

A narrow gangway seemed to hang precariously from a square opening carved into the side of the ocean-going mastodon and they filed their way up it, amongst a stream of advancing passengers, leaving the island behind them. Cornelia imagined she was moving away from paradise, and her heart was overcome with a feeling of dread, as if a dream she could no longer control was being punctured by the approach of cold reality. Nervously secure in the knowledge that a point had been reached and passed and they could never return to the easy-going simplicity they had enjoyed between their initial, seemingly innocent encounter and their departure for the West Indies.

The journey would take eight days, she knew, including the two stop overs.

As much as she was looking forward to what was going to be yet another totally new experience, she couldn't help but wonder why he had chosen to sail rather than fly home.

But she resolved to enjoy the short cruise and banish her fears away for now.

Life on the huge ship quickly fell into easy routines: late breakfast in the Brasserie on Deck 10 followed by an hour or so of wallowing in the sun that rained down from the eternal blue skies, a dip in the busy pool, and then lunch in one of the two restaurants, where they alternated between the Waldorf and the Buckingham. Then afternoons in a choice of luxurious lounges, spent reading while watching the waves break against the ship's side as it parted the waters at even speed in its inexorable journey home, their leisure interrupted at irregular intervals by the cruise director's overly jolly reminders on the tannoy of events taking place for the idle: bingo, yoga, talks, line dancing lessons, quizzes, games, lectures. Until it was time for their dinner again, at the table for two he had reserved, away from other passengers who preferred to socialise at large tables of six or eight. Hopley had declined to sit on any of them, preferring to spend time with just her, separate from the on-board crowds, who were mostly older than them and with whom he felt they had little in common.

As the days ticked by, she noted that he was becoming more and more taciturn; a man of fewer words now reduced to long streaks of silence when they just sat or relaxed in their cabin.

'What are you thinking of?'

'Nothing, really.'

'You're very quiet …'

'Not much to say. Just pleased to be here with you …'

Late afternoon.

'I have to wash my hair,' she explained. 'Want to be presentable in the restaurant tonight.'

'That's fine. I'll go up to the sun deck for a while.'

'Bring some mineral water when you return,' she asked.

'I will.'

He disappeared down the long corridor, that reminded her of the haunting ones in Kubrick's *The Shining*, at the Overlook Hotel, avenues of metal punctuated by lines of identical cabins all the way down the length of the ship.

She switched the shower on and undressed.

Noted his computer standing on the stateroom's small table.

She was tempted to spy on it again but there was no light on and she knew it would be password protected.

Walked into the shower and squeezed the shampoo into her hair.

The jet of hot water streamed over her shoulders, dividing into an infinity of rivulets that streaked down her body. She rubbed the scented cream into her hair until it permeated her scalp. Her eyes stung and she washed the soapy water away. When she opened her eyes, she had a shock. He was standing by the bathroom door, silently watching her.

'I didn't hear you return to the cabin,' she muttered. 'I thought you'd be away a while longer.' She shivered, thinking how he could have found her messing with his computer. She had no idea what his reaction might have been.

'I've brought your mineral water,' he said.

'Thanks.'

He kept on standing there, watching her intently. By now she was accustomed to being naked in his presence, and enjoyed his evident admiration, but presently she found it unsettling.

Truly she reckoned, she would never quite fully understand him or the thoughts that went through his mind. His unpredictability. But then she had to weigh this up against his tenderness, his generosity, the way he enjoyed looking after her; voluntarily dealing with all the logistics of the surprise trip, the way he arranged all the documents, kept her passport, filled out immigration forms, not allowing her the least preoccupation or responsibility. Spoiling her. The way he concealed his true nature from her, not that that was a sin seeing she was doing likewise. A man of two worlds. A woman with two lives. After their initial encounter, she had entertained flimsy hopes he could be the person to make her change, help transform her into just an ordinary woman.

'I could join you in the shower,' he suggested.

'It's a bit narrow,' Cornelia said, her elbows rubbing against the glass walls of the cubicle. 'Not sure if we'd both fit in, let alone if …'

'I was only kidding.' He moved back into the cabin. 'Join me when you're ready.'

By the time she had dried her hair, it was almost time for dinner on one of the higher decks, together with the now familiar dilemma of what to wear, something presentable that she hadn't yet worn on previous evenings. He really should have warned her in advance that on this stage of the holiday, other women tended to dress so much more formally than Cornelia had expected.

Dinner again was a menu of interrupted silences and pregnant looks she found difficult to interpret, his smile inscrutable, his manners impeccable, the food delicious all the way to the passionfruit sorbet she finished off with.

The moment they reached the cabin his hands swept through her newly washed hair, his nose burying itself against the crook of her neck, smelling her, analysing her fragrance. She remembered how, by the window in Chelsea, as midnight neared, he had done the same, shortly before their first kiss, and had immediately recognised the scent she always wore: Anais Anais.

And she had known, from that moment onwards, that a man who knew women's perfumes must surely be a man worth bedding, worth even loving.

His hands now lingered all over her body, touching, teasing, caressing, lifting her skirt, unbuttoning her blouse, dexterously unzipping her, moving across her bare skin with expert assurance, mapping the contours of her rising desire.

Cornelia surrendered willingly.

Offering herself.

Opening herself.

All the while hoping against hope he might say something, some magic words that would appease the pain digging dagger-deep into her heart that was no longer fully satisfied by their slow, exquisite bouts of lovemaking. She wanted peace. At any cost. The impossible happy ever after scenario. But she knew it was something all her flaws would ever keep out of her reach. A mirage.

Eventually, they separated, extricating their limbs from each other.

Each pausing for breath.

Anchored again in reality.

Cornelia heard him sigh. His head was turned away from her.

'What is it?'

'It can't get any better, can it?' he said.

Maybe those weren't exactly the words she had been praying for, but they would do for now, she guessed, as she shuffled against him, to shelter in his warmth.

'It will,' Cornelia said. 'Tomorrow, I will dance for you. In private. Like I do on stage.'

'I'd like that. You always said you didn't want me to come and see you should you ever perform again.'

'That's true. But this is different.'

'No time like the present?'

She asked him to close his eyes and went through the drawers to find the skimpiest of her G-strings and an opaque flesh-coloured A-cup bra. She plugged in her iPhone charger, called up iTunes and selected a couple of suitable songs. Melodies she enjoyed, slow, languorous, melancholy. Music to undress by. *The Light Goes On* by The Walkabouts and Sharon Van Etten's duet with Angel Olsen *Like I Used To*. She dimmed the ceiling light and twisted both the bedside reading lights upwards to where she was now standing in an approximation of a cone of theatrical spotlight.

The music began.

'You can open your eyes now.' And then danced her heart away.

He found the spectacle a thing of sheer beauty. It was poetry in motion and obscene and personal and moving.

One he would never forget. And that tiny tattoo within half a finger's length of her cunt almost came to life, hypnotising him, killing him with lust.

27
The Bermuda Triangle Killings

It was well past midnight. The sky outside their state room window a dark mass occluding any stars, merging with the choppy sea and its spittle of cresting waves.

The captain's final bulletin of the day ran through the ship's public announcement system and the cabin's TV set even though they always kept it switched off. An intrusion on their search for total isolation from the outside world while they were sailing.

Longitude. Latitude. Wind speed. Time and knots from departure port to destination. Height of wave swell: 4.5 meters. Depth below the keel: 4,000 meters. It sounded endless to Cornelia.

'Did the bulletin wake you up?'

'Not really. I wasn't sleeping.'

'Thinking of anything special?'

'No.'

In truth, yes: him, them, fears, seeds of doubts, that damn folder on his laptop screen. Revisiting every dialogue, each successive event in their story. Possibly interpreting things in a new light.

'I can't seem to sleep either.'

'What time is it?'

Fumbling for his watch which he'd left on the bedside table.

'Around three in the morning. It'll be nice to set foot on land again.'

'One more day to Bermuda. Might be interesting. Have

you ever been?.'

'Yes.'

'I hear the seafood there is wonderful.'

'That would be nice.' She could eat oysters, raw or grilled, until the cows came home. Often felt she could happily live without meat as long as seafood and fish were on offer.

A prolonged silence.

'Fancy a walk?'

'Where?'

'Anywhere. Everyone on the ship is no doubt deep asleep, I guess. The lounges, the decks will be totally empty. Some privacy. As if we were the only passengers ...'

'Won't it be cold outside?'

'Wear something warm. With sleeves.'

'Why not?'

The overhead lights came to life, blinding her briefly. She staggered out of bed. He already was slipping into his jeans.

She shrugged off her nightie and grabbed a pair of shorts from the chair and burrowed into the cupboard for a long-sleeved grey sweatshirt.

The corridors. Empty, ghost-like. Not a soul around. No stragglers. Neither passenger, nor crew. The stewards for each section usually disappeared around 10 pm.

The aft elevator.

He pressed the button for deck 12, the sun and observation deck. Top of the ship. Top of the world.

Past the casino section and the Captain's Lounge where most of the daytime activities took place, until they emerged onto the wooden deck. It was nowhere as chilly as she had expected. Just a gentle breeze breathing across her face and legs as the boat steadily cut through the north Atlantic. It took her a moment to find her balance, to acclimatise her body to the ship's gentle but steady up and down movement.

'Look!'

Ahead, in the direction they were sailing, the dark clouds draped over the sky were shifting, a curtain being pulled open to reveal a desert of stars. Cornelia had never learned to read the map of the sky as a child, distinguish between Polar star or North star, name any constellations or was it galaxies? Not an essential gap in her education, but one she sorely regretted. They were all just random dots in the heavens.

'It's beautiful,' she remarked. 'Can you name any of them?'

He did. In wonderful, intricate detail.

Her heart weakened there and then as he enumerated the stars on display, Latin and Greek names, often weird names she had barely come across before but all seductive and magic. Even more so coming from his lips, warm, hypnotic.

'You should have been an astronomer,' she remarked.

'Who says I'm not?' he joked.

He'd never really explained to her the sort of work he did. Or tried to lie about it. Always understandably so vague in his responses.

'Come,' he asked.

Extending his hands and guiding her towards the forward section, beyond the vessel's principal, monstrously squat funnel until they reached the low-railed V-shaped frontier that separated the boat from the sea. The crescent-shaped observation deck which was always crowded in daytime.

'That's it,' he said. 'We can't go any further.'

Cornelia chuckled.

'Don't tell me that you're thinking of recreating the scene from 'Titanic'?'

'Why not?'

'It's just corny.'

'Even more of a reason to do so,' he pointed out. 'Come on, please …'

Cornelia tried to recall what the actors, Di Caprio and Winslet, had said in the iconic scene, but all she could remember was how the young woman had leaned over the railing held back by Leonardo –yes, Jack, he was called Jack -

and extended her arms to the sky as if hoping to fly.

But that had been in full daylight.

Now it was the dark heart of the night.

'Kiss me first,' she asked him. 'Make it wonderful, make it memorable. And then we'll do *Titanic*. Promise.'

'How can I refuse?'

He brought his hand to her hips and pulled her against himself and it was like their very first kiss all over again.

Their lips met, softness against pliant softness, she felt his tongue making its slow, deliberate way through the barrier of her lips, grazing the hills of her teeth and venturing beyond, finally their tongues meeting.

She inhaled the taste of him, felt his cheek rubbing rough against hers, he needed a shave, the hard bulk of his body pressing against her. She closed her eyes. She didn't want the kiss to end. Never mind *Titanic*. To stay like this with him forever in the very middle of the Atlantic, below the heavy black skies with no moon in sight. No longer having to think of her orders, the Bureau, the killing life. Could it ever be possible: him and her books. Was it too much to ask?

The kiss lasted forever.

Now I truly can fly, she thought. And came to her senses.

He relaxed his grip on her but kept her pressed against the railing, its wooden bar digging into the small of her back.

Cornelia opened her eyes. She had this habit of always closing her eyes when she was kissed. Silly, she knew.

His gaze was distant.

Hard.

He raised a hand to her shoulder.

'I'm sorry,' he said. 'It can't get any better, can it?'

This time, there was something final about his words. Cornelia froze, allowing her basic instincts to take over, her body turning rigid, all heat draining from her.

She sustained his gaze.

And then he pushed her firmly against the low railing. Still dazed, she initially failed to offer any physical resistance and almost lost her equilibrium and stumbled backwards like a dismembered puppet sundered from its strings. There was nothing to break her descent. But just as Hopley shifted his weight from foot to foot to get a better balance and complete his assault, Cornelia slid sideways, almost a dance move from her repertory and his weight against her lessened. He hesitated briefly. She adjusted her stance and with her left leg fully extended she kicked his heel, making him stumble.

His eyes glassed over as, in a flash, he realised he was no longer in control of the struggle and was now vulnerable in turn, with just the flimsy wooden bar between him and the fall.

Was it fear or just resignation she read in his face right now?

'I'm sorry, Hopley,' she whispered and lunged towards him, as he still was trying to regain his initial balance. She'd calculated the angle just right and had the element of surprise on her side.

His body toppled over the guardrail, the roar of the sea below loud and hungry, eager to eat him up in its wet claws.

In his panic, she thought he cried out her name but the sound was swallowed by the rumbling murmurs birthing beneath the surface of the cold waters.

Racing through his mind, in the brief time it took for him to hit the surface of the swirling sea, a whirlwind of questions, thoughts and questions again, and just a hint of despair, disappointment. Fear came when he hit the water.

He was normally a good swimmer, but these were choppy, hungry waters and he was no match for them.

Depth: 4000 meters.

Hopley drowned before any answers reached his struggling mind.

Cornelia's throat had tightened, and she was struggling to breathe properly. It had felt easy, but so unreal.

She was frozen to the spot. Paralysed.

She became aware of the strong wind buffeting her, and the cold sea air creeping through her thin layer of clothing. She began to shiver uncontrollably. Wiped a tear from one eye. And finally took a step backward, with a final glance at the churning sea below.

As she swivelled around to make her way off the deck and back into the ship's interior, she caught a slight movement to her left, close to one of the hanging lifeboats. She squinted. Cigarette smoke? A sketchy movement in the darkness. She stepped forward, approached. There was a woman cowering in the narrow space between the mass of the tender embarkation and its elaborate jumble of thick ropes and pulleys.

Cornelia recognised her.

It was the waitress who often served them drinks in the Botanical Lounge. She visualised her badge. Sladjana. Eastern European. Seldom smiled. Compact and efficient. Dark-haired with blonde streaks in her ponytail. She held the final inch of a cigarette in her right hand. Had sneaked out for a puff.

And from the panicked expression on her face, had no doubt fully seen what had just occurred with Hopley.

A witness. An inconvenient witness.

Cornelia approached her. Even if both women had been standing, she would have towered above her, but Sladjana was crouched, trying to make herself as diminutive as possible.

'I won't tell anyone …' she pleaded. Her lips quivering from the cold and the fear.

'I know,' Cornelia said. She gestured at her. 'Get up.'

The waitress did so. Hesitantly standing. She wore a thick woollen pullover over her regulation white shirt and grey trousers.

Gave Cornelia a sorry look.

As if she knew already that Cornelia's mind was made up. Resigned to the fact.

Cornelia nodded at her to come closer to the extremity of the observation deck. Sladjana allowed herself to be positioned exactly where Hopley had fallen to his death by the guardrail. She was sobbing.

She was half Hopley's weight and toppled over the bar with just a mild push.

She made no sound as she hurtled down.

As Cornelia walked back into the stateroom she and Hopley had shared, she felt as if her mind had been wiped blank. It was done. But an extra kill was something of a nuisance, might attract undue attention. She had calculated she could account for his disappearance with some sleight of hand with the electronic cruise cards when they disembarked, but the absence of a crew member would be noticed as early as the next morning and might create something of a stir, she guessed. She would dispose of his clothes, luggage, and laptop overboard under cover of darkness the following night, she decided. And as for Manhattan, he had perversely seldom taken her out to places where others would remember them as a couple and his apartment building didn't have any doorman so there was little to associate her with him. She had a spare key and would discreetly comb through the rooms to wipe out any trace of her past presence there, not that she expected anyone to launch much of an investigation when he did not reappear.

The best of plans, she sighed …

28
In Which Ramona Finds New Employment

Ramona's heart missed a beat at the very same moment that hundreds of miles away, Hopley's body disappeared below the rumbling waves of the Atlantic as the brief memory of him came racing through her brain.

Ramona was by vocation and character an accountant. She sometimes imagined her life along the lines of a profit and loss ledger. The brief encounter with Hopley in New Orleans fitted into the left-hand column but his sudden desertion undeniably belonged in the other category. Of course, she never used handwritten ledgers these days but relied on computers. The encounter had been a pleasant surprise and she had briefly entertained amongst the throes of passion which the smells and sounds of the French Quarter only multiplied in her mind that it could prove to be something that lasted. It was not to be.

But Ramona was a practical sort of woman and soon wrote Hopley and his memory off and continued with her orderly life. He had been most likeable -and skilful- but also something of a mystery when she realised that in all their hours together he had never volunteered the slightest bit of information about himself or his life. It must have been quite deliberate and negated against the possibility of trying to pin him down back in New York. She filed him away under profit and losses!

So, she was surprised when at the oddest of times, thoughts of him would come flooding through the mist of her feelings. Like right now. So out of the blue and a powerful flash of almost bodily pain, which woke her up in the dead hours of night. She found it difficult to find sleep again, which annoyed her intensely as she was having her annual appraisal the following morning and wanted to be at her best, hoping for a substantial promotion. She tossed around in the bed. She knew she had drawn a final line under Hopley weeks ago so why were these little stabs in the hollow of her stomach still taking her by surprise?

She'd been at her present company for going on four years – had joined straight after qualifying, four months following the New Orleans encounter - and there were rumours that one of the founding partners would soon be retiring, allowing for someone at her level of seniority to possibly be elevated to the upper floor.

'Ms. Taylor, do sit down. Can I call you Ramona?'

'Of course, Sir.'

He had never done so before. Was this a good omen?

'I have bad news and good news.'

'Oh ...'

'You may have heard that one of our managing partners, Mr. Khan is soon hoping to retire.'

'I have.'

'Well, I can confirm it.'

'I've never had the opportunity to work directly with Mr Khan or the specific accounts he looks after, but he has always been pleasant to me. I'm sure the company will miss his expertise and wisdom.'

'Oh, we will.'

'At the risk of being forward, might I enquire about the bad news?'

'Well, Mr. Khan has long been looking after a very specific account on a confidential basis and we have been advised by the client that on his departure they wish to bring the account back in house. It will be a substantial revenue loss for the firm, I fear.'

'I'm sorry to hear that. How might this affect my own position?'

'The client has suggested we recommend someone who could move with the account and run it from their own premises and be employed by them. We thought you might fit the bill well.'

'I don't know what to say.'

Ramona was uncertain whether they were in fact trying to sack her, and this was just an excuse. She felt a flush of anger.

'The renumeration package they are offering is considerable. Much superior to what we have been in a position to pay you here. We've put your name forward as you have always shown both loyalty and a high regard for business confidentiality.'

'Who is the client, if I might enquire?'

'All I can say at this stage is that it is a non-governmental organisation where discretion is a must. Even I am not a party to much further information. Mr. Khan is the only person in the firm who has ever had contact with them.'

It sounded odd to Ramona. But the prospect of both a change and the enhanced salary on offer was dauntingly attractive. And she was intrigued. She had a final query before agreeing to her name being put forward to the mysterious client.

'Do they work within legal parameters?'

'I can only assume so. That's all I can say. As you know Mr. Khan is presently unwell or he would have been able to clarify matters further. So, what do you say?'

'I'm happy for my name to be considered by the client, but would be grateful for more information should I be granted an interview. Should I prepare an updated CV to be forwarded to them?'

'That won't be necessary. The client has done its own background check and your name is high on their wish list.'

Curiouser and curiouser.

It was another two weeks before she was invited to a

formal interview. It was an anonymous if well-maintained brownstone on the upper West Side. There was no plaque on the door or indication of even the name of the company on the door or outside the building.

The crewcut middle-aged man who answered the bell wore a conservatively cut light brown suit, a white buttoned-down shirt, and a Harvard fraternity necktie. He had the sort of features you forget in an instant, as if he had the ability to blend into his surroundings like a chameleon. Ramona's first gut feeling was to think of the CIA; something about his appearance, the whole secrecy involved, but she had been told back at her firm that the organisation interested in her talents was not linked to the government. But of course, people lie for a reason.

Inside the brownstone was a maze of corridors and circular stairs. Every door in view was closed. There was a hush of silence that descended like a curtain over the whole place, a hint that voices here should never be raised and that the work done on the premises took place in a harbour of quietness.

She was guided to the upper floor. The office she found herself delivered to was functional but expensively furnished. Not governmental then.

She was left on her own. Her interviewer would be joining her shortly. She sat herself down in a plush leather designer armchair and waited.

'Taylor?'

The voice was behind her. The man must have entered through another door carved into the wall of law books. He had taken her by surprise.

'Ramona Taylor, yes.'

'We only use the surname here.'

'Ah ...'

'I'm Jones.'

'Good to meet you.'

His manner was terse as if he wanted the whole thing over as soon as possible. She thought he was a most dislikeable man.

'You come highly recommended. And our background checks have proven most positive. We feel you would fit well into our organisation.'

'I'm flattered.'

'As you may know we have decided to bring all our accounting functions in-house. Partly because of Mr Khan's impending retirement but also the fact that the workload is growing and it makes more sense centralising here at our New York headquarters. You will run the department and also oversee similar functions in Los Angeles, Berlin and Singapore, where we have regional offices. But there will rarely be any need for travel. I gather accounting work these days principally takes place over computer screens and networks?'

'It does. It can.'

'Excellent. I'm personally a bit old school; always remember that sort of work and associating it with ledgers and dusty old books. And being done by crotchety old men wearing glasses. It will be nice to see a woman doing it.'

And flattery will get you nowhere, Ramona thought.

'So, what sort of work would I be controlling the accounts for?' she asked.

He pulled a sheet of paper from his jacket and handed it over to her.

'Before we get to that, I must get you to countersign this non-disclosure agreement though.'

She glanced at the form. It was both standard and punitive. Any breach of confidentiality would lead to her financial ruin. And should she ever break the agreement, she might be hounded to the ends of the earth in retribution. Not an uncommon sort of document in the cut throat world of modern finance.

But her curiosity had been fired and she agreed to sign it. Jones handed her a chunky silver Parker pen. She scribbled her name down at the bottom of the page, and Jones folded the document and returned it to his inside pocket.

She sat there in total amazement while Jones explained what the organisation they hoped she would join was involved in. How it met a specific need, generally had the blessing of governments as well as underground groupings and, when necessary, came under their umbrella for protection. How wide its activities ranged and how its departments were strictly compartmentalised for reasons of confidentiality. As to the morals involved, Jones reassured her; advising that in most of the cases the targets only had themselves to blame, were either on the wrong side of the fence or seldom totally innocent. He paused as Ramona's eyes stood wide open in sheer shock and surprise as she digested the information. At the end of the day, he justified their existence by the fact that if they didn't do it, others would and they had, over centuries now, displayed a measure of independence, discipline and standards that were unequalled. There were only a dozen and a half staff at these headquarters and a similar number scattered overseas, and the overall bulk of the people employed were sub-contracted as freelance operatives and go-betweens, if that reassured her as to the scale of the accounting burden and funds released to them were on a job per job basis and only the lump sum needed to appear in the accounts.

'Not too overwhelming?'

'A little. It sounds like something you'd read about in a thriller novel.'

Jones laughed. 'Which you enjoy reading, I gather?'

'Well, you certainly have good researchers to know that ...'

'We only employ the best, Taylor.'

'Count me in.' She reckoned it would be an adventure and not just a job. She had read too many books!

He smiled in approval.

'And is there a company name?'

'Not really, we use several entities, registered in a diversity of countries, to muddy the waters, and in your new function we'd expect you to rationalise that side of things somewhat, but people on the outside just call us the Bureau.'

Within a year, Ramona had risen to the challenge and totally reorganised the Bureau's accounting infrastructure, streamlining, and improving it. She was even made a partner or its equivalent. It helped that all she had to contend with were figures and codenames, shielding her from the cold reality of death as a transaction.

One day, she would even accidentally come across old records that listed the late Hopley's past engagements and now finally understood why he had left her high and dry in New Orleans. But that was ages ago now, and she felt nothing personal after all. Not that it any longer meant anything as his name had a completed termination code attached to it, but the numbers queen of the Bureau forgave him.

29
Cornelia in the City

Cornelia's found her herself both mourning and being so damn angry at Hopley. Could he have not come clean about the nature of his work and they would have maybe laughed out aloud at the sheer, improbable odds of their meeting and engaging in a relationship? They could have conspired in ways to make it work and damn the Bureau.

It felt as if she was now stranded in between lives, adrift.

No one from the Bureau had been in touch for ages and the rule was that operatives should never initiate contact. When the time was right, a call would happen, a meeting arranged and the job assigned, discussed and planned. One way traffic. Not that Cornelia felt she was ready for a further hit. It wasn't something she needed right now; she had never been the blood thirsty type. If she had to live without, she would manage. She had her books, the dancing, her memories. She could always gratifyingly relive the thrills, if that was what her soul called for. All else was superfluous.

She trawled the internet, weekly checking out antiquarian and rare book dealer listings in hope of a title she coveted surfacing somewhere as well as catching up on eBay auctions. During her interlude with Hopley, she saw she had missed out on a couple of volumes she would early have loved to acquire, which she estimated had gone for well under market value. She was particularly sorry to have lost out on a first of John Irving's *Garp* and a signed Emily St John Mandel *Last Night in Montreal*; a title which had lingered in obscurity before the success of *Station Eleven*. It was also a novel which had affected her deeply, even though she had little in common with its heroine; or at least that's what she thought.

She took long, slow walks through Central Park, Harlem, all the way up to the Cloisters, Washington Square Park, Battery Park and wandered endlessly from one end of Broadway to the other, even made incursions over the bridge into Brooklyn, briefly considering moving there, before concluding she had no appetite for the disruption of having to pack all her books and belongings.

Still, the hours of day slowed to a glacial pace as Spring approached and the phone refused to ring while her inclination to resume the dancing showed little resolve.

Neither did sex appeal any longer; the stuff of anonymous encounters or pick-ups with men whose faces she wouldn't recall the next morning. On her wanderings, she would often pause for coffees or drinks in random bars and cafés, and even though she now made a habit of dressing in public in shapeless pullovers or cardigans and tracksuit bottoms with well-worn sneakers, her wild hair concealed under a bonnet or a scarf, she would still be hit upon regularly., as much as she wanted to feel unattractive and unremarkable.

On several occasions, as if attracted to the locale like a magnet, she found herself passing by the shabby building on the Bowery where the dreaded basement was, but the front door was always closed, padlocked, and giving the place the appearance of being derelict it invariably gave her food for thought.

At night, she dreamed of the sea.

Its muted roar, its ever-present swells fading into the distance to a line where sky and sea converged, merged, blended as if they were just the one uncontrollable element.

Just five minutes previously, she had halted, lingered more than necessary by the Bowery basement, and walked slowly away in the direction of Union Square where she thought she might visit the Strand Rare Book Room, Cornelia glanced at a store window on St Mark's Place, partly hidden by displays of tourist-bait gadgets and baseball caps, advertising a tattoo parlour.

On the spur of the moment, she walked in. The air inside stank of weed. It was narrow and claustrophobic. She remembered it had previously been a comics store. Or had that been on the other side of St Mark's, close to Kim's Video, the legendary video emporium that had once been hipper than hip and bursting with music, foreign videos, bootlegs and DVDs that you couldn't find anywhere else in the US? This store had seen better days as the East Village of old slowly gentrified and lost its personality.

Cornelia glanced at the right-hand wall festooned with photographs of past elaborate ink jobs, patterns of flowers, demons, skulls and every imaginable animal from the annals of creation onwards, including no doubt extinct ones.

'Miss?'

The assistant who greeted her had a coloured Mohawk, a prominent nose ring and her eyes disappeared in a well of kohl and lack of sleep. She was dressed all in black leather and wore battle-scarred Doc Martens.

'I want a wave,' Cornelia said.

'A wave?'

'Yes, like a wave in the sea.'

'OK. I think I could manage that. Have you brought your own sketch, maybe?'

'No. I think something stylised. Like in Japanese prints. A wavy line, with maybe a thin white crest. Out of Hokusai?' Cornelia said.

'I've heard of him. He's the guy who does these great pictures of octopuses fucking women, isn't he? Cool.'

'I was thinking more of mountains and seascapes, actually.'

'Sure.'

'Have you a computer. We could Google some images. I can show you the sort of thing I'm after.'

'No problem, lady.'

'You'd be the one inking me?'

'For sure. I can show you more examples of my work, if you want. And if you need it somewhere private, you know, better to have a woman do it, right?'

'Not that private. I have one of those already,' Cornelia commented.

'Wow. I'd love to see it. Between girls, you know …'

'Maybe later.'

'Sure.' She stepped through a curtain into what must have served as a back office and emerged holding a laptop. 'Here we are.'

They quickly settled on a stylised version of a single wave inspired by a Hokusai print. Cornelia found it elegant. A statement of sorts.

'Great. That's an easy job.'

They agreed on the dimensions and a price.

Cornelia stood and pulled off her grey sweatshirt, her mass of blonde curls fell across her pale shoulders. She wore nothing underneath. The young tattoo artist gazed at her, assessing her future canvas.

'I thought you wanted it on your wrist or ankle,' she said.

'No,' Cornelia stated. 'Here,' she pointed to the underside of her left breast, close to her heart.

'You're the customer. I just follow instructions.'

She slathered Cornelia's skin with alcohol to clean the area where she would be working.

She did a good job. As Cornelia observed her reverse image in the small mirror the young woman was holding in front of her breasts, it was exactly what she had imagined it would be. Simple, elegant, to the point.

'You've done great.'

'Thank you. I think that looks really classy on you. A lady with style.' She applied some protective gauze to the now permanent image gently carved into Cornelia's body and taped it down. 'Just keep it on for three or four days. Then wash carefully over the area at first. Keep it disinfected.'

'I know.'

'Of course, not your first tattoo … May I ask about your other … intimate inking? I'm sort of curious …'

'No problem.'

Cornelia straightened and pulled her tracksuit bottoms down, revealing the miniature but realistic image of the gun aimed at her cunt.

'Wow, wow … that is so … I was going to say groovy … unique, that's it. Never seen that one before.'

Cornelia smiled indulgently before pulling her loose trousers back up to her waist and adjusting the in-built belt holding them up.

'Wow again, Miss. I liked That Very much. Are you a model, or something?'

'No, just a book collector.'

'A what?'

'That was a joke.'

'I see. I once had to work that close to a woman's privates before. This awful guy brought in his girlfriend. Wanted me to ink her just above her slit with the word 'slave'. I managed to talk them out of it. He ended up changing it to just 'slut'. The poor woman couldn't help blushing throughout and averting my eyes as I worked that close to her opening … Quite an experience. But a tat is a work of art, you know, it's for life, a statement and not something you should ever live to regret. Most gals they just want flowers or dolphins, or the name of a partner or boyfriend. The guy I apprenticed with once told me he'd been asked to ink a woman with the word 'whore' around her butthole, with the 'o' coinciding with her actual anal sphincter. Maybe he was a pimp and he owned her? I think that's just going too far, you know.'

'Fascinating,' Cornelia said as she slipped her woollen top back on and paid the tattoo artist.

A gun and a wave. Forever. She knew she would not indulge in further tattoos. She was done, now. Indelible memories of Tallinn and the north Atlantic. She had no wish ending up as the female equivalent to Bradbury's *Illustrated Man* or that supernatural queen in another novel that had left a mark on her, Vina Jackson's *Mistress of Night and Dawn*, who would find a brand-new image added to the landscape of her skin following each orgasm she experienced until her whole epidermis was covered by art from the tip of her toes to her chin with just her face spared. Cornelia, however, mostly found orgasms out of reach, with a few rare exceptions.

Cornelia was angry at herself. After bids and counterbids over the past week, she had not succeeded in winning an online auction for a copy of the Centipede Press edition of *Dune*. She was not a science fiction fan and had in fact failed to finish reading the novel on two separate attempts, but this particular iteration of the book was, by all reports, eminently beautiful and valuable, a veritable *Objet d'art*. The final bid had upped her previous one by just a hundred dollars, and she had been hesitant in counterbidding for just too long and had lost out. She still had sufficient funds in her savings account, even if her stash was at an all-time low since she hadn't danced or killed in ages.

She spent the following days in a blue funk, unwilling to leave her apartment, surviving on the few items of food left in her fridge and too lazy or unwilling to order in.

She switched her small flat-screen TV on. Discovered her Netflix account had been suspended as she had failed to renew her subscription. Threw her remote at the wall, missing a framed sketch of her six-year-old self, done by a boardwalk artist on Coney Island on a summer vacation in years gone by. It just dropped down to the old Persian rug that had seen better days and which she had picked up for a song in a Goodwill store back in Pasadena. One of the few things that had followed her from coast to coast. As had the portrait. Her parents had sworn by it but Cornelia had never seen the resemblance but still somehow held on to it for sentimental reasons. A link to her distant past.

Cornelia lifted her camisole up and peered down at the rectangle of thin gauze protecting her new tattoo. It no longer itched underneath. Maybe she could get rid of it now? Allow her newly acquired wave full exposure. But to whom?

A puzzling sense of disaffection was running through her veins, colonising her thoughts, making her feel both guilty and grasping for her sense of self. She'd been resisting it, but finally gave up and pulled out her laptop, scrolled through its distant history and, once again, giving in to a combination of curiosity and temptation descended into the murky worlds of the chat rooms. This time she no longer logged in as Zelda, an incarnation she felt was better left forgotten. She was now Bad Girl.

Some of the earlier protagonists were still around, including Master of Pain. She noted how he kept regular hours on certain days of the week, and how his spider's web of infamy spread its wings, initially inquisitive, then inviting, then menacing. It became clear he was a predator. A clever one. Often using gay men of a submissive nature to actually do his calling. Offering them what they sexually sought in an attempt to drag younger, initially reluctant women, into his grasp. There was a clear agenda in full view, now that she understood his methods. By soliciting couples, if only of a temporary and purely sexual nature, he supplied some form of reassurance that weakened resistance or doubts in the mind of his victims. The gay men were his unwitting pimp troops in trawling for new flesh.

Cornelia was repelled but also couldn't fully conceal her attraction, to the risk, the danger, the possible high of the experience. She still recalled how she felt, her mind in turmoil, almost begging to be mounted as poor Maxwell groaned under the other man's thrusts, her wanting to be in his place, to be annihilated, humiliated, degraded, seeing the punishment as something she deserved. For her sins, past and future. For the very fact she existed and craved to be someone with a single purpose, instead of a castaway in her own life.

Master of Pain was a brute, a supreme manipulator but he also connected with the deepest part of her soul. He was a bad man, and made no pretence of hiding the fact. Was she truly a bad girl?

She came out of the shadows of the chat room and joined the fray. Went into private mode with him.

MASTER OF PAIN:/WELCOME TO THE REAL WORLD BAD GIRL … IF YOU ARE A WOMAN OF YOUR WORDS THIS IS TRULY WHERE YOU BELONG …

BAD GIRL:/THIS BAD GIRL IS LOST … SHE WISHES TO BELONG …

MASTER OF PAIN:/OUR WORLD OF PAIN GREETS YOU BUT HENCEFORTH YOU WILL ALWAYS CALL ME SIR, GAL … IS THAT CLEAR?

BAD GIRL:/YES SIR …

MASTER OF PAIN:/GOOD GAL …

BAD GIRL:/ I CAME HERE ONCE BEFORE, SIR … A FRIEND BROUGHT ME … I HAD ANOTHER NAME …

MASTER OF PAIN:/AND YOU COULDN'T KEEP AWAY …

BAD GIRL:/NO SIR …

MASTER OF PAIN:/THE SIGN OF A LOST SOUL WHO HAS ALREADY GIVEN IN TO HER DEVILS … ACCEPTS HER CONDITION …

BAD GIRL:/YES, SIR …

MASTER OF PAIN:/YOU WILL BE USED … THE WORD 'NO'

WILL NO LONGER BE A PART OF YOUR VOCABULARY …

BAD GIRL:/YES, SIR …

MASTER OF PAIN:/YOU WILL BE PUBLICALLY DISPLAYED FOR OUR PLEASURE … YOU WILL BE SHARED … YOU WILL BE WHORED … DO YOU UNDERSTAND?

BAD GIRL:/YES, SIR …

MASTER OF PAIN:/WHEN IN OUR PRESENCE YOU WILL HAVE NO PRIVACY WHATSOEVER … NO REASONS TO BE SHY …

BAD GIRL:/I UNDERSTAND, SIR

MASTER OF PAIN:/YOU WILL BE OWNED WITH NO LIMITS AND IF YOU PLEASE US, YOU WILL BE PIERCED AND MARKED AS PROPERTY AND YOU WILL TAKE PRIDE IN THE FACT …

BAD GIRL:/IT'S WHAT I CRAVE, SIR … TOTAL SUBMISSION … I THINK IT'S THE REASON I WAS MADE TO EXIST …

MASTER OF PAIN:/YOUR NEW LIFE IN THE WORLD OF PAIN WILL TAKE PRECEDENCE ON YOUR CIVILIAN LIFE AND YOU WILL COME WHENEVER SUMMONED WITH NO HESITATION …

BAD GIRL:/YES, SIR …

MASTER OF PAIN:/EXCELLENT … YOU REALISE THIS NOT A GAME FOR SPOILT BRATS … IT'S FOR REAL.

BAD GIRL:/I AM FULLY AWARE OF IT, SIR

MASTER OF PAIN:/YOU WILL SUPPLY A FULL NUDE

BODY SHOT SO I CAN ASSESS YOUR ASSETS, YOUR SUITABILITY ...

BAD GIRL:/I WILL, SIR ...

Cornelia recalled the fact she had a few such pictures in an old file somewhere in the depths of her laptop. They had been taken when she was trying to break into the stripping circuit in Los Angeles and had to demonstrate her physical credentials to club owners. All taken long before she had acquired her tattoos. She didn't want him to recognise her quite yet. When she had joined Maxwell for the sinister basement playdate, a photo had not been required. Just the boy's word that she was suitable meat for the envisaged feast.

MASTER OF PAIN:/EXCELLENT ... EXCELLENT ... SO, LAST TIME, WERE YOU FULLY BROKEN IN?

BAD GIRL:/NO, SIR ... YOU FUCKED MY MALE COMPANION FIRST ... YOU INDICATED YOU WOULD ENJOY ME ON THE FOLLOWING OCCASION ...

MASTER OF PAIN:/GAL, I DON'T FUCK MY SLAVES, I USE THEM ... REMEMBER THAT ... THAT'S WHAT YOU ARE THERE FOR ... BUT INDEED I ENJOY TAKING POSSESSION OF THE MEN FIRST WHEN IT COMES TO COUPLES ... INSTILS BOTH FEAR AND ENVY IN THE MARE ... PUTS HIM IN HIS PLACE AND KEEPS THE BITCHES IN A STATE OF DREAD AND WANT ... SO WHAT HAPPENED TO HIM, HE COULDN'T BEAR YOU FOLLLOWING IN HIS FOOTSTEPS? HAD COLD FEET?

BAD GIRL:/WE LOST CONTACT ... I DON'T KNOW WHY ...

MASTER OF PAIN:/NO MATTER. SEND ME THAT PHOTO SO I CAN PLAN WHAT CAN BE DONE WITH YOU ... JUST

A SEX SLAVE … A BREEDING COW … OR MERE DOMESTIC SERVITUDE … I HAVE A WHOLE MENU OF WONDERFUL CHOICES AND PRIDE MYSELF IN FINDING THE PERFECT FIT …

BAD GIRL:/YES, SIR …

He promptly supplied Cornelia with an email address and she obeyed his imperious orders. Only a few hours passed, and she was duly provided with a day, a time and a place to present herself. He appeared eager to get the measure of her. It was not the Bowery basement.

30
Flirting with the Devil

A thought occurred to Cornelia that she might not survive the assignment arranged for the following day. If something did go wrong, she knew there was one last thing she wanted to do.

She rang the manager of the Bali Bali Club, a place she had often danced at, in the shadow of the Brooklyn Bridge. Unfashionable, old school, the sort of joint she had long ago left behind.

'I'd heard you'd retired.'

'I was thinking of it.'

'So, what brings you along this sunny morning?'

'I want to do a set.'

'When?'

'It has to be today.'

'A bit short notice, no?'

'I'll do it for free. Just fit me in. Quarter of an hour is all I need.'

'For free?'

'Yes. I lack practice. Want to rehearse some new moves.'

Cornelia wanted to perform a final dance.

'It would have to be mid-afternoon. There won't be many punters around, though, at that time of day.'

'It's not for them. It's for me. I don't mind.'

'Deal, then. For free, just for the tips?'

'Just for the tips.'

The place was almost empty, although the smell of sweating bodies, stale beer and a Sargasso Sea of cigarette smoke still lingered in the air like persistent, invisible mist.

Cornelia had put her make-up on at her apartment, having no wish to linger backstage amongst the other dancers working that particular shift. She had showered, hurriedly washed her hair and not blow-dried it. Her mess of curls hung limply, luxuriant, making her look feral and wild. Mascara, highlighting her prominent cheekbones, white shader around her eyes, emphasising the steely grey of her gaze. A deep red lipstick which she then also used to rouge her nipples and the contours of her sex. All the war paint she required.

She had brought neither accessories nor lingerie of any kind. She had decided she would dance nude from the outset. The bare essentials of her pale body. No stripping, just dancing. Her, the stage, the pole.

The spotlight focused on her solitary form.

The music launched.

She was like a statue frozen in the pool of light. On offer. Both innocent and an object of temptation.

She began to move, her mind on another planet altogether, distant, detached, indifferent to her surroundings, a hostage, a pawn in the great comedy of life.

There were barely half a dozen men in the audience and everyone was immediately transfixed. Even those who had only ventured into the lowlife bar for a drink.

Cornelia danced. She twirled. She flew. Limbs akimbo, sprawled, torn into impossible configurations, no inch of her body spared the indignity and joy of complete revelation. Nuder than nude, obscene, gaping, joyful in the obscenity of her beauty.

The Author had walked into the club as a second thought. He had been walking the Manhattan streets for hours on a personal pilgrimage of grief and felt the need for a drink. He hadn't even realised there would be a floor show. He paused mid-sip as Cornelia appeared and was hypnotised. For the next ten minutes he was unable to take his eyes off her.

He'd lost his wife to a devastating illness and was bone tired, of life, of writing. Revisiting past haunts despite the memories they evoked, the places they had been, the streets and cities of their common past, felt like necessary penance for all the wrong things, the bad things he had done in his life. He'd flirted with the dark side, sometimes given it to its temptations. His own career was at a standstill, and he doubted his talents, felt he had no longer anything worthwhile to say. Dark thoughts were increasingly clouding his mind.

He watched Cornelia with lust and awe.

Finally, the spotlight died abruptly, the beat of the music faded into an oppressive silence, the beautiful dancer disappeared to thin applause and, still, the author stared at the empty and now dark circular stage.

He badly wanted to know more of the wondrous performer but realised it would be a thankless task to investigate and made no attempt to do so. The truth would prove disappointing, he felt. Better stay with the memory of her on stage. The time was past for grand gestures. Or getting fixated on younger, unattainable women.

He finished his drink and lost himself in the rush hour crowds on the way back to his hotel room fifteen blocks away.

She danced in his dreams that night.

Lightning struck.

He resolved to attempt writing one final book. And it would be about a dancer. Something to wipe the slate clean. Maybe he could provide her with a better life than the one she had lived through the artifice of fiction?

Cornelia checked the slip of paper on which she had scribbled the address she had been asked to report to. The residential property was a block away from the Metropolitan in a leafy, tree-lined street, an opulent and well-kept stone-fronted three-storeyed building with high curtained windows. Certainly a step up from the Bowery.

She rang the bell.

Master of Pain opened the door.

Today he was not in BDSM gear but wore a well-tailored three-piece pinstripe suit, his barrel-shaped torso straining against the buttons of his waistcoat. His silk blue necktie was loose.

He looked her over.

Immediately recognised her.

'Ah, Zelda … I was wondering what had happened to you … I regretted opting first for your little faggot companion … Should have availed myself of you while I had the opportunity. So glad we meet again.'

He waved her in.

The house reeked of old, establishment money. Heavy, dark, wooden furniture and framed paintings of country scenes, horses, trees, hunters, thick curtains and brocade. The place a third-generation wealthy stockbroker would own, passing from generation to generation. That hadn't changed its appearance and style for years. Was this where he actually lived or a momentary rental being used for the occasion?

'A marked change in scenery, I note,' Cornelia said.

'Let's say that I guessed you deserved a classier kind of décor to our traditional basement arena.'

'I'm flattered.'

'Only the best for new flesh …'

'Must I still call you Sir? It feels somewhat old-fashioned in this environment.'

He had led her from the hallway down a long corridor that took them to a door which he opened wide.

A large salon, with barred windows looking onto a probable urban garden, leather sofas, chairs and a thick carpet in patterns of brown swirls.

And a wall of standard regulation issue torture paraphernalia: whips, leashes, spreader bars, canes, paddles, alongside a pommel horse, an elaborate lattice of leather straps which formed a swing fixed to the ceiling by pulleys, a wooden cross, a variety of chokers, masks and instruments of restraint scattered across a low glass table.

'Yes. To you I will always be Sir, Cornelia.'

She held her breath.

'How do you know my name?'

He smirked. 'All your other names too, my dear. Carla, Zelda, Bad Girl. And C the Gun, of course. So many identities to conceal your sins.'

Cornelia held her anger in, but she was both livid and furious. This was not how she had planned for matters to unfold.

'That lovely little image of a gun lower down, dear. Rather unique. I made enquiries …'

Surely he was not connected to the Bureau? Who else would have the resources to identify her from such an obscure clue?

'I …'

'Best stay silent, girl. Your time for words has come to an end.'

Cornelia nodded. Inside, she was steeling herself for what was to come. Master of Pain might have plans, but she had too.

'Undress. I wish to inspect the goods.'

She proceeded to shed the flimsy summer knee-length cotton dress she was wearing. It had a floral pattern and was zipped down the side. She wore no bra underneath. Her pink G-string followed. She allowed her attire to fall to the ground where it crumpled up in a pile.

'Your shoes.'

She kicked off her sneakers.

'Excellent. As I remembered.' He moved closer to her, examining her body.

'I see that's a new feature,' he said, indicating the pattern of the wave by her left breast.

'Yes, Sir.' For now, she would go along with his whims.

'Tasty.' His fingers grazed one of her nipples. It was pinker in shade than usual, as not all the lipstick she had smeared on it for her dance had fully washed away. Cornelia shuddered. And was admonished to stand still. He lowered his hand down to her stomach, brusquely kicked her legs apart, and delved between her thighs. Purred, like a cat in heat.

She stood motionless.

'It's going to be a joy to break you, Cornelia or whatever you prefer to be called, because break you I will. And when all is said and much has been done, you will become the perfect whore, believe me.'

He stood back, taking her all in. She withstood his gaze.

'So, you like tattoos, do you? I can think of some more decorative ones to have you marked with, believe me. Would you like that?'

Cornelia meekly nodded.

He pulled his necktie off and threw it over the nearby divan.

'So much I wish to accomplish with you, to you, my dear slut. But where oh where to begin. Maybe you could with the right treatment, training and care become my ultimate masterpiece? What a quandary, hey?'

He took a step back, approached the wall, hesitating over which implement to use on her first. Deep in thought. Kept on muttering to himself, like the parody of a movie villain. But he was the real thing, she knew and there was nothing comedic about the situation she was in. Soon, the point of no return would be reached, beyond which she knew she couldn't ever return to any form of normality. She wasn't unduly bothered by the likely sex and its nature. She had always accepted sex as a part of life, and something of a necessity on the occasions when it had facilitated a kill job. It was a means to an end. But with a twisted man like this, she knew her mind could be seduced, and the darkness she was aware lay deep inside her soul, her grey cells or wherever it harboured, sometimes overwhelmed her and she couldn't resist that fatal call towards oblivion.

Still with his back to her, he shouted out 'Get on your knees, bitch.'

Cornelia obeyed. There was a mirror on the wall where the man could follow her movements. But as she settled her knees on the thick carpet and adjusted her body to the new position, she discreetly reached for the crumpled dress and swiftly pulled out the length of piano wire she had brought along and concealed from its otherwise empty side pocket. She had been ordered to come as she was and not bring along any handbag or tote. Which would have made it awkward for her to smuggle in a knife or even her smallest gun into the building. The silk necktie he had thrown off was just a few inches away by her sneakers. Cornelia quickly grabbed it and wrapped it around her hand between the thumb and her other fingers. It would help avoid the wire cutting into her own skin.

He was still lingering by his busy wall of torture implements, holding a spreader bar in his left hand and weighing up some sharp metal pegs in his other hand.

It was perfect timing.

Cornelia sprang up and rushed at him, her strong dancer's leg kicking out and aiming straight at the lower part of his crotch.

He swore loudly but couldn't prevent himself from bending over.

In an instant, still benefiting from the element of surprise and the minor pain he was experiencing, she wrapped the length of piano wire around his neck and threw herself back, applying pressure, tightening the noose around his carotid. A strangled sound escaped his lips, but Cornelia leaned further back, now holding her right foot against the arch of his back. She could feel a rush of adrenaline rushing through her own body as she withstood his frantic attempts at shrugging her off. She heard one of his ribs break and a sound of panic journeying up his bruised throat. He was stronger than her but she had the element of surprise and knew the exact geometry to apply to the angle of her attack, and very soon the strength went out of him and, Cornelia still panting, sweat running under her arms and between her breasts, felt his life ebb away until he was the one who just broke, collapsed on himself, the wire now deeply embedded into the flesh of his neck which now profusely shed blood. A widening stain began to discolour his trousers. As he managed a final gurgling squeal before falling inert, his whole body doubling up, seeming to shrink in size as he expired. Still, she kept on garrotting him, maniacally not letting go.

Soon, the room fell silent again and she finally let go, gave the dead man a few kicks for good measure, caught a sight of herself in the mirror. She looked properly wild, her hair surrounded by a halo of light, blood smeared across one shoulder, naked and truly feral. A vision she would long remember, as if the moment had briefly released the animal inside her into the wild of civilisation.

Finally, she dressed. Then meticulously retraced all her steps from the moment she had rang the doorbell and carefully wiped every single surface she had come into contact with. Cornelia had been cautious in that regard and avoided as many as she could, just timidly following in Master of Pain's footsteps.

She then saw herself out, desperate for a shower, but unhurried. She could still smell him all over her skin, alongside her own sweat. She mistakenly felt that every passing stranger in the street and on the avenues was giving her odd looks as if they all knew what she had just done, shockingly aware that she had reverted briefly to the status of beast, a wild, naked woman on the bloody rampage. The return of an unbridled Amazon killer warrior from the depths of the past.

The following day saw the beginning of Spring.

31
Death and the Author

Unlike Hopley, Cornelia kept no record of her past assignments, but she had a vivid memory of each and every one of them, and knew that this year Easter fell on the fifth anniversary of her initial hit, back in California.

It was neither a cause for celebration nor one for regret. It was just the way she was wired.

She had just shopped at Century 21, close to the site of the old Twin Towers for stuff she might use as future accessories in her set. It was best to renew her garde-robe on a regular basis. Couldn't be predictable, could she, to keep the tips coming?

She was crossing Houston by the corner of Wooster Street when, for the first time, she thought she recognised someone she had once killed. It took her aback. It certainly looked like him. She was walking north in the direction of Union Square, where she was hoping to browse through the new hardback arrivals at the Barnes & Noble flagship store.

Cornelia remembered the man well.

She had slit his throat, taking him by surprise while he was pouring drinks, pre-bedroom he had hoped, in the vast penthouse space he occupied on the Upper East Side just a few blocks away from the Met. It had only been a year and a little ago, so it was still very clear in her mind. She also recalled it was the day the translation of the final Elena Ferrante novel in the *Naples Quartet* had been published and she had earlier in the day picked up a copy and rushed back to the Airbnb she had been renting for the duration of the assignment to change into the required evening wear to meet up with her target. He was an expansive man with vulgar manners, who openly advertised his profound lack of taste with unfeigned pride, an enormous Rolex watch, gold medallions pouring down the front of his silk shirt, garbed in an expensive tailor-made three-piece suit which no honest citizen would wear in so shiny a fabric. Cornelia now attempted to recall his name, but it evaded her. All those dead people were ciphers, not names. She always tried to draw a line once a kill had been successfully completed. Once and for all. But the faces remained, as much as she tried to avoid those images being stored away in the back of her mind.

She stood still for an instant, watching the man hailing a yellow cab, thinking it must surely be someone else who looked like him, but he was wearing the same stupid silk necktie, with a pattern of gold embroidered hawks against a night black background. Certainly not a memento of his alma mater, more likely his clan.

Surely this could not be the same man? Or an identical twin? The hit had been successful. You don't come back from a slit throat. She had checked for pulse, and had later been paid accordingly, which the Bureau wouldn't have done had she botched the job.

There was nothing else to do but dismiss the preposterous idea and forget. Just some eerie coincidence, she decided. Or maybe she should have her eyes tested? Might all those hours centre stage in the fiery glare of the stage spotlight be insidiously harming her sight?

Or maybe it's just that I'm getting old, she sighed. Her faculties beginning to fail.

Time passing by, wasting her life, but were there any credible alternatives?

By evening she had dismissed the strange apparition. The familiar man had hailed the vehicle, rushed in, slammed the door behind him and the car had driven away uptown at speed towards the zone where the alignment of the skyscrapers turned Manhattan into canyons. It had been so fleeting a sighting. Just an illusion, surely.

He went on a pilgrimage. To places he had known, travelled with her, spent time he now wanted to impossibly recapture. All those lost hours he had not appreciated enough until she was no longer at his side.

Now that she was lost to him forever, he was bereft and left with few valid reasons to live. His family and friends did their best to console him, to lavish dutiful love on him, but it couldn't do the trick. They had their own lives to live and he felt guilty imposing on them, despite all their best intentions.

Maybe he sought some form of absolution.

For all the things he had done wrong. The lies, the infidelities, the half-truths, the thoughts he shouldn't have harboured, his selfishness. He knew he had never been a perfect man. Never would be. More often than not he felt of himself as an imposter, a fraud. The Author no longer liked himself.

In one of the movies that had proved a major influence on both his life and the books he had written, Louis Malle's *Le Feu Follet*, based on the novel of the same name by Drieu la Rochelle, a man spent his final 24 hours wandering familiar streets, meeting acquaintances and more particularly women he had known. Some he had briefly possessed; others had scorned him. He never said anything explicit to them, but it becomes clear that by seeing them again he is asking not just for their forgiveness, but maybe a word, a gesture to change his mind about the terrible decision he has already committed to. To take his own life.

An urban *Danse Macabre*, throughout which he remains misunderstood.

Before he takes that final step from which there is no coming back.

The theme had resonated inside him. He was just that kind of misguided romantic. Had he not once written a novel titled *Confessions of a Romantic Pornographer*? He had often traversed life imagining he was in some kind of foreign art movie, humming an improvised theme tune as he ambled along. Plaintive strings or melancholy piano straight out of

Erik Satie. Sometimes he would do public readings of his stories accompanied by a mix tape he had prepared to accompany the words. It wasn't an original idea; he had borrowed it from another writer he had once seen performing on stage.

He sat in a Starbucks sipping organic lemonade that had no taste, not enough to provide him with his addictive sugar kick. He took a five bucks bill from his wallet. His thoughts lingered. He didn't return the wallet to his jacket pocket. Instead, he pulled out a few photos from one of the compartments. Evoking memories.

Images fixed in time.

When they roamed the Caribbean, explored China, and navigated down the Yangtze River, even once sailed halfway round the world, taking nearly three months to reach Sydney where they stayed in a boutique hotel off Bondi Beach before flying back to London. On Bondi she suffered from a bad toothache, and they had to locate an emergency dentist. They'd swept down Dutch canals, the Douro River, and the Danube.

Some of the photos were only six years old but, God, how they both looked so much younger. Different. Her hair was lustrous and swept back, she wore her pale blue jacket and skirt outfit from that fashion store in Covent Garden in one of the photographs, and in the other, taken on a separate evening, an embroidered top with swirling lace patterns which conjugated perfectly with her smile and offered a hint of cleavage. A minute gap between her top front teeth that he had always found profoundly endearing was unveiled for the camera through her half-parted lips. In the same photo, he was wearing a dark blue tie against a similarly pale blue shirt and a beige jacket, looking unusually dapper for him. Not the true him. These days he lived mostly in T-shirts and cargo pants.

His heart hiccupped that perennial beat seeing her again.

Fuck, she was so beautiful.

They had travelled so much. As if a secret interlocutor

was already warning them their days together were counted and they had to make the most of it.

They once lived in Italy, where the fog raced down daily through the valley at the point where the motorway between Milan and Venice ran, just ten kilometres from Lake Garda. The small village where they were based only screened a movie once a week in the local church, and every foreign film was dubbed, so they had to drive an hour or more to Milan to view something in English with subtitles. He still remembered how there was always a sudden break halfway through the film, at a moment you least expected, interrupting the flow, the storyline, the suspense. Attending, for business purposes, a trade conference in Venice, they had visited the casino on the Lido, where a security guard wouldn't initially allow her in as he didn't believe she was of legal age until she presented him with her passport; she was actually twenty-nine. The guard blushed, while she was delighted to be considered still so young in appearance.

They had children.

They had grandchildren.

They once flew back from Mauritius and floated above the Sahara. Peering through the windows of the aircraft cruising at low altitude, witnessing the endless dunes shimmering like a sea of sand, ever in motion, wave climbing over wave, a mineral ocean in constant flux, alive, slithering, boiling, a vision that had never abandoned him.

At sea for over five days between exiting the Panama Canal and reaching the islands of French Polynesia – Nuku Hiva, Tahiti, Bora Bora – watching the endless vistas melting into the distant, curved horizon, experiencing the sheer magic of human existence on a planet so full of water and unexplored depths, the calm but undulating sea like a repository of profound knowledge, watching through their state room porthole, feeling terribly small and unimportant in the eyes of creation and literally stranded voluntarily in the middle of nowhere.

But, already, she was forgetting small things. Getting

confused.

He took another reluctant sip, memories unavoidably bubbled up again.

Another year in their incessant journeys: the Viking Sky seemingly moving at a snail's pace through the becalmed Stockholm Archipelago in bright summer sunlight, slaloming lazily in low gear around its 24,000 islands, she on their balcony, topless, her breasts tanned and still high and firm, on offer to the cloudless, untroubled sky, long blonde hair cascading down to her shoulders.

On the photographs taken at the 6 pm first sitting dinner on Magellan, her smile is luminous, as if she has not a care in the world. In ignorance of the future, barely bothered by her now regular lapses in memory, just blaming the incidents on absent-mindedness.

There are other photos he does not carry with him, filed away back home in albums and folders. Or maybe the images have just nested inside his imagination, growing tendrils of pain and heartache, simulacra of memory that feel all too real and treacherous for his own mental health. A naked beach in Jamaica or possibly it was the South of France where they would drive every summer down to the Languedoc. But it struck him now in the middle of a crowded downtown Manhattan Starbucks, weren't they places where cameras were strictly banned from? So how come the visions he recalls are so vivid? The two of them standing proudly, feet moored in the warm sand, their skin tanned, their genitals shaven one morning in an act of amused compliance to the assumed etiquette of the resort and initially feeling like plucked chickens, more naked than nude, and in no way sexual direct descendants of Adam and Eve in the Garden of Eden.

The Author felt a dizziness take control of his body and mind.

Shards from times past.

Distractedly drifting down the placid Yangtze River, passing through the gorges that rose on both sides of the boat, gazing out to catch sight of the ancient tombs carved into the mountain side, where souls sat forever and both of them held their breath, in awe at the sheer power of nature. He had turned towards her, seeking her eyes out. Her glasses had turned dark, but he had recognised how pensive she was and imagined they might well be thinking the exact same thing. Like old established couples do in stories.

On an ill thought-through vacation to Mauritius, during the wrong season when the light faded too early and the days were short and evenings interminable, they had swum in the infinity pool that rose above the Indian Ocean and watched in communal silence as the sun climbed down the line of the horizon, a fleeting vision of gold and fire drowning in savage splendour.

New Orleans had become their city of adoption. The smell of beer in the gutters of Bourbon Street; the festooned balconies; bougainvillea in bloom spreading through the trellis with its odorous smell of honeysuckle and sun; the glossy green leaves and delicate white blossoms of the magnolia trees, and endless feast for the senses. New Year's Eve on the balcony at Tujague's watching the ball drop on the façade of the Jax Brewery to trigger the fireworks exploding on the barges spaced out on the nearby, wide Mississippi. The crawfish boils releasing their spicy aromas, the fat, greasy oysters on their bed of ice, followed by gumbo; gospel brunch at the House of Blues on Decatur, just across from the dusty warrens of Beckham's Bookshop over the street where the Author would spend hours hunting down collectibles through a maze of spines of all colours and textures.

He closed his eyes, almost in tears.

His heart was falling apart, split right in the middle, shattering into a million fragments.

The world, their world, was no longer what it used to be. Gone were the Water Margin on Golders Green Road, the Ganges on Gerrard Street, that couscous restaurant in Paris off the Boulevard Saint Michel, the cavern-like bodega here in New York where they had been served succulent seafood tacos and which he'd discovered yesterday had become a tourist store selling electronic gadgets and fake designer handbags. The sushi restaurant on 13th Street was also gone. They'd kept on visiting it for several years, despite nearer Japanese eateries closer to their hotel and Manhattan base. He blamed it on familiarity and sentimentality.

In Tahiti, in a large mall in Papeete, the Author had bought his wife a splendid necklace of black pearls and got his currency conversion rate wrong and paid ten times more than he had initially believed he was doing. By the time he had realised his mistake, they had sailed away and were already skirting the coast of New Zealand.

They had honeymooned in Desenzano on the shores of Lake Garda, following a brief stopover in Nice on the Côte d'Azur. He remembered watching her intensely against the background of the still, green waters of the lake bordered by snow-topped mountains. Thinking she was the only woman in the world and that he just didn't deserve her, her long straight blonde hair cascading down her back, slim but wonderfully curvy, and with a smile so full of intelligence that he would have happily allowed her to lead him to eternal damnation. His father, on their wedding day, had predicted to his pals that the marriage wouldn't last a year. They'd proved the bastard wrong.

He checked his watch. Still early in the day. Too many hours ahead to kill.

The Author closed his eyes. Pictured them sitting in a thousand restaurants, across from each other, tasting the silence, the complicity. Lentil and barley soup at Veselka in New York, just a few blocks from where he was sitting now, on the Avenue full of Ukrainian businesses; the sizzling, chargrilled oysters saturated in an herb and butter sauce at the Acme Oyster Bar in New Orleans where you had to earn the right to eat by queuing for ages outside; the boiled beef tongue at the Dostoyevsky Restaurant in a suburb of Cologne. It was an endless list.

Why couldn't he have made time stop to capture those moments, imprison the two of them in their bubble, making the them last forever?

He had come to the city to remember.

He had come to this city to forget.

It could have been any city. They'd travelled to so many.

It was New York, where he could find it easier to hide amongst the multitude of boroughs, skyscrapers and desolate tenements and the milling crowds the Big Apple continued to attract from all over the world: loners, refugees, romantics and outlaws. Widowers who didn't have the grace to accept their fate. It could have been London or New Orleans, other cities teeming with life and memories too, where he could merge with the crowds, become invisible in broad daylight. It could never have been San Francisco, a place celebrated by the movies but that, despite *Vertigo* he had never quite connected with intimately enough, although to his surprise it appealed to so many others who swam in the same waters as him.

He'd now managed almost eighteen months on his own. Feeling as if he lived on borrowed time, unable to enjoy what was certainly the final chapter in his own life. He'd idly thought of attempting one more novel, but he had no inspiration. Hadn't he said all he had to say? Written all the words he had at his disposal? Who out there wanted more dark streets and femmes fatales? He was finding it increasingly difficult to read books written by others, in the clandestine knowledge that he might never know how they ended if he made his exit stage door before he reached that point. Or began binge-watching a TV series, with the final episode shielded by future clouds possibly never to be viewed. He had never lived this way before. The Author had always been a man who made plans, lists of things to do, and invariably ticked them all off in descending order. He'd never missed a deadline. There had always been a future ahead of him: a new movie to see, a CD to listen to by musicians he loved, a holiday in an exotic place yet unvisited, a meal in a familiar restaurant where he would inevitably mostly order the same items from the menu he had enjoyed before. It was like a strange sensation of running in place.

He did not have to work. He still had enough money set aside from a fortuitous piece of hackwork he'd delivered some years before. Days rolled by; some ever so slowly, dragging along, thoughts lazing through his head and never quite achieving fruition; others raced by until darkness came and he realised he had accomplished nothing for days on end.

His stomach reminded him he hadn't had any food since the garlic bagel with salmon and cream cheese he had eaten for breakfast.

The Author looked up.

It was a simple diner on a street corner, straight out of an Edward Hopper painting and life had stood still since its lines and colours had been conjured into life. He sat himself on a high stool by the zinc counter and ordered a burger with fries and a glass of cold home-made lemonade. He was down to his last handful of fries, his mind in neutral gear, his eyes focused on a squabbling middle-aged couple in a booth at the far end whose arguments he could barely hear although the simmering anger that hung between them was betrayed by their body language. He enjoyed observing people, casually building up stories about them in his imagination. When they finally turned silent and began to concentrate on the plates of steaming food on their table, he noticed that someone was now sitting on the stool to his right. It was a woman. Her perfume was quietly fragrant. Elusive, shifting notes of green and citrus. She was blonde. Oozed class in a cool sort of way. Steel-grey eyes. Her hair, a tangle of curls, fell to her shoulders, its tendrils draping themselves across the top of her brown leather jacket. He initially thought she looked a bit like Taylor Swift. She was perusing the laminated menu.

He had always been partial to blondes. His first blonde had broken his teenage heart and caused him to lacerate his wrists in a clumsy, forlorn attempt to retain her; it hadn't worked but he still had the small scar that reminded him of Lois Elizabeth. The next blonde he had married; her name was Laura. The final blonde had been called Katherine and their affair had lasted six months and almost broken up his marriage.

The young woman turned towards him. Maybe not Taylor Swift, he thought. There was something steely and glacial about her that made her appear even more alluring, less apple pie, more ambiguity, polished like a diamond. Deadly beautiful.

'How's the burger?' she asked. She had a slight accent that didn't quite sound American. Canadian maybe? He couldn't quite pinpoint it.

'Decent, actually.'

She had grey eyes and the moment he looked deep into them the Author both fell in lust and immediately realised she was his angel of death. The beautiful spectre he had often dreamed about. Written about. The time had finally come. It wasn't at all what he had expected, but he rather enjoyed the thought that this would be the woman who would kill him.

She smiled at him. He smiled back.

Words unsaid; particulars kept in the dark. He could read her. She offered a flash of recognition.

By the following morning, he was dead. In his hotel room. Hotel rooms were always the places where both wonderful and terrible things happened in his stories and books.

Knife? Gun? Poison? Pills? Overdose? Fall from a great height? Strangled?

It mattered not in the order of things.

32
Faces in the Crowd

Two days later, sitting in Washington Square Park and sipping a tepid coffee from a paper cut while reading a book in which a ballet dancer in Montreal was turned into a wooden puppet, Cornelia's attention was drawn to a nearby nanny chiding her curly-haired, cherubic-like ward who was throwing pieces of the cupcake he had just crumbled towards the marauding squirrels. As she looked across the path, a woman in loose dungarees and outsized sunglasses jogged by, pulling a dog on a leash behind her. Cornelia had never been animal friendly and could not for the life of her distinguish between canine breeds, but she recalled having had to lock the animal into the bathroom on the night she had killed Sicilia Ann. Who right now was running past her bench, her sneakers hitting the ground in metronomic rhythm.

Sicilia Ann. It was the only hit she had ever undertaken against someone she had previously known in her private life. Until Hopley, of course. Sicilia Ann had worked as a stripper in the same club where Cornelia was under contract that particular summer, was the undisputed queen of the pole and had incredible, natural breasts which were the envy of all the other dancers. Cornelia's chest dimensions were more modest, not that it had ever bothered her. Sicilia Ann had once worked as a microbiologist and, when dancing, billed herself as Doctor Ann. She was always dragging her fellow performers out of hours along to obscure street food eateries where she was always familiar with the cooks. Cornelia never wanted to know why someone was designated as a hit but assumed Sicilia Ann had stumbled into some voluntary or maybe even involuntary involvement with illegal drugs and was now having to pay the price for theft or betrayal of some sort. Strip tease artists were often on the periphery of the shadow world. It came with the occupation. When she had received the large manila envelope with details of the assignment, it hadn't initially clicked until she had torn it open and glanced at the familiar face in the photograph; she had never been aware of her erstwhile fellow dancer's family name and the fact she was of Italian descent. The Sicilia moniker hadn't properly registered with her.

It had been one of her easiest kills, with little need for subterfuge; just a drunken night out with a friend. Cornelia had wanted the death to be painless and had simply twice injected Sicilia Ann with an air bubble directly into her veins, cutting off the blood supply to the brain. She had read about the process online. *Maybe*, Cornelia had thought, *when my time comes, that's the way I'd like it to be.*

And there was Sicilia Ann rushing out of Washington Square Park, on the corner of Waverly Place, crossing past the boutique hotel that had once hosted Bob Dylan and many other cult figures, with her dog in tow, yapping away. There was no doubt it was the same person; Cornelia clearly recognised the distinctive striped black and grey leotard she was wearing. Along with the familiar pink colouring of Sicilia June's pigtail ends. She rubbed her eyes, uncomprehending. This made no sense. She had even attended the young woman's funeral. Out of a sense of duty and compassion.

Her mind was fuzzy. In normal circumstances, she would have quickly stood up and followed the unlikely jogger, but she wasn't thinking clearly right now, her faculties blunted by the shock appearance of someone she clearly knew she had killed. Who shouldn't have been there. No way.

Cornelia wondered whether this was a message. Either her mind or the world out there was giving her a hint that she should put an end to her killings. It wasn't as if she needed the cash right now. She had all she wanted and enough set aside for rainy days or new books and she had never taken any particular pleasure in undertaking the hits, getting kicks from it; it had just been a job. One she did well and took pride in, but no more. Not like an addiction she couldn't shake. She could easily turn the page, if she truly wanted to do so.

She looked down at her feet and caught sight of a brown squirrel negligently ambling along the narrow path, making its way to the patch of grass behind which Cornelia was sitting on the wooden bench.

Wrong animal, she wryly remarked to herself. She was not being drawn into a remake of *Alice in Wonderland*, and following it, or the jogger who looked like Sicilia Ann, down some existential rabbit hole in the ground. She was staying put. She took a final sip of her coffee. It was now cold. She dismissed the jumble of thoughts and emotions running around her brain like a turbulent tide and attempted to go back to the book she was reading. The lines on the pages now blurred and she couldn't presently recall which character had disappeared through the enchanted shop window or whether the wife had been a dancer and the husband a translator or the other way around. Thrillers were so much easier to follow. Just a panoply of killers and victims.

Cornelia rose from the bench, dropping the half-read paperback to the ground and abandoning it.

She was determined to clear her mind.

'I am sane,' she remarked to herself as she stepped away from the bench and took off in the direction of Greenwich Avenue, 'It's all an illusion, a form of dizziness, maybe a virus that I've caught which is distorting my perception. I am not in a film or a book, because that is where these sorts of things happen. This is real life.'

She sighed.

Back at her apartment, she enjoyed a leisurely bath, her body submerged in the warm water, its surface a landscape of fragrant bursting bubbles, while Bruce Springsteen's *Born to Run* played on the hi-fi and she tried to sing along to *She's The One*. She had put the song on repeat, her attention hypnotised by its insistent piano riff. Finally, the blanket of shimmering rainbow bubbles slowly faded away and she watched as the contours of her body became visible through the surface sheen of the water, the way her legs stretched away, long, shapely, her best asset she knew. As she shifted her position, her nipples came up for air, dripping bath water, their distinct shade of pink and light brown a familiar sight. They had always been coloured slightly differently, and, when she was younger, she had briefly thought of herself as a freak: the girl with different coloured nipples, but then one day she had come across photographs of the singer David Bowie and noted how his eyes came in distinctly different shades, and she had accepted her oddity, even taken it to heart as a proof of her individuality. Her gaze wandered further down to her delta. She kept herself shaven; it was something of a professional obligation for the job as an ultimately nude dancer. Initially she had felt something like a target for paedophiles, being bare down there but had long since become accustomed to the smoothness of her mound, and the way it divided cleanly, her labia peering through with restrained discretion down its centre. Between her sex and her navel, where she displayed the image of a small gun. And then there was the thin line of the Hokusai wave breaking against the soft pale underside of her breast.

Stepping out of the bath, she towelled herself dry and slipped on a white oversized T-shirt, then tiptoed to the main room of the apartment where all three walls were heavy with packed bookshelves. Remembering the puzzling sighting of her first kill a few days earlier, she walked over to the shelf where she kept her signed advance proofs, meaning to take a peek at the Le Carré *The Night Manager* rarity she had managed to purchase thanks to that initial kill of the mob-related guy. She froze. It wasn't in its usual place. For the next hour, she kept on browsing through every single shelf in the room and was unable to locate the book. Cornelia was extremely organised. Considering her double life, she had to be, and she was inordinately proud of the excellence of her tidiness and her attention to detail. She had never misplaced a book before. Maybe she'd scour the shelves tomorrow again when her mind was less preoccupied by the recent improbable appearances of those disturbing ghosts from her past as a hit woman?

She tried to clear her mind of the troubling vision of Sicilia Ann jogging with her dog down through the pathways of Washington Square Park. Tried to recall which book she had acquired with the resulting fee that had rewarded that kill. It came to her: a dust-jacketed copy of Cornell Woolrich's sixth novel *Manhattan Love Song*, the final book in his Scott Fitzgeraldian career phase before he turned to pulp and noir. She had never got round to reading it, always meaning to do so next and, anyway the cover was in a fragile state, as few copies had survived the weight of years past since its publication, which made it a coveted rarity wrapped in its transparent plastic book protector sleeve.

Again, she failed to find it, despite a meticulous, quasi-forensic search through her collection.

After a whole afternoon of frantic searching, Cornelia gave up in despair. Again, it made no sense: her apartment had not been broken in to that she could see, and what about the troubling coincidence of these two particular titles which were strangely linked to the impossible reappearances of her two victims?

Having taken up her former stripping career once more, she was doing two shifts at one of the clubs she was currently working at that evening. She quickly packed her gear: the diminutive outfits she wore at the onset of each dance, her make-up bag, her music tapes. She slammed the door behind her and checked twice she had properly locked the apartment up.

Every time Cornelia felt she had succeeded in blocking the memories of the sightings of her two phantom victims and her mind attained some form of peace, her focus returned to the disappearance of the two matching books from her collection. Appearances and disappearances.

The strip club operators were always critical of the music she selected to dance to. They would have preferred her to choose more popular, familiar hits but Cornelia had idiosyncratic tastes, veering towards the obscure and her movements were always in perfect synchronisation with the music she had brought along, whether tunes by Aldous Harding, Leonard Cohen, Sharon Van Etten or The National. Not for her the bump and grind obligations of *We Are the Champions* or *Hey, Big Spender*. They stank of vulgarity. Too obvious. Not for the sorts of her. Anyway, her choices of music made her stand out from the other working girls, didn't they?

'They're all a bit gloomy, don't you think?' the club operators kept on complaining. 'You should give the punters something they know. Are familiar with, expect ...'

But once the music played she was at one with it, and the way her body moved in harmony with its melody and rhythm, how she orchestrated the unpeeling ritual of her clothes until she stood swaying totally bare in the spotlight on the elevated stage, paler than pale in the sheer glare of both the lighting and the eyes of the men who lusted for her was a thing of absolute beauty. Revealing, obscene and triumphant in the knowledge that every man in the room was captivated by the sight of her enigmatic smile, the gentle curves of her breasts and arse and the sexual heart at the crux of her body, the cunt of a hundred lustful attentions.

Her final set of the day.

She was now fully naked, winding down her movements to the final chords of *Candy's Room* when a man stood up from the shadows of the sparse audience and threw a banknote towards the stage. His face briefly traversed the beam of the spotlight and she recognised her last kill. It was without a doubt the man she had inadvertently come across at the Franconia Diner and later despatched. It had been a curious evening. He had greeted her as if he already knew who she was and was resigned to it. Accepting of his fate. He had never struggled, almost offered himself up to her, not even going through the pretence of trying to seduce her to justify her readily following him back to the hotel room where he happened to be staying nearby.

The music faded away. The lights went off. Cornelia departed the stage, with a final look at the audience, anonymous faces scattered in the dimness that came in the aftermath of every dance. She sought out the face of the man who had stood up to tip her, noticing in passing that it was unusually a hundred-dollar bill which she held crumpled in her fist as she stepped down and made her way to the backstage area where she could dress again. He was no more to be seen. Had it even been the same man?

'Did you see the guy in the audience who stood up to throw me a bill at the end of my set?' she asked Teresa, who served at the bar and was afforded a clearer view of the small auditorium.

'The customers all look the same to me,' Teresa answered. 'All perverts, every single one of them, if you ask me.'

Cornelia returned straight home, calling an Uber. She slept badly that night. First she dreamed, then she remembered every single person she had killed. By morning, the bedsheets were damp with her sweat.

Over the following weeks, she chanced across further random sightings of past victims.

It was like facing a growing conspiracy.

At Chelsea Pier, a fleeting vision of the couple whose car she had sabotaged. On the down escalator at the Union Square Regal as she journeyed up on the opposite side, a middle-aged man with a ponytail, wearing a shabby linen three-piece suit and scuffed shoes; he had struggled and almost got the better of her and it taken several days for the scratches he had inflicted on her back to fade away. On the same day, crossing Broadway after the movie, she had to step back toward the pavement when a car raced around a corner and almost took her out; she caught a glimpse of the driver: it was a guy she had been forced to sleep with before she could get the opportunity to dispose of him; he had been rough and unpleasantly verbal and she had taken extra pleasure in discharging the whole barrel of the SIG Sauer in close contact into his heart. On the subway, briefly noting a familiar face on the platform as her Sixth Avenue Line train pulled out; a guy she had avoided the imposition of sleeping with, having managed to slip a pill into his drink and knocking him out before smothering him with a pillow while he still dozed; she had a clear memory of that evening, having departed the hotel room with a swoop on its complimentary toiletries, having taken a shine to the fragrance they stocked in each bathroom, which she had been using ever since.

But the books kept on mysteriously disappearing from her shelves. Cornelia could now predict in advance which would have faded away into oblivion as she returned to the apartment following yet another sighting, equating titles with certain hits she had been involved in. She began to despair.

Her whole world was turning into a Philip K. Dick novel. It wasn't funny, either. She had never even collected him as his more valuable titles were all initially issued in paperback format.

There was no sense or reason to it. She felt as if she had been plunged into the heart of a bad pulp story, but then even those have an ending of sorts. She wondered how hers would conclude.

The one thing she was certain about was that it wasn't guilt that was causing this disarray to her life. Cornelia did not believe in guilt. Just in books, sex and death.

She ceased working. Phoned around the clubs she had been dancing in and advised them she was taking an indefinite break from the trade. Could no longer concentrate on her moves and knew she lacked grace when she danced on automatic pilot.

She felt adrift and forlorn, mourning her lost books and increasingly troubled by these regular apparitions of unlikely ghosts. Surging back into her life with worrying, clockwork regularity.

Unable to find sleep or peace, she finally reached a decision. She had always been proud of her lack of display of emotions and it was with a certain detachment that she went about her business.

Cornelia knew she had reached the end. She had had a good run, but time was running out and she'd rather leave the stage on her own terms.

She called Jones at the Bureau.

'This is highly irregular. We're the ones to contact you. I do not appreciate this call.'

'I'm aware of that. 'But I'm calling to advise I'm quitting. You haven't put any jobs my way for ages, anyway, so what's the point of remaining at your beck and call? Was it something I did wrong?'

He sounded as if he was trying to restrain his temper.

'You were never this inquisitive, Cornelia. You were once one of our best operatives. Some people here even thought that, with your talents, we could have brought you in house. On permanent retainer.'

'You learn and live.'

'Is it because you are still resentful about the Hopley job you were given?'

'Well, you could say I wasn't over the moon. But I did it. I didn't complain, did I?'

'It was a loose end and could not be allowed to remain that way.'

'You knew about him and me?'

'Of course.'

Cornelia held her breath, simmering with quiet anger that it had come to this. Aware that in a battle of wills between the Bureau and her, there was no possibility of a happy ending.

'Well, I said it: I want out. I'm retiring. Full stop.'

'It's not the way we do things.'

'No matter.'

'I daresay that makes you a loose end too, then ...'

'I'm aware of that. I'll take my chances. Although I would respectfully point out that, unlike Hopley, I have not held on to any physical records of the jobs I did for you lot.'

'It doesn't have to be physical evidence, Cornelia. It's in

your head and, you recall every single hit. And face. Am I mistaken?'

Were the bastards even monitoring her dreams?

'The disappearing books. Is it you? Trying to warn me? If it is, I want them back. Every single one of them. They have nothing to do with you. Nothing. I worked hard to acquire them.'

'What disappearing books, Cornelia? I don't know what the hell you are talking about. Are you ill, by any chance?'

She tried to read into his tone whether he was pretending or not. But his voice was impassive, not giving an iota away.

'Fuck you, Jones. I never liked dealing with you. Irish Ivan had more soul than you ever will.' She disconnected.

That should do the trick.

Her initial thought had been to use whatever money she had left in the bank to contact the Bureau anonymously and purchase a hit on herself. Anonymous bankers draft. Fake name in the dossier. But the plan wouldn't hold up. They would quickly see through it.

And why should she pay for her own elimination? She was now curious which operative they might commission to take care of her, not that she had ever met any others in the Bureau's employ. Apart from Hopley.

Jones called Ramona and explained the situation.

'Most unfortunate,' she concluded, after a moment's reflection. She had no need to consult Cornelia's personal file. She had read through it many times. 'But the rules are the rules.'

Later in her top floor office with an undisturbed view of Central Park, she reflected how her own life had briefly intersected with Cornelia's in New Orleans.

'Could it have been me?' Ramona wondered.

But the answer was a negative one. She couldn't dance even if it was to save her life. But she did collect books and her own collection was growing rapidly since she could afford coveted titles now that she worked for the Bureau.

She opened her laptop and entered the proper termination code. Making things official. Jones would take care of the practicalities. She was a stickler for adhering to the proper procedures.

Cornelia sat in her Village apartment and waited.

She was aware the outcome would not be immediate. There were administrative procedures. Logistics and personnel would have to get involved. The inexorable system grinding into gear. The cogs. The telephone calls.

There were so many books she owned she still hadn't read. Of those that remained. Maybe she would have time to complete a few more before her killer came. And listen one final time to her favourite music by Counting Crows, Grant Lee Buffalo, Townes Van Zandt and others, wondering where it had all gone wrong.

She knew the hit would be fast and painless. Even the best of assassins harbours some form of compassion. It came with the job, didn't it?

She didn't even lock her front door.

ABOUT THE AUTHOR

Maxim Jakubowski published his first book at the age of 16 and has worked for several decades in book publishing. He has written 21 novels, 5 short story collections and edited over 100 anthologies in the Sf & fantasy, erotica and crime genres.

A winner of the Karel, Anthony and Red Herrings awards, he has also featured regularly in the *Sunday Times* bestseller lists under a pseudonym.

He was until recently Chair of the Crime Writers' Association and ran Crime Scene, London's mystery film festival for 10 years while reviewing crime for *Time Out* and *The Guardian*. He once wrote a *Doctor Who* outline, which Douglas Adams rejected.

Also by Maxim Jakubowski

NOVELS

It's You That I Want To Kiss (1997)
Because She Thought She Loved Me (1998)
The State Of Montana (1998)
On Tenderness Express (2000)
Kiss Me Sadly (2002)
Confessions Of A Romantic Pornographer (2004)
Skin In Darkness (omnibus edition of revised versions of *Because She Thought She Loved Me, It's You That I Want To Kiss* and *On Tenderness Express*) (2003)
I Was Waiting For You (2010)
Ekaterina And The Night (2011)
The Lousiana Republic (2018)
The Piper's Dance (2021)

SHORT STORY COLLECTIONS

Life In The World Of Women (1998)
Fools For Lust (2006)
A Washington Square Romance (2011)
The Music Of Bodies (Ebook only) (2011)
We Mate In The Dark (Ebook only) (2011)
Hotel Room Fuck, The Best Of Maxim Jakubowski (Ebook only) (2012)
Death Has A Thousand Faces (2023)